DON'T WORRY. THESE SECURITY GRUNTS CAN ROAST A FEW MARSHMALLOWS... WHEN THEY WAKE UP.
--WHOOOAAAA--!
HE'S GOT GLASS BALLS.
FAR WARNING: THE CONCEPTS OF LIFE AND DEATH ARE BEYOND ME NOW.
OR SO I'VE BEEN TOLD.
--THEY'RE SIMPLY A WAY TO INSURE THAT YOU DO.
BIG DEAL, AND OBVIOUS, TOO. I'VE NEVER MADE ANY SECRET OF MY TASTE FOR THE FINER THINGS.
I SHOULD TELL THESE TOOLS TO TAKE THEIR FRESH MEAT BEIBE AND FUCK RIGHT OFF.
CHASIN' THE DRAGON ACROSS A NERVE-CELL NIGHTMARE...
MAYBE THIS TIME, I CAN ACTUALLY--
N-NOW HOLD ON, YOU SUMBITCH...
BAKER! DAT PIECE A' SHIT!
TOO MANY TIMES HE KNOCKED MY DICK IN THE DIRT...
... HERE I FUCKING AM.
RIGHT.
ENOUGH TIME SPENT FEELING SORRY FOR MYSELF, LOOKING DOWN AT THESE POOR BASTARDS... THE INSTINCT THAT KICKS IN... THE PURE ADRENALINE RUSH...
... THIS IS BETTER THAN SEX.
YEAH, FOR A SUPERHERO, HE WAS A SADISTIC SON OF A BITCH.
EVERY TIME I GOT INTO IT WITH HIM...
"...OH, YOU DIDN'T KNOW THERE WAS A PRESIDENT OF REALITY? WELL, YOU SURE AS HELL CAN'T VOTE FOR HIM, BUT HE EXISTS, JUST THE SAME...
"BIT OF AN EGO ON THIS GUY. NOT THAT I BLAME HIM...
GUESS I CAN HAVE A LITTLE PRE-GAME FUN.
GODDAMMIT... I GOT A MILLION VOICES IN MY HEAD...
... NONE OF 'EM FAMILIAR.
--OH SHIT!
...ESPECIALLY COMPARED TO HER GLORY DAYS AS MS. MAYHEM. AS A SUPERHEROINE, SHE WAS IN A CLASS BY HERSELF.
ASK ME, SHE'S GOTTEN BETTER WITH AGE.
--AND I AIN'T GETTIN' NO JUSTICE?!
NO SATISFACTION?!
GYAAAHHHH--!!
ON THE OTHER HAND...
... WHEN OPPORTUNITY KNOCKS...
TALKING ABOUT OLD TIMES--

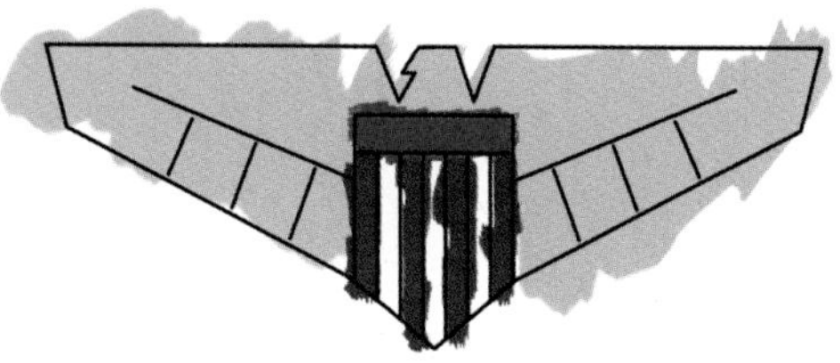

JOE CASEY
WRITER
+ BOOK DESIGN

BUTCHER THE RIGHTEOUS MAKER

MIKE HUDDLESTON
ART + COLORS

BAKER

RUS WOOTON
LETTERING

SONIA HARRIS
DESIGN

BUTCHER BAKER THE RIGHTEOUS MAKER.
FIRST PRINTING. DECEMBER 2012.
ISBN: 978-1-60706-652-1

PUBLISHED BY IMAGE COMICS INC.
OFFICE OF PUBLICATION: 2134 ALLSTON WAY, 2ND FLOOR, BERKELEY, CA 94704.

FOR INTERNATIONAL LICENSING, WRITE TO:
FOREIGNLICENSING@IMAGECOMICS.COM

PRINTED IN CANADA.

WWW.MANOFACTION.TV

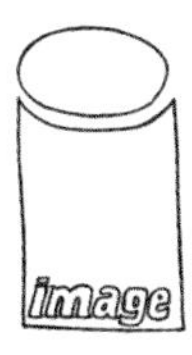

IMAGE COMICS, INC.

ROBERT KIRKMAN
CHIEF OPERATING OFFICER
ERIK LARSEN
CHIEF FINANCIAL OFFICER
TODD MCFARLANE
PRESIDENT
MARC SILVESTRI
CHIEF EXECUTIVE OFFICER
JIM VALENTINO
VICE-PRESIDENT

ERIC STEPHENSON - PUBLISHER
TODD MARTINEZ - SALES & LICENSING COORDINATOR
JENNIFER DE GUZMAN - PR & MARKETING DIRECTOR
BRANWYN BIGGLESTONE - ACCOUNTS MANAGER
EMILY MILLER - ADMINISTRATIVE ASSISTANT
JAMIE PARRENO - MARKETING ASSISTANT
SARAH DELAINE - EVENTS COORDINATOR
KEVIN YUEN - DIGITAL RIGHTS COORDINATOR
JONATHAN CHAN - PRODUCTION MANAGER
DREW GILL - ART DIRECTOR
MONICA GARCIA - PRODUCTION ARTIST
VINCENT KUKUA - PRODUCTION ARTIST
JANA COOK - PRODUCTION ARTIST

WWW.IMAGECOMICS.COM

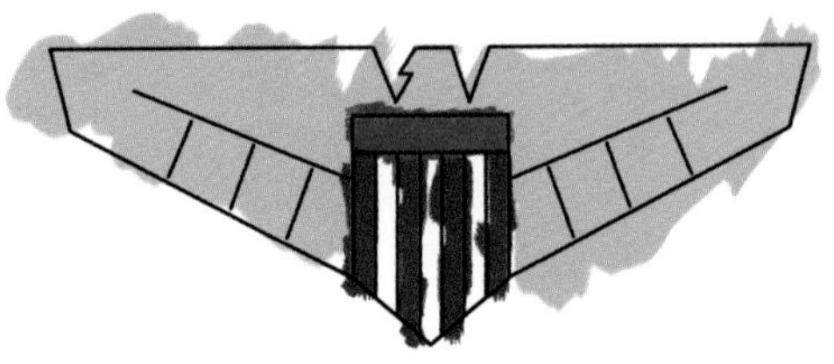

PART ONE
OKAY, LET ME SAY UP FRONT HOW ASHAMED OF MYSELF I AM OF THIS IDEA... ...AND HOW PROUD I AM... I THINK THIS ONE IS PRETTY SELF-EXPLANATORY.
LOGO + CREDITS
OF COURSE, WE'RE GOING FOR A MID-70'S HUSTLER MAGAZINE KIND OF VIBE. DON'T BE AFRAID OF THE BODY HAIR ... IT'S ABSOLUTELY NECESSARY.
PAINTING ALL?

AGE BEFORE BEAUTY.

HOW MANY POOR BASTARDS ACTUALLY *BELIEVE* THAT?

LIKE SHEEP TO THE SLAUGHTER...

NOT NECESSARILY. BESIDES, WE BOTH KNOW HE'S EXACTLY WHAT WE *NEED*...

... LET'S JUST HOPE OUR INTEL IS *ACCURATE*. NEITHER *ONE* OF US WANTS TO BE CAUGHT IN A PLACE LIKE *THIS* EMPTY-HANDED.

YEAH, WELL... I'VE *HAD* MY SHARE OF PR FIASCOS. I DON'T NEED *ANOTHER* ONE.

JUST KEEP THE SQUEAK TO A *MINIMUM*.

HE CAN SMELL *INSINCERITY* A MILE AWAY.

WHAT'RE YOU SAYING...?

-- SUPERHERO.
HOLY SHIT.
SO I KNEW THEY'D COME AROUND EVENTUALLY. AFTER ALL, THE WORLD DOESN'T GET SIMPLER. IT DOESN'T
JUST LEAVE YOU ALONE TO YOUR OWN DEVICES.
THINGS DON'T WORK LIKE THAT.
AND I WATCH ENOUGH CABLE NEWS TO KNOW... WHEN SHIT GETS WEIRD, PEOPLE GET DESPERATE.
I KNOW I DID.
MAYBE YOU TWO DIDN'T SEE THE SIGN OUTSIDE THE LOUNGE. NO PRICKS ALLOWED.
EXCEPT MINE, OF COURSE.
LUBE
MAGNUM
MAGNUM

AHHH... BUTCHER BAKER, I PRESUME.
OBVIOUSLY, WE'RE INTRUDING ON A PERSONAL MOMENT. MAYBE WE SHOULD INTRODUCE OURSELVES --
I KNOW WHO YOU ARE.
THAT DRESSER MERGER STILL A STICKING POINT ON YOUR CV, DICK...?
LIFE'S A BITCH, EH?
SAY WHAT?
ANCIENT HISTORY.
MISTER BAKER, YOU MAY KNOW WHO WE ARE, BUT IN REGARDS TO WHY WE'RE HERE, LET ME JUST --
HOLD ON...
... I WANNA SAVOR THE MOMENT.
THIS IS QUITE THE OCCASION. MY HERO HOTLINE DOESN'T RING AS OFTEN AS IT USED TO.
THEN AGAIN... YOU WOULDN'T BE HERE IF IT DID.
HERE'S TO THE GOOD OL' DAYS --
-- THE DAYS WHERE COLLATERAL DAMAGE WAS RE-BRANDED AS "ACCEPTABLE LOSSES" --
-- THE DAYS OF EVIL EMPIRES AND FEMME FATALES --
-- THE DAYS OF METHODIZED MAYHEM --
-- THE DAYS WHERE MIDDLE MANAGEMENT FUCKHEADS LIKE THESE TWO ATE THE PEANUTS OUT OF MY SHIT.
WELL... ERRR...
... WE DO HAVE SOMETHING YOU MIGHT BE... POSSIBLY INTERESTED IN...

HEY! DON'T ASSUME WHAT YOU THINK I'D BE "INTERESTED" IN, CHUCKLES...!
THINK MY TICKER NEEDS A TUNE-UP? I'M THE GODDAMN RIGHTEOUS MAKER HERE, GET IT?!
AND WHO'S THE FUCKIN' TRENCHCOAT MAFIA LURKING IN THE BACKGROUND?
YOU ACTUALLY PLAN ON TRYING TO MUSCLE ME IF I DON'T DRINK THE KOOL-AID?
NO, NOT AT ALL...
... THIS IS MORE LIKE... WELL... AN INCENTIVE.
THAT IS... WELL, WE'VE HEARD...
AHEM!
I-I MEAN... THAT YOU HAVE AN APPRECIATION FOR --
WE JUST WANT YOU TO HEAR US OUT --
-- THEY'RE SIMPLY A WAY TO INSURE THAT YOU DO.
BIG DEAL. AND OBVIOUS, TOO. I'VE NEVER MADE ANY SECRET OF MY TASTE FOR THE FINER THINGS.
I SHOULD TELL THESE TOOLS TO TAKE THEIR FRESH MEAT BRIBE AND FUCK RIGHT OFF.
UNLESS WE WERE MISINFORMED ABOUT YOUR REPUTATION AS A PUSSY HOUND. BUT I DON'T THINK WE WERE.
ON THE OTHER HAND...
... WHEN OPPORTUNITY KNOCKS...

... I KICK THE GODDAMN DOOR IN.
THAT'S HOW I ROLL, MOTHERFUCKERS.
HEADS UP OUT THERE -- THIS IS THE RIGHTEOUS MAKER BEHIND THE WHEEL OF MY BELOVED LIBERTY BELLE!
I'M BACK ON THE BLACKTOP! MAKING THE TRIP ONCE AGAIN! BROADCASTING ON ENCRYPTED CHANNEL ZERO --
-- SO ALL YOU ROAD HOGS KEEP ME UP ON THE LATEST SHENANIGANS FROM MY TWENTY, STRAIGHT DOWN TO THE HINTERLANDS.
IN THE MEANTIME, YOU CAN IMAGINE MY SURPRISE WHEN I HEARD WHAT MY IMMEDIATE FUTURE HOLDS...
"... THEY HAD IT ALL WORKED OUT FOR ME."
GO AHEAD, THEN. WHADDYA' NEED...?
WELL, UMMM...
COULD WE MAYBE WAIT UNTIL... YOU'RE FINISHED THERE...?
BUTCHER, THE NEW ADMINISTRATION WANTS TO START THINGS OFF WITH A CLEAN SLATE. THEY DON'T WANT OLD GHOSTS HANGING AROUND.
"ONE THING I'VE LEARNED OVER THE YEARS... GOVERNMENT STOOGES ALWAYS SPOUT THE SAME RAP."
"THEY NEVER SEEM TO REMEMBER WHAT SUPERHEROES ACTUALLY DO..."

... WE'RE WAY *BEYOND* THEIR SUBURBAN STANDARDS... THEIR *NEED* TO MAINTAIN THE STATUS QUO...

... BUT I GET IT. IT'S THE WORLD WE LIVE IN. THEY JUST PLAY DEAD WHEN THEY GET A GLIMPSE OF HOW WE SEE THINGS.
THESE TWO HAD BALLS, THOUGH...

AS YOU KNOW, QUITE A FEW OF YOUR ADVERSARIES ARE STILL INCARCERATED IN A FACILITY THAT SPECIALIZES IN...
... WELL... ITS SPECIALTY IS IMPRISONING INDIVIDUALS OF YOUR...
... RARIFIED PROFESSION.
WHAT JAY IS TRYING TO SAY IS THAT ALL OF YOUR ENEMIES CONTINUE TO SERVE TIME AT THE BERTRAND INSTITUTE FOR META-CRIMINAL CONTAINMENT...
OF COURSE, MOST PEOPLE KNOW IT BY ITS OTHER NAME...

"... THE CRAZY KEEP"

TAXPAYERS ARE FED UP WITH SUBSIDIZING THREE SQUARES A DAY FOR THESE GODDAMN DEVIANTS.
CONGRESS FINALLY LISTENED.
WE WANT YOU... TO GET RID OF THEM ONCE AND FOR ALL.
DO IT HOWEVER YOU PREFER. WITH OUR FULL SUPPORT.

TOOK 'EM LONG ENOUGH.
THING IS, I WAS MADE FOR THIS KIND OF WORK FROM THE VERY BEGINNING...

"... I AM THE AMERICAN DREAM --
"-- NATIONAL INGENUITY COLLIDING WITH SCIENTIFIC CHUTZPAH --
"-- A PROTOTYPE ENGINE HEART WITH MORE HORSEPOWER THAN A BIG VALLEY STI --
"-- NOT TO MENTION A HEALTHY DOSE OF NAIVITE ADDED TO THE MIX --
ALRIGHT, LET'S CUT HIM OPEN...

"-- AND WHAT DO YOU GET?
"THAT'S RIGHT, ALL YOU RUBBER BANDERS... YOU GET A BONA FIDE SUPERHERO! A MODERN-DAY WARRIOR FOR OUR TIMES!
"YOU PAINT ON YOUR COLORS AND YOU GET OUT THERE AND YOU FIGHT EVIL IN WHATEVER FORM IT HAPPENS TO COME IN! YOU FIGHT FOR WHAT YOU BELIEVE IN --
"-- WHATEVER THAT HAPPENS TO BE.
"I'VE BEEN TOLD IT WAS AN HONOR AND A PRIVILEGE TO SERVE YOU..."

... FOR A WHILE, ANYWAY.
TIME PASSES. THINGS CHANGE. AND HERE WE ARE TODAY.
SO, WHATEVER. LIVE FOR THE MOMENT, I SAY. BITTERNESS IS FOR THE WEAK.
IN THE MEANTIME...
... I'M TAKIN' IT UP.

127
FUCK ME--!

AIN'T SEEN A RIG MOVIN' THAT FAST IN AWHILE --

-- LET'S SEE WHAT THIS SUMBITCH HAS TO SAY FOR HIMSELF...!

... SO, THINK ABOUT IT, WHEN SOMEONE LIKE THAT RINGS YER BELL --
THE FUCK?!
THOUGHT IT MIGHT BE A SMOOTH RIDE TO BERTRAND, BUT HERE WE GO --

-- BUBBLE GUM MACHINE TRYIN' TO SLIDE RIGHT UP MY ASS.

GUESS I CAN HAVE A LITTLE PRE-GAME FUN.

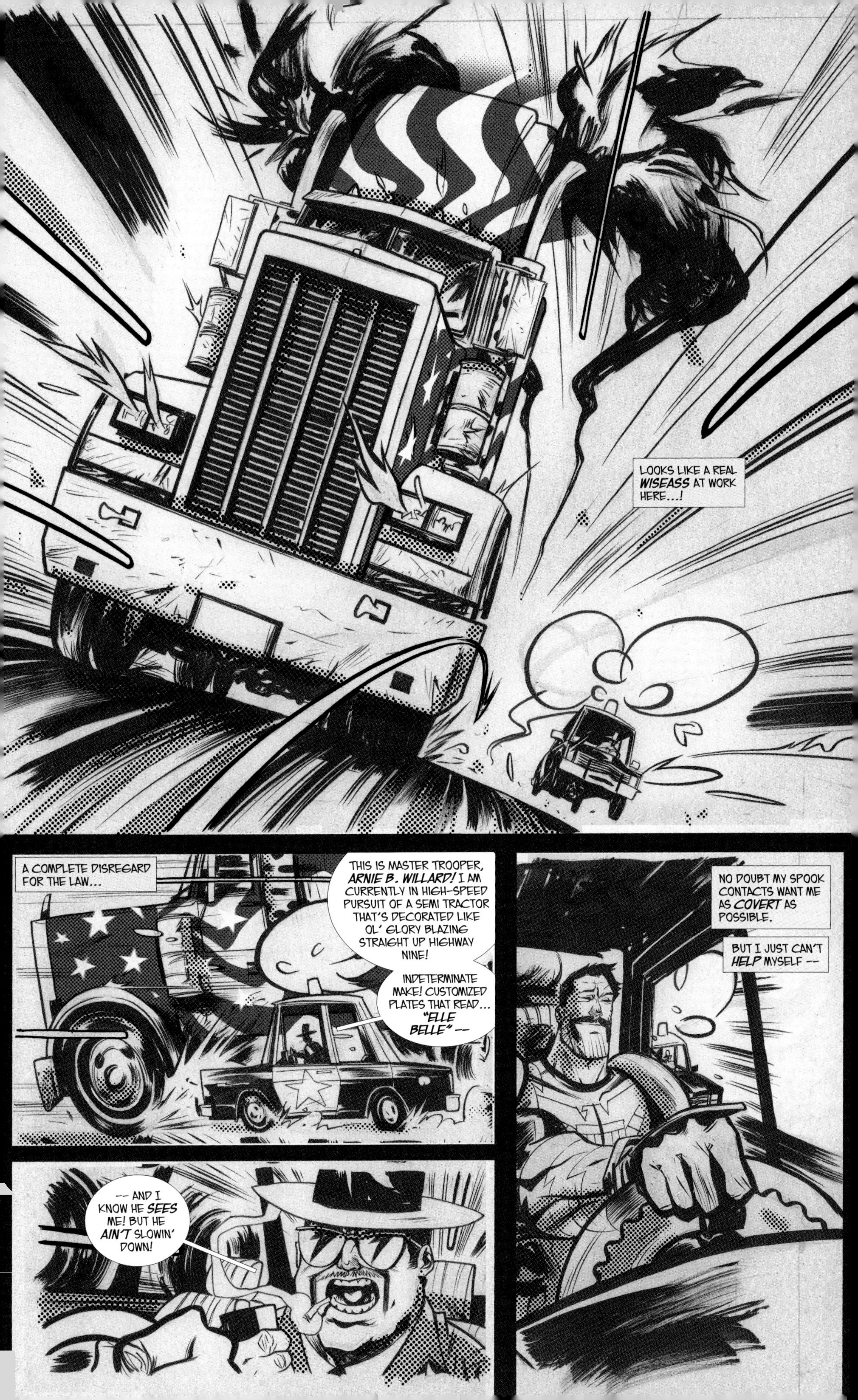

LOOKS LIKE A REAL *WISEASS* AT WORK HERE...!

A COMPLETE DISREGARD FOR THE LAW...

THIS IS MASTER TROOPER, *ARNIE B. WILLARD!* I AM CURRENTLY IN HIGH-SPEED PURSUIT OF A SEMI TRACTOR THAT'S DECORATED LIKE OL' GLORY BLAZING STRAIGHT UP HIGHWAY NINE!

INDETERMINATE MAKE! CUSTOMIZED PLATES THAT READ... *"ELLE BELLE"* --

-- AND I KNOW HE *SEES* ME! BUT HE *AIN'T* SLOWIN' DOWN!

NO DOUBT MY SPOOK CONTACTS WANT ME AS *COVERT* AS POSSIBLE.
BUT I JUST CAN'T *HELP* MYSELF --

-- JUST A LITTLE LOVE TAP.
HE'S TRYIN' TO KILL ME!
CONTROL! DO YOU COPY--?!
AS A REAL AMERICAN ICON ONCE SAID...
... "RUBBER BULLETS. HONEST."
GODDAMMIT--!

-- GONNA' TEAR HIM A NEW SHITHOLE --
ARNIE B. WILLARD HERE AGAIN! THIS PURSUIT HAS TURNED NASTY --
-- SOMEBODY BETTER SEND SOME BACK UP BEFORE I USE LETHAL FORCE ON THIS COCKSUCKER!
HOLD ON! I'LL BE GIVIN' YOU A DRIVER DESCRIPTION IN ONE HOT SECOND--!
SHIT...!
CAN'T QUITE SEE --
BOOOOM!
GAH--!
FUCK-FUCK-FUCK --

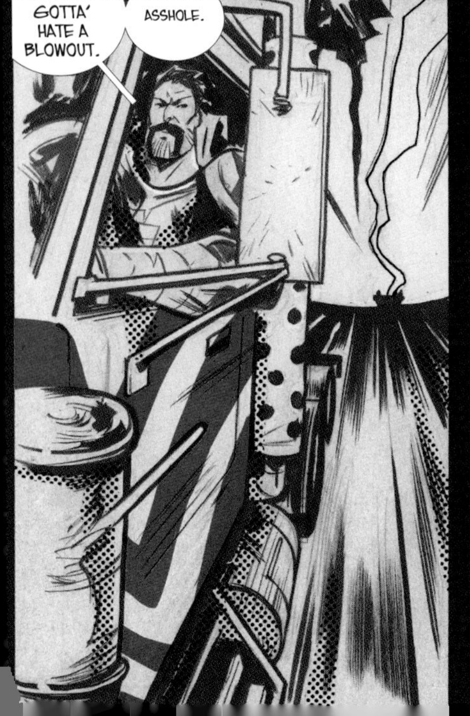
GOTTA' HATE A BLOWOUT.
ASSHOLE.

ONE THING ABOUT *ME*...
...I *NEVER* FORGET.

THIS PRICK --
-- WHO*EVER* HE IS --
-- JUST MADE MY *SUPREME SHIT LIST*.

TWO HOURS LATER:
GOOD OL' BURTRAND.
IT HASN'T CHANGED ONE BRICK.
FRANKLY, SOMEONE SHOULDA DONE THIS A LONG TIME AGO...
... PUT THESE SAD BASTARDS OUTTA THEIR MISERY.
I'VE GOT MY MANDATE --
-- LEAVE NO TRACE BEHIND --
-- AND DEAL WITH ANY AND ALL *RESISTANCE.*
NOT A PROBLEM. NOT *THESE* RENT-A-COPS.

DON'T WORRY. THESE SECURITY GUARDS CAN ROAST A FEW MARSHMALLOWS... WHEN THEY WAKE UP.
I DON'T MIND BUSTING A FEW HEADS ON THE PERIMETER.
PART OF ME WISHES I WAS DOING THIS ONE-ON-ONE...
... MORE THAN A FEW OF THESE DICKHEADS COULD USE ONE MORE BEATING BEFORE I SEND THEM INTO THE NEXT LIFE.
THE STAFF, ON THE OTHER HAND --
-- I NEED TO GET THEM OUT CLEAN --
ALERT
-- LUCKILY MY ASSHOLE BENEFACTORS SUPPLIED ME WITH A SPECIFIC ALERT CODE.

OVERRIDING EVERY TERMINAL, EVERY HANDHELD, EVERY CELL PHONE... THEY'LL GET THE MESSAGE:
"DROP EVERYTHING. GET THE FUCK OUT. *NOW.*"

HELL, I'M BETTING MOST OF THESE GUYS HAVE BEEN *WAITING* FOR THIS...

... AND THERE THEY *ARE.* EVERY LAST ONE OF THEM.
THAT'S THE KIND OF SUGAR PAPA LIKES. MAKES MY JOB THAT MUCH *EASIER.*

I HEAR THE CRICKETS IN THE BUSHES AND I FLASH BACK...

... TO A FEW *POST-COITAL* MUSINGS BACK IN PLATO'S RETREAT:
YOU LADIES HAD A JOB TO DO. YOU DID IT WELL.
WORD OF WARNING, THOUGH: MY *REFRACTORY PERIOD'S* ONLY SEVEN OR EIGHT MINUTES. SO ENJOY THE RESPITE.

YOUR BOSSES KNEW BETTER THAN TO USE GOD AND COUNTRY ON ME. DOESN'T WORK LIKE THAT ANYMORE.
I'M A SUPERHERO. WE SEE THE *BIGGER PICTURE.*
LIKE THE TIME I SAVED THE *PRESIDENT OF REALITY...*

"... OH, YOU DIDN'T KNOW THERE WAS A PRESIDENT OF REALITY? WELL, YOU SURE AS HELL CAN'T VOTE FOR HIM. BUT HE EXISTS, JUST THE SAME.
"BIT OF AN EGO ON THIS GUY. NOT THAT I BLAME HIM...
"... THE PROBLEM BEING, HE GOES THROUGH SECURITY DETAILS LIKE SHIT THROUGH A GOOSE.
PAN-DIMENSIONAL AFFIRMATION PARADE (AUTHORIZED)
"LUCKILY, I WAS THERE WHEN IT COUNTED. HE WAS THREE SECONDS AWAY FROM FRENCHING A BABY BOMB.
TALKING ABOUT OLD TIMES --
... BUT THANKS TO ME, 'TWAS NOT TO BE.
"Y'KNOW, OFFING THE PRESIDENT OF REALITY WOULD'VE BEEN A FEATHER IN THE CAP OF ANY RETRO-TERROR CULT...
-- ALMOST ALWAYS A TURN ON.

THESE DAYS, IT'S PRETTY MUCH ALL I HAVE.
MEMORIES... STORIES... MOMENTS...
... THE GREATEST LIFE EVER LIVED.
BUT WAS IT ENOUGH?
DID IT ALL ADD UP TO SOMETHING GREATER?
OR WAS IT REALLY SO UNFINISHED...
... WAITING FOR THIS MOMENT TO PUT IT ALL TO REST?
WHO THE FUCK KNOWS?
GUESS I'M NOT ONE FOR SYMBOLISM.
SUCH AS IT IS.

THE INSTANT WHEN IT'S REAL --
-- THE HEAT ON MY FACE... THE THUNDER IN MY EARS... THE FIRE IN MY EYES --
-- THAT MOMENT ISN'T QUITE THE CATHARSIS I THOUGHT IT MIGHT BE.
I IMAGINE ALL THE SCUMBAGS AND THE SHITHEADS STILL HELD INSIDE... THE MOMENT OF INCINERATION... THE MOMENT WHERE THEY REALIZE THEY'VE FINALLY LOST THE WAR...
... I THOUGHT IT MIGHT FEEL DIFFERENT.
BUT I DON'T FEEL ANYTHING.
HERE I FIGURED IT MIGHT END UP AS MY GREATEST TRIUMPH... A FINAL ACT OF PURE RIGHTEOUSNESS...
... BUT IT'S NOT.
NOT EVEN CLOSE.
BUT IF THIS AIN'T IT... I COULDN'T TELL YA WHAT IS.
AND I SURE AS HELL DON'T LIKE THAT HOW THAT FEELS.

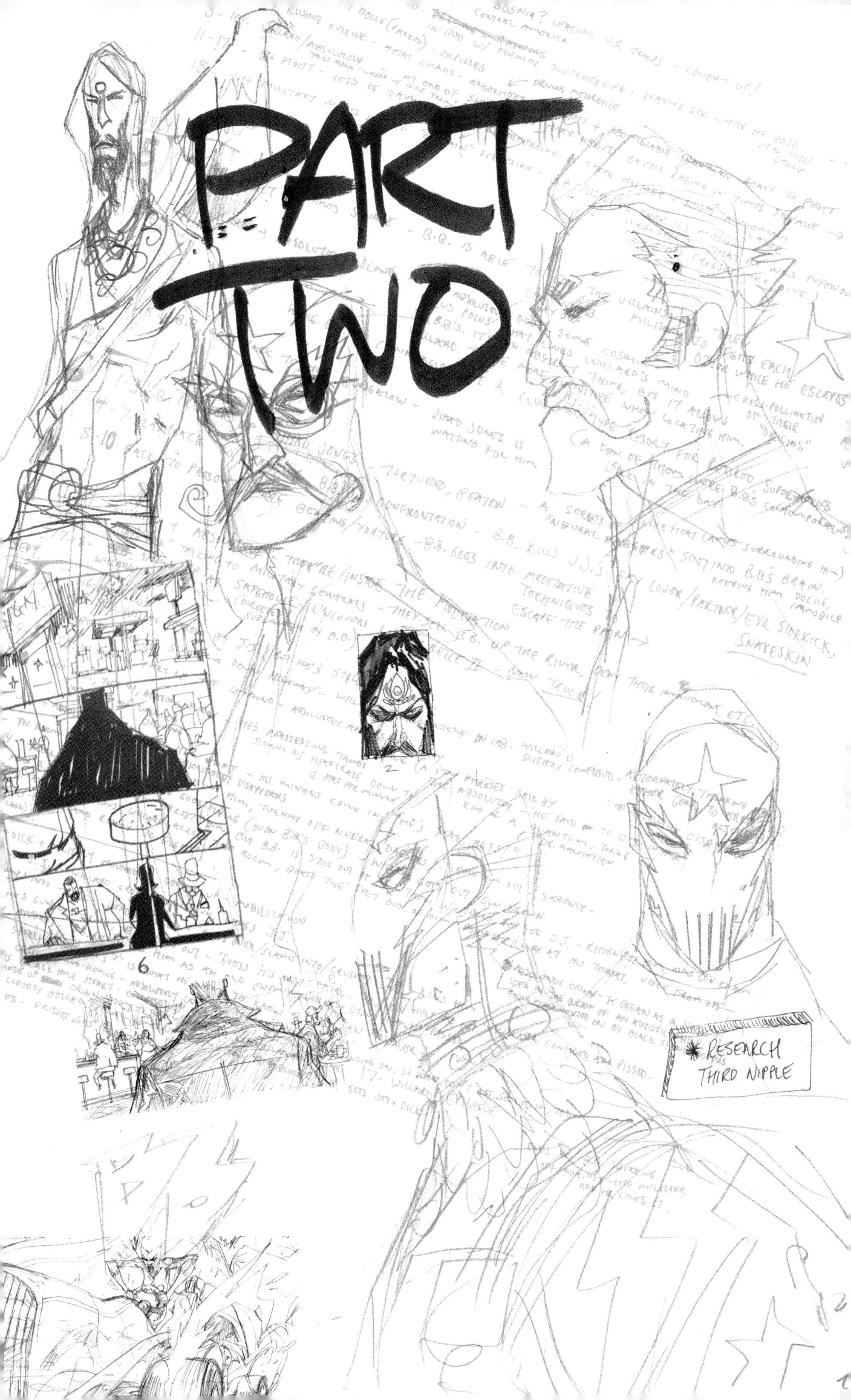
PART
TWO
*RESEARCH
THIRD NIPPLE

MISSION ACCOMPLISHED.
TEN MINUTES AGO, IT WAS THE BERTRAND INSTITUTE FOR META-CRIMINAL CONTAINMENT -- COLLOQUIALLY KNOWN AS THE CRAZY KEEP -- FILLED TO THE BRIM WITH SUPER-VILLAINS OF EVERY SHAPE AND STRIPE.
THE WHITE MEN IN THEIR BLACK SUITS WANTED THEM GONE.
AS IN, FOR GOOD.
AND, AS IT'S ALWAYS BEEN FOR AS LONG AS I CAN REMEMBER, WHEN YOU WANT SOMETHING DONE RIGHT --
-- THAT'S WHEN YOU CALL ME.
SO I BLOW'D THE MUTHAFUCKA UP REAL NICE.
EVERY ONE OF THOSE COCKSUCKERS SENT TO A FIERY GRAVE...
... JUST LIKE THOSE GOVERNMENT FUCKNUTS ASKED ME TO.
BUT IT STILL FEELS...
I DUNNO...
WHATEVER. IT WAS A CLEAN KILL.
BY THE NUMBERS. EXACTLY HOW IT SHOULD BE...
... LEAVE NO TRACE BEHIND.
OWW! WHAT THE FUCK--?!
DAT WASN'T SUPPOSED T'HAPPEN...

... WUZ IT?!
≥KAFF!≤
SOMEONE LIGHT A MATCH IN DA MAXIMUM SECURITY HEAD OR WUT...?!

SHUT THE FUCK UP, EL SUSHI. SOMEBODY JUST --
≥NG!≤
FOUND MY GEAR, AT LEAST...
CLEARLY THIS WAS A PLANNED EVENT...

... THE CRAZY KEEP -- OUR PRISON -- HAS BEEN TARGETED FOR TERMINAL DEMOLITION. AND, TO SOME DEGREE, IT WAS A SUCCESS.
AND, IF YOU'LL NOTICE, NONE OF OUR CAPTORS SEEMED TO BE PRESENT WHEN THE FIERY SHIT HIT THE FAN...

... ONLY OUR BRETHREN SUFFERED THE ULTIMATE CONSEQUENCES OF THIS ATTACK.
FAREWELL, SNAKESKIN. MAY YOUR JOURNEY IN THE NEXT LIFE BE LESS FRAUGHT WITH PERIL

SNAKESKIN? TOTAL PUSSY.
HE NEVER MADE A SCORE HE DIDN'T BITCH ABOUT AFTERWARDS.
SURVIVAL OF THE FITTEST.
ANYONE EVER WORK WITH ARTHUR BLUDD? HERE'S YOUR CHANCE TO SAY YOUR GOODBYES...

WE ARE BOUND BY EXPERIENCE. ALL OF US... FORGED IN FIRE.
WE LIVE TO FIGHT AGAIN.

AMEN, JONES. I WANNA FIND OUT WHO DID THIS... LET 'EM KNOW I DON'T APPRECIATE ATTEMPTED EXECUTION.
RIGHT. UP CLOSE AN' PERSONAL.
REVENGE IS A DISH THAT'S BEST SERVED COLD.

YOU'RE A MASTER OF THE POP CLICHÉ, SNOWMAN.
HOW 'BOUT WE KEEP LOOKING FOR SOME KIND OF CLUE INSTEAD OF MAKING USELESS PROCLAMATIONS...
THAT'S ABOMINABLE SNOWMAN, LADY. GET IT RIGHT NEXT TIME.
WHATEVER.
AND IT'S WHITE LIGHTNING, NOT "LADY".

SIGH
WHERE ARE YOU WHEN I NEED YOU, JETBOY...?

ANY OF US STILL OUT THERE WHO MIGHT'VE --
QUESTIONS AND ANSWERS...
... TRUTH AND LIES...

... ONLY PERSPECTIVE SEPARATES THEM.
HOW DID I GET HERE?

SELF-ACTUALIZATION. LIMITLESS POTENTIALITIES. A HIERARCHY OF NEEDS.
I REMAIN WHAT THEY SAY I HAVE ALWAYS BEEN...
WHOA... THE EXPLOSION MUST'VE DAMAGED THE NULL FIELD CELL BLOCK...
SO... HE REALLY GOT OUT, DIDN'T HE...?
FUCK ME.

... THE ABSOLUTELY.

JIHAD JONES.
A WORD.
MAKE IT A GOOD ONE.

YOU KNOW THEY'RE AFRAID OF YOU...
YET YOU DO NOT SHARE THEIR FEAR. YOU PRESENT YOURSELF AS A KINDRED SOUL TO THE PLIGHT OF THE AFFLICTED --

-- BUT YOU ARE NOT ONE OF THEM.
WE ALL HAVE OUR PAIN.
I SEE THE SIMILARITIES. CERTAINLY, AFTER THIS, WE SHARE A COMMON ITCH. I DON'T NECESSARILY VIEW IT AS REVENGE...

... IT'S MORE ABOUT CLOSURE.
SOMETHING THEY WILL NEVER UNDERSTAND.
SHIT. THEY'RE TALKIN' ABOUT US, AREN'T THEY...?

DEMOTION OF EMOTION. THE NEED TO EVOLVE IS STRONG INDEED...
HOW POETICALLY OBTUSE. YOU HAVEN'T CHANGED A BIT DURING YOUR PERIOD OF INCARCERATION.

NOT ALTOGETHER TRUE.
I SAW MYSELF IN THE ABYSS. COLD EYES STARING BACK AT ME.
SOMETHING STIRRED...

... A COMPULSION TO COMMUNICATE.
AS USUAL, YOUR TIMING IS IMPECCABLE.
PERHAPS YOUR "COSMIC INSIGHT" COULD ACTUALLY BE OF SOME USE TO US.

PERHAPS YOU'RE RIGHT.
THERE IS ALWAYS SOMETHING WORTH CONSIDERING IN THIS WORLD...
WAIT --

INCOMPREHENSIBLE CREATURE...!

HEY, JONES --

-- WE'RE GETTIN' THE FUCK UP OUTTA HERE!
YOU WITH US?

Casey's
CHOKE N PUKE
DINER
EVERY ENGINE NEEDS FUEL. EVEN MINE.
I PARK IN THE BACK. NO NEED TO ADVERTISE.
BACK IN THE SHIT NOW.

IT'S EASY TO *LOSE YOURSELF* IN A DIVE LIKE THIS. PROBABLY WHY MOST OF 'EM COME HERE.
ME, I JUST NEED A *DRINK*... OR TWO...

... OR *TEN*.

PATRON.
DOUBLE.
AND KEEP 'EM COMING.
YOU NEED TO SEE SOME I.D....?
STILL NOT ENOUGH.
MY GODDAMN BRAIN STILL ITCHES.

LOOKS LIKE THIS BULLDOG'S GOT AN ITCH OF HIS OWN...
YOU'D BETTER SLOW IT DOWN, PARDNER. A WORLD OF REGRET'S WAITIN' FOR YA...
?
...THAT THERE ROCKET SAUCE DON'T MESS AROUND.
KINDA THE IDEA. I'M LOOKING TO FORGET MYSELF FOR A FEW HOURS.
I'VE HAD A HELLUVA NIGHT.
HMMF. YOU AN' ME BOTH.
I PLANTED MY ASS TO DO A LITTLE FERGETTIN' MY OWN SELF...
...BUT, Y'KNOW WHAT? THAT AIN'T NEITHER HERE NOR THERE.
I MAY BE DRINKIN'... BUT I'M STILL THINKIN'.
WELL, THEN... FER CHRISSAKES, LET'S HAVE OURSELVES A TOAST.
TO... THE BEST LAID PLANS...
...EVEN WHEN THEY END UP FUCKIN' YOU IN THE ASS.
POWERFUL FORTUNE COOKIE SHIT.
I CAN DRINK TO THAT, STRANGER...
...HERE'S TO YA.
WHATEVER YA DO, WILLARD OL' BOY...
...DON'T TELL HIM WHAT HAPPENED.

LOOKIE HERE... I'LL TELL YA WHAT THE REAL PROBLEM IS NOWADAYS...
...NO RESPECT FER A MAN WEARING A BADGE.
THIS IS ONE SAD FUCKER...
...WHOEVER HE IS.
C'MON, NOW! DON'T GO GETTIN' DOWN ON YOURSELF...!
SOMETIMES IT'S WAR OUT THERE! YOU CAN'T JUDGE VICTORY ON ANY SINGLE BATTLE Y'MIGHT WIN OR LOSE!
IT'S ONE OF THOSE -- WHADDYA CALL IT? -- CUMULATIVE EFFECTS THAT HAPPENS OVER TIME.
AS MANY TIMES AS I'VE BEEN KNEE-DEEP IN IT, IT'S THOSE EXPERIENCES THAT MAKE A MAN THE MAGNIFICENT BASTARD HE CAN BE.
WELL, THIS WAS DEFINITELY AN EXPERIENCE. LEMME TELL YA... I AIN'T OVER IT YET.
STILL PISSES ME OFF JUST TO THINK ABOUT IT.
MY RECORD AS A LAWMAN WAS SPOTLESS...
...BUT THAT WAS BEFORE TONIGHT.
HOLD ON THERE, COWBOY. WHAT EXACTLY HAPPENED...?
SIGH...
FUCK IT.
HIGH-SPEED PURSUIT. ME AND THIS MOTHERFUCKER OF A RIG I'D CLOCKED AT AROUND ONE-TWENTY.
GAVE ME A BIT OF CHIN MUSIC. NUTHIN' I COULDN'T HANDLE.
BUT THEN IT GOT NASTY...SENT ME HEAD-OVER-ASS AND LEFT ME LIKE A GODDAMN USELESS PAPERWEIGHT IN THE MIDDLE OF THE ROAD...

HOLY CHRIST.
...SOME RED, WHITE AND BLUE HIPPIE MOBILE WITH ABSOLUTELY NO REGARD FOR THE LAW...!
THE DIPSHIT I FUCKED WITH ON THE WAY TO BERTRAND...!
I'LL TELL YOU RIGHT HERE AN' NOW...I'LL MAKE IT MY LIFE'S MISSION TO TRACK THIS SUMBITCH DOWN...!
WITH ALMIGHTY GOD AS MY WITNESS --
-- I'LL TEAR THE TONGUE OUTTA HIS HEAD AND THE BALLS FROM HIS BODY!
NOBODY MAKES AN ASS OUTTA' ARNIE B. WILLARD AN' GETS AWAY WITH IT!
JEEZUS.
OLD MAN'S ON A TEAR NOW...
AH HELL... MY BACK TEETH ARE FLOATIN'...
NICE TO SHARE A DRINK WITH A SOMEONE WHO GETS IT...
BE BACK... Y'KNOW... MOMENTARILY...
I'LL BET YOU WILL.
BETTER TO LET THIS POOR BASTARD WALLOW ALONE.
HE'D NEVER PUT TWO AND TWO TOGETHER ANYWAY...
BUT JUST IN CASE...
...NNNNNN...
AAHHHH...

AWWWW YEAH...
SO, I'M THINKING WE SHOULD MAYBE ORDER SOME *GRUB* TO HELP SOAK UP ALL THIS --
-- BOOZE...?
NOW WHERE THE HELL DID HE --
WHU...?

WELCOME TO ONE OF MY OLD SAFEHOUSES...

... IT'S BEEN *YEARS* SINCE ANYONE'S *BEEN* HERE, BUT MAKE YOURSELVES AT HOME.
CHRIST... THIS STUFF IS STILL *STATE-OF-THE-ART...*
JIHAD JONES DON'T MESS AROUND...!

QUIT KISSING ASS, SUSHI.
AND KEEP YOUR MUSHY BUTT OUT OF MY WAY WHILE I CRACK SOME BLACK BOX FILES TO TRY AND FIND OUT WHO *DID* THIS TO US...!

GUESS WHITE LIGHTNING'S GOT HER HACK ON...
Y'KNOW, IT COULDA BEEN *TERRORISTS* TRYIN' TO --

WHAT'RE YOU *TALKING* ABOUT?! *WE'RE* THE TERRORISTS...
... WHY *ELSE* DO YOU THINK THEY LOCKED US UP AND THREW AWAY THE KEY?!

YOU'RE LIKE A GHOST WHO WILL NOT ENTER THE LIGHT.

FAIR WARNING. THE CONCEPTS OF LIFE AND DEATH ARE BEYOND ME NOW.
OR SO I'VE BEEN TOLD.

BY WHOM, I WONDER...?
SO ARE WE THE FLAME TO YOUR MOTH? YOU SEEM TO BE MUCH MORE SOCIABLE THAN ANY OF US ARE USED TO...

YOU AIN'T GETTING ANYWHERE, ARE YOU, SWEETHEART?
HOW 'BOUT LETTING OL' ANGERHEAD TAKE A PASS AT --

-- OWWW!
FUCKIN' HELL, LADY--!
WELL, I'M STILL TROLLING THE PENTAGON DATABASE! SO BACK OFF--!

THEY SMELL A CONSPIRACY. I THINK THEY'RE GIVING THEMSELVES TOO MUCH CREDIT.
MY INSTINCTS TELL ME THIS IS MORE... PERSONAL.
DEFINE "PERSONAL"...

YOU WOULDN'T UNDERSTAND. IT TOOK ME YEARS TO EMBRACE REALITY...!
TRUE CONFLICT DOES NOT HINGE ON NATIONAL IDEOLOGY OR POLITICAL IDEALS...
... IT HINGES ON THE FIRE BURNING IN ONE MAN'S EYES!
INDIVIDUALISM AND THE WILL TO PILFER.
THE SEARCH FOR MEANING IN CHAOS. ALL FOR NAUGHT. NOTHING IS RANDOM, YOU KNOW.
ALLOW ME TO INFLUENCE THE OUTCOME...
SHIT.
COMPUTER'S FREAKING OUT... LOCATING DATA FROM SOMEWHERE...!
I DON'T GET IT. HOW DID --
-- MASTER TROOPER, ARNIE B. WILLARD! I AM CURRENTLY IN HIGH-SPEED PURSUIT OF A SEMI TRACTOR THAT'S DECORATED LIKE OL' GLORY BLAZING STRAIGHT UP HIGHWAY NINE!
HIGHWAY NINE! THAT LEADS STRAIGHT TO BERTRAND--!
INDETERMINATE MAKE! CUSTOMIZED PLATES THAT READ... "ELLE BELLE" --
-- AND I KNOW HE SEES ME! BUT HE AIN'T SLOWIN' DOWN!
"ELLE BELLE"...
... THE RIGHTEOUS MAKER...!

OUR OLD ENEMY... FINALLY RETURNED TO ATTEMPT A --
-- VICTORY LAP...?
...

AND YOU KNEW THE ENTIRE TIME, DIDN'T YOU...?
"ABSOLUTELY".

YOU HEAR THAT?! THAT SMOKEY JUST DESCRIBED THE LIBERTY BELLE!
BUTCHER BAKER'S RIDE!

BAKER! DAT PIECE A' SHIT!
TOO MANY TIMES HE KNOCKED MY DICK IN THE DIRT...

"... AND, GODDAMMIT, I THINK HE LOVED DOIN' IT!"

YEAH, FOR A SUPERHERO, HE WAS A SADISTIC SON OF A BITCH.
EVERY TIME I GOT INTO IT WITH HIM...

"... HE SEEMED TO GO OUT OF HIS WAY TO HUMILIATE ME AS HE WAS KICKIN' MY ASS."

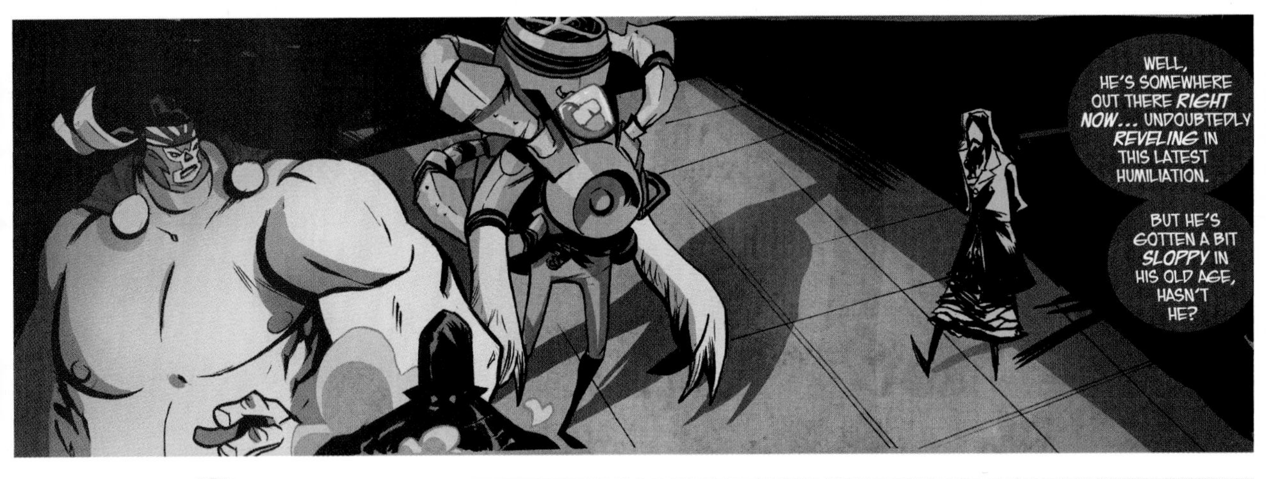

WELL, HE'S SOMEWHERE OUT THERE *RIGHT NOW*... UNDOUBTEDLY *REVELING* IN THIS LATEST HUMILIATION.
BUT HE'S GOTTEN A BIT *SLOPPY* IN HIS OLD AGE, HASN'T HE?

OUR *SURVIVAL* IS TESTAMENT TO THAT.
AND OUR SUBSEQUENT *FREEDOM* WILL BE HIS UNDOING.

I CAN *FEEL* IT EMANATING OFF YOUR SOULS. THE LONGING. THE YEARNING.
YOU ALL WANT *REVENGE*...
... BUT WHO AMONG YOU WILL HAVE IT *FIRST?*

WE HAVE THE *NUMBERS*... BUT NOT THE *ORGANIZATION*.

QUITE THE DILEMMA.

WELL, NOW THAT WE KNOW WHO WE'RE *UP AGAINST*, I'VE ALREADY GOT A PLAN TO --

HEY--! WHERE THE FUCK DID *WHITE LIGHTNING* DISAPPEAR TO...?!

GODDAMN IT! SHE'S ALREADY ON THE *HUNT--!*

THAT WAS AN ODD COINCIDENCE.
AND I DON'T BELIEVE IN COINCIDENCES.
I HOPE I'M BREAKING THE NEEDLE ON THIS ONE, BECAUSE THIS REALLY NEEDS TO BE SAID --
-- THAT CHOKE N' PUKE OFF THE SEVENTY-SIXER, THEY NEED TO START SCREENING THEIR CLIENTELE.
THEY'LL LET ANYONE UP IN THERE THESE DAYS! IT JUST AIN'T THE EYEBALL IT ONCE WAS...!
NOW MY MIND DOESN'T GENERALLY LEND ITSELF TO MICROCOSMIC THOUGHTS, BUT I COULDN'T HELP BUT THINK TO MYSELF --
-- DO ANY OF US REALLY KNOW WHEN IT'S THE END OF AN ERA?
I'LL ADMIT, SELF-AWARENESS WAS NEVER MY STRONG SUIT...
... BUT I'M STARTING TO WONDER IF THIS FUNNY FEELING I'VE BEEN HAVING IS ACTUALLY --
EH...?
DÉJÀ VU.
ONE THING I'LL SAY FOR HIM --

-- HE'S TENACIOUS AS HELL.
THERE YOU ARE, YOU GOOSE-PRICK!
BREAKER-BREAKER! THIS IS ARNIE B. WILLARD WITH A MESSAGE ON ALL AVAILABLE CHANNELS AN' I AIN'T JUST BLOWIN' MUD --
166.8
THIS SHOULD BE GOOD...
KKKKKK
-- IF YER LISTENING, MR. NO-REGARD-FOR-THE-LAW... I WANT YOU T'KNOW THAT I'M COMIN' FOR YA!
I'M CRAWLIN' RIGHT UP YER ASS RIGHT NOW --
HE'S A POET AND HE DOESN'T KNOW IT.
-- AND I'M GONNA BURY MYSELF IN YER COLON LIKE CANCER!
I'M GONNA BURN THROUGH YER PROSTATE AND FEED YER BALLS TO THE SHARKS --
-- AND WHEN THAT'S DONE, I'M GONNA --
WUT THE HELL--?!

YEEOOWWW--!
WUT THE MIGHTY FUCK IZZAT?!
NOW... THE EASY PART.
EAT ME, BUTCHER BAKER.

PART THREE
GLORY HOLE TECNOLOGY
A
B

WELL, *THIS* IS A FUCKIN' PICKLE...!

EVERY FEW HOURS, THEY WALTZ IN HERE AND REPLACE MY GODDAMN *MORPHINE DRIP*...

...ACTIN' LIKE I AIN'T EVEN *HERE*.

THEY ASKED ME WHAT I WANNA *WATCH* TO TAKE MY *MIND* OFFA THINGS.
LESBIAN PORN.
WELL, WHAT WOULD *YOU* SAY?

I'LL TELL YA *THIS* MUCH... SOMEONE SHIT ON THE *WRONG LAWMAN*.
ARNIE B. WILLARD DON'T JUST LAY DOWN AN *DIE* FOR *NO ONE*.
ALTHOUGH, CONSIDERING WHAT *HAPPENED*...

... YOU'D THINK I MIGHT AS WELL HAVE.
I WAS BACK ON THE SCENT. BACK IN MY ELEMENT. HIGH-SPEED PURSUIT ON THIS GREAT NATION'S BYWAYS.
I HAD THAT LAW-BREAKING FUCKFACE IN MY CROSSHAIRS...
... BUT SOME FORCE O' NATURE WAS TRYIN' TO SNAKE HIM OUT FROM UNDER ME--!
BREAKER-BREAKER, CONTROL --
-- GOT A BRAND NEW BOGEY IN THE MIX! NO VISIBLE TAGS!
I AIN'T LETTIN' "ELLE BELLE" OUTTA MY SIGHT! BUT I MAY NEED SOME BACK UP--!
OH YES!
THIS IS WHAT I'VE BEEN MISSING--!

I SEE YOU IN THERE, RIGHTEOUS MAKER --
-- YOU'RE NOT LOOKING SO GOOD, Y'KNOW THAT?!
NO KIDDING...
YOU'RE SWEATING ME! IT'S SO OBVIOUS!
I THINK YOU REALLY WANT SOME OF THIS--!
OH, YOU GOTTA' BE SHITTING ME--!
NNGG!

I STARTED GETTIN' A BAD FEELING...
CONTROL! WE GOT LOW TRAFFIC RIGHT NOW, BUT THIS THING IS HEADED FER THE I-12 INTERCHANGE --
-- AND WE GOT OURSELVES A GODDAMN STUNT DRIVER HERE!
YEEEAAHHH--!
RIGHT THERE!
GODDAMMIT, LIGHTNING --
-- CRAZY BITCH--!

FIRST, I'M GONNA' FRY YOUR BALLS! AND THEN --
-- OH SHIT!
LIKE IT WUZ HAPPENIN' IN SLOW MOTION...
THE HAIRS ON MY NUTS STARTED VIBRATIN'...
MUTHAFUCKA --

NOW, I AIN'T MUCH OF A FIRE N' BRIMSTONE KINDA' GUY --
-- BUT IF THAT WASN'T HELL, THEN I DON'T KNOW WHAT IS.
BUTCHER --
-- YOU COCKSUCKER!
ALL THESE YEARS --
-- YOU NEVER FIGURED OUT HOW TO FUCK ME RIGHT!
THERE I WAS.
LIKE DOGSHIT ON THE SIDE OF THE ROAD...

... WAITING TO BE *STEPPED* ON.

KNOCKY-KNOCK!

EL SUSHI IN DA HOUSE!

SUBTLE.

WHAT'S THAT SMELL...?

... BUT I CAN TELL BY YOUR *FACES* THAT NONE OF YOU HAD *THIS* IN MIND.
AH WELL.
HORSES FOR COURSES.

JIHAD JONES. YOU GOT HERE FIRST.
SO... BUTCHER'S NOT AROUND.
OR DID YOU ALREADY...

WHATEVER WORKS.
YOU HAVE AN OPINION YOU'D LIKE TO *EXPRESS?*
THIS IS ***BULLSHIT,*** JONES!

ME, SUSHI AND SNOWMAN... WE'RE WORKING ***TOGETHER*** TO FIND THIS FUCK AND ***SQUASH HIM*** LIKE A BUG!
THAT'S WHAT WE ***AGREED*** TO -- IN ***YOUR*** SAFEHOUSE, EVEN!

NOW YOU WANNA ACT ALL ***HOT SHIT*** ON US --
-- GLK!
MY DEAR ANGERHEAD. I FIND MYSELF CONSTANTLY REASSESSING THE VERY IDEA OF A ***"SUPER-VILLAIN TEAM-UP."***

-- SIGNAL MATCH: 89.33% AND RISING...
A-HA...
... PERFECT TIMING.
GYUH--!
KAFF--!
IF THE RIGHTEOUS MAKER HAS MADE LIKE A GHOST... THEN THE OBVIOUS MOVE IS TO TRACK THE BEST GHOST HUNTER.
IN THIS CASE, OUR SISTER-IN-ARMS, WHITE LIGHTNING. NOW THERE'S SOME TEAM-UP MOJO AT WORK...
... WOULDN'T YOU AGREE, ANGERHEAD?
S-SURE...
... WHATEVER YOU SAY.
C'MON, JONES!
YER GONNA PUT YER TRUST IN DAT WACKY BITCH OVER US?!
WELL, SHE DID FIND HIM FIRST...
"TRUST" IS A RELATIVE TERM, EL SUSHI.
AND FINDING HIM IS ONLY PART OF THE OVERALL EQUATION.
AS I'M SURE OUR FAIR LADY IS DISCOVERING AS WE SPEAK...

OH BAAYY-BBEEEE--!
I WANNA CHAR-BROIL YOUR BURGER, BAKER!
FUCK ME.
SHE'S GOT THE JUICE TO DO IT, TOO --
IT'LL TAKE MORE THAN THAT TO KNOCK THE LIBERTY BELLE OFF THE BLACKTOP --

-- THIS OL' LADY LOVES TO STAY ON TOP.
TRAFFIC'S ALWAYS A BITCH, THOUGH.
SHE DON'T GIVE A GODDAMN.
SHE AIN'T JUST OUT FOR BLOOD --
-- SHE'S HORNY OVER THIS SHIT.
I WANT YOU TO WANT ME, BAKER!
YOU WANNA' SEND ME TO HELL --

-- I'LL BE TAKING YOU WITH ME!
RARE TO BE AROUND A CHICK I HAVE NO INTEREST IN FUCKING --
-- *THIS* IS ONE OF THOSE TIMES.
I HATE TO *DO* THIS --
-- BUT I'M ON A REAL *SELF-PRESERVATION* TRIP.

BELLE'S FIGHTING ME. THIS IS MORE OF A WORKOUT THAN SHE WAS EXPECTING.
STATIC ELECTRICITY. I CAN FEEL IT -- THE HAIRS ON THE BACK OF MY NECK...
I NEED TO TOUCH YOU --
OH DAMN --
-- WITH MY ELECTRIC DIM MAK!
SHE'S GOT THE DEATH TOUCH. NO DOUBT ABOUT IT --
-- BUT THIS AIN'T OVER YET.

YOU CAN'T SHAKE ME, BAKER!
I'M THE SCAB THAT WON'T HEAL--!
WHATEVER.
BEING A PROFESSIONAL SUPERHERO... THERE'S NO FORMAL TRAINING FOR THAT JOB.
IT INVOLVES A HELLUVA LOT OF IMPROVISATION --
-- NOT TO MENTION INSTINCT --
-- AND A BIT OF HOPE THAT THE ANGELS ARE SMILIN' ON YA' --
NO--!

-- AND THE CONFIDENCE THAT YOU'RE DOING THE RIGHT FUCKIN' THING.
ELECTRICITY AND WATER. NOT A GOOD MIX.
ELECTROCUTED THIS BITCH RIGHT OUTTA HER MISBEGOTTEN LIFE.
A SINKING FEELING IN THE PIT OF MY STOMACH BRINGS BACK WHAT LITTLE I KNEW ABOUT HER...
... ORPHANED RUNAWAY PLUCKED OFF THE STREETS, SUBJECTED TO BLACK MARKET GENETIC EXPERIMENTS. AND WAY TOO YOUNG TO HANDLE IT.
NO IDEA WHAT HER REAL NAME WAS...
... BUT SHE CALLED HERSELF WHITE LIGHTNING.
AND THERE IT IS.
UNDENIABLE PROOF THAT I FUCKED UP.
STUPID OLD MAN.
SO WHO ELSE MADE IT OUT OF THE CRAZY KEEP ALIVE?
WHO ELSE IS GUNNING FOR ME?

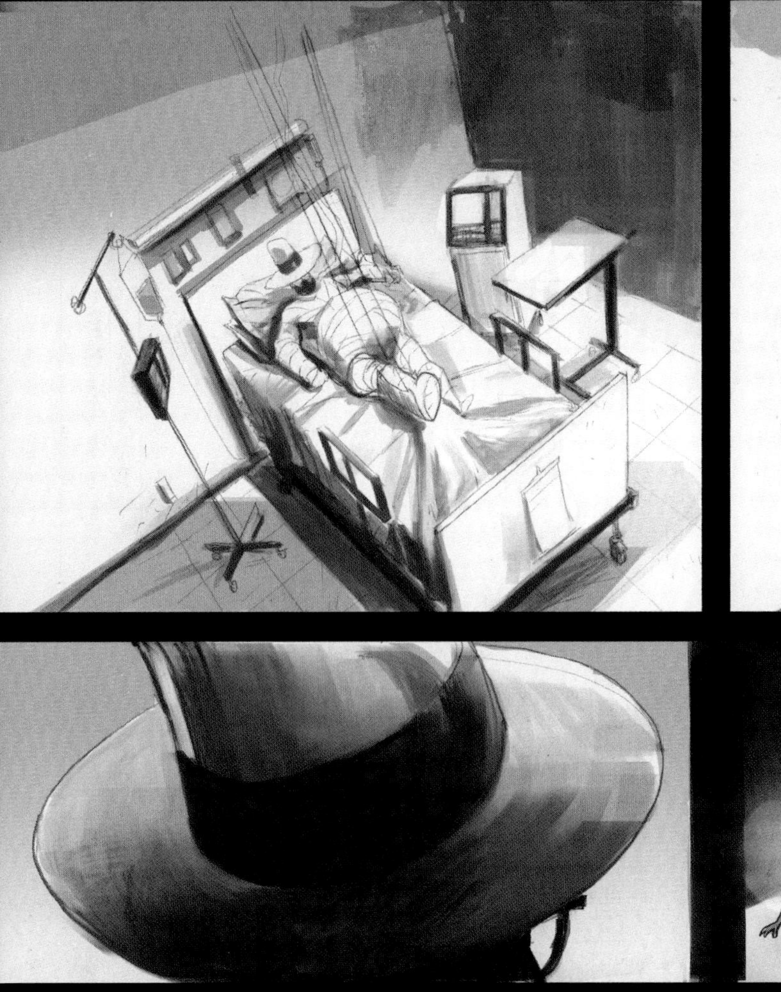

THE INFIRMED AND THE INJURED...
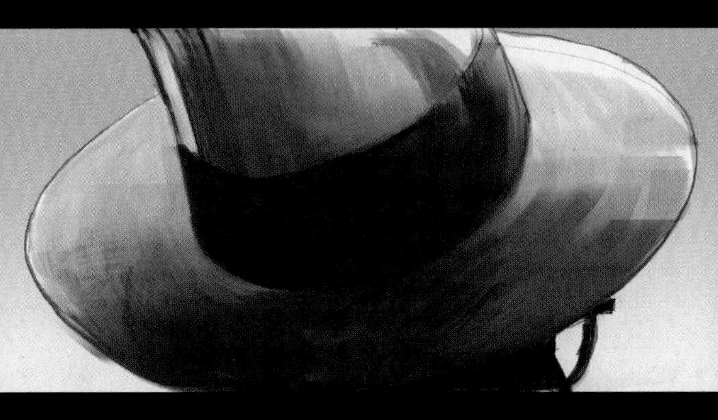

... AT WHAT POINT WILL *THEY* INHERIT ALL OF EXISTENCE?
WE ARE ALL SO *BROKEN*... EACH IN OUR OWN WAYS.

SAY WHU--?
WHO THE FUCK'RE *YOU*...?!
A QUESTION I OFTEN PONDER. FOR *NOW*, I AM WHAT I HAVE ACCEPTED MYSELF TO BE...

... ALBEIT WITH A SLIGHT DEGREE OF *RELUCTANCE*...
... *THE ABSOLUTELY.*
ALLOW ME TO *DEMONSTRATE* WHAT IT IS I AM *CAPABLE* OF...
GAAAAAAHHH--

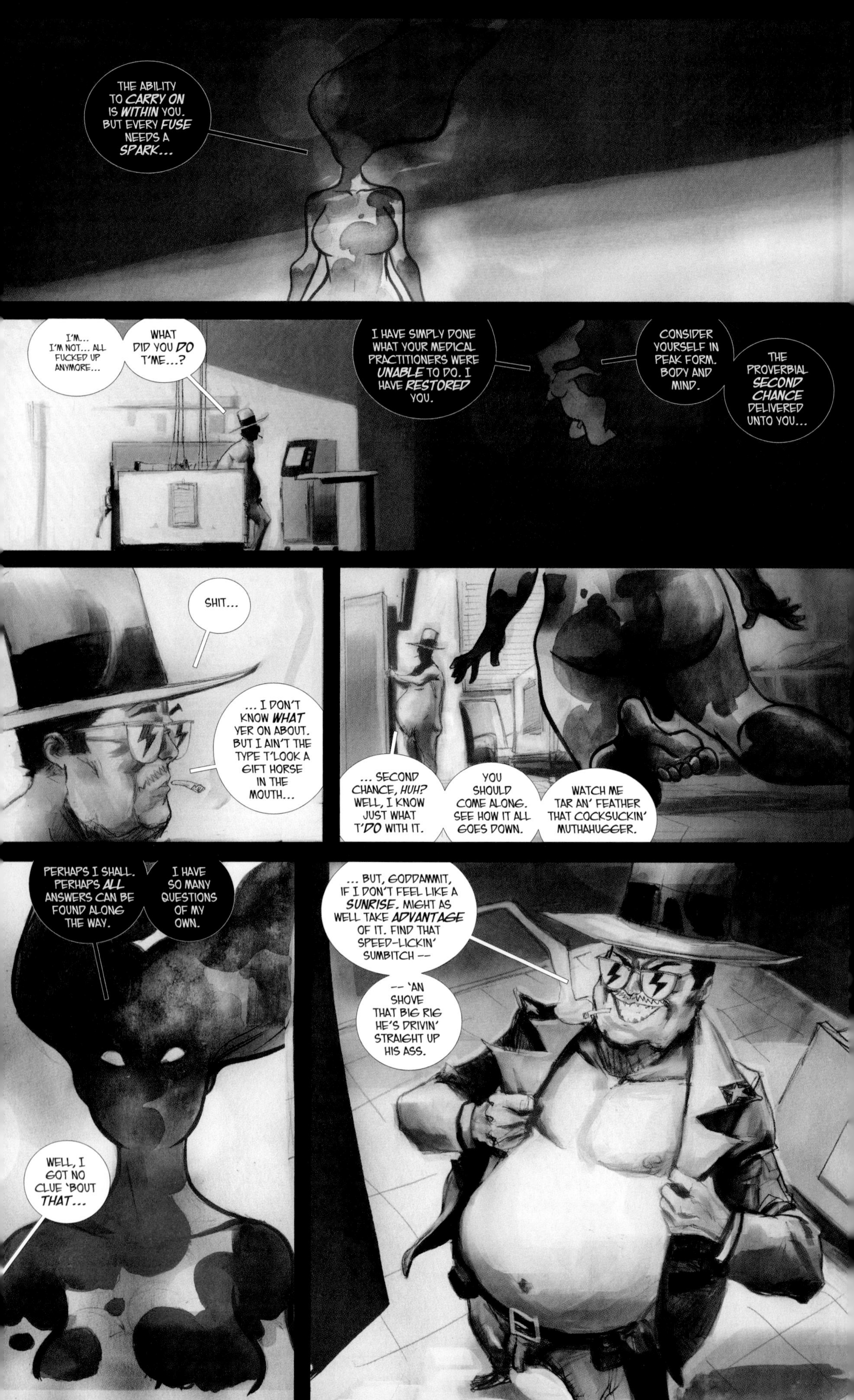
THE ABILITY TO CARRY ON IS WITHIN YOU. BUT EVERY FUSE NEEDS A SPARK...
I'M... I'M NOT... ALL FUCKED UP ANYMORE...
WHAT DID YOU DO T'ME...?
I HAVE SIMPLY DONE WHAT YOUR MEDICAL PRACTITIONERS WERE UNABLE TO DO. I HAVE RESTORED YOU.
CONSIDER YOURSELF IN PEAK FORM. BODY AND MIND.
THE PROVERBIAL SECOND CHANCE DELIVERED UNTO YOU...
SHIT...
...I DON'T KNOW WHAT YER ON ABOUT. BUT I AIN'T THE TYPE T'LOOK A GIFT HORSE IN THE MOUTH...
...SECOND CHANCE, HUH? WELL, I KNOW JUST WHAT T'DO WITH IT.
YOU SHOULD COME ALONG. SEE HOW IT ALL GOES DOWN.
WATCH ME TAR AN' FEATHER THAT COCKSUCKIN' MUTHAHUGGER.
PERHAPS I SHALL. PERHAPS ALL ANSWERS CAN BE FOUND ALONG THE WAY.
I HAVE SO MANY QUESTIONS OF MY OWN.
WELL, I GOT NO CLUE 'BOUT THAT...
...BUT, GODDAMMIT, IF I DON'T FEEL LIKE A SUNRISE. MIGHT AS WELL TAKE ADVANTAGE OF IT. FIND THAT SPEED-LICKIN' SUMBITCH --
-- 'AN SHOVE THAT BIG RIG HE'S DRIVIN' STRAIGHT UP HIS ASS.

PART FOUR
NO BACKGROUN
LOGO IN DIFFERENT PLACES ON EACH COVER
LOGO + CREDITS
TOO TALL CABIN
STRETCH
IT SHOULD BE CENTERED ON THE COVER, SO WE GET A HEALTHY AMOUNT OF NEGATIVE SPACE, ESPECIALLY AROUND THE EDGES OF THE COVER
MOVEMENT ... POWER ... BADASS-NESS

"Y'KNOW, SOME SAY THAT LOSING A WAR IS AN ART UNTO ITSELF.
"THE IRAQIS KNEW HOW TO GIVE A FINAL 'FUCK YOU' AS THEY HAULED THEIR ASSES BACK ACROSS THE BORDER. THE OL' SCORCHED EARTH POLICY OF RETREAT.
"ME? I WAS TOTALLY IN MY ELEMENT."
YOU THINK YOU CAN HIDE OUT HERE, BUT IT'S STILL COWBOYS AN' INDIANS...
THIS PLACE... KINDA' LIKE THE WILD WEST, EH, GATOR?

... WHILE THE GODDAMN WORLD ENDS ALL AROUND US.
SIR...?
IS THE TARGET INCAPACITATED?
AND THEN SOME. YOU CAN FINALLY CROSS THE PALE GATOR OFF THE FEDS' MOST WANTED LIST.
JUST DON'T TALK TO ME ABOUT EXTRADITION LAWS. THIS SHITHEAD DOESN'T APPLY.
HOLD ONTO THIS FOR ME, WOULDJA?
SH-SHOULD WE ARRANGE FOR YOUR TRANSPORT BACK TO --
-- THE STATES?

NOT THIS TIME.
"SO, YEAH. I DIDN'T COME BACK FOR A WHILE.
"A *LONG* WHILE.

"CHASING SUPER-VILLAINS HALFWAY ACROSS THE GLOBE HAD ME FEELING LIKE I WAS TRAPPED IN A *ROADRUNNER CARTOON...*
"FUNNY TO THINK *NOW...* HOW MUCH *SIMPLER* LIFE WAS BACK IN NINETY-ONE. HOW *EASY* I HAD IT THEN.
"IT TOOK A FEW MORE YEARS FOR ME TO ACCEPT THE *OBVIOUS...*

... MY LIFE *IS* A FUCKIN' CARTOON, ISN'T IT?

COME ON, BAKER...

... YOU WOULDN'T WANT IT... ANY OTHER WAY...

PANT!

HFFF!

UUHH --

KINDA' SURPRISED SHE CAN PUT TWO WORDS TOGETHER, CONSIDERING...

-- HERE IT COMES AGAIN...

... OOOHHH FUUUUCK--

I LET YOU *REMINISCE*. OUT LOUD.
GOOD POINT. DOESN'T MAKE ME FEEL MUCH BETTER ABOUT HOW *SLOPPY* I'VE GOTTEN...

...IS *THIS* WHAT IT'S LIKE TO GET OLDER?
OKAY, BETSY, YOU PICKED THE *PHYSICAL CHALLENGE*. NOW, YOU KNOW HOW THE GAME *WORKS*...

...THE *MEDIEVAL DEVICE* YOU'LL BE PLACED INTO SHARES A NAME WITH A CLASSIC *HEAVY METAL BAND*...
...FOR *ONE MILLION DOLLARS*, NAME THAT BAND'S *ORIGINAL* LEAD SINGER...!
UHHH... WHAT...?

LISTEN, I WOULDN'T KNOW ABOUT GETTING OLDER. COMPLETELY FOREIGN CONCEPT.
AH, RIGHT. TOTALLY FORGOT. MY BAD, BABY DOLL.

NO PROBLEM. BESIDES, THERE ARE *BETTER* THINGS TO CELEBRATE BESIDES *BIRTHDAYS*, DON'T YOU THINK?
HARD TO BELIEVE HOW MUCH SYLVIA'S *MELLOWED OUT*...

...ESPECIALLY COMPARED TO HER GLORY DAYS AS *MS. MAYHEM*. AS A *SUPERHEROINE*, SHE WAS IN A CLASS BY HERSELF.

ASK ME, SHE'S GOTTEN *BETTER* WITH AGE.

NOT LIKE ME.
WELL, THIS WAS *SUPPOSED* TO BE A CELEBRATION... INSTEAD OF ME LICKING MY WOUNDED *EGO*.
I BLEW MY GIG, SYLVIA. SO *NOT* BUSTING A NUT...

... IT'S NO LESS THAN I *DESERVE*.

I'VE NEVER KNOWN YOU TO BE A MAN WHO HARBORS *REGRETS*...

DIDN'T *HAVE* MANY UNTIL JUST RECENTLY.

ANOTHER SIDE EFFECT OF FACING YOUR OWN --

FIGURED IT WAS JUST A MATTER OF TIME. AFTER *WHITE LIGHTNING*, I'D ASKED THE QUESTION, *"WHO ELSE?"*
HERE'S MY *ANSWER*...
HOW YA LIKE US NOW, COCKSUCKA --

-- WE JUST FLAMBÉD YER RIDE!
HE AIN'T GOIN' NOWHERE NOW.
ANOTHER THREE I MISSED WHEN I TORCHED THE CRAZY KEEP.
EL SUSHI... ANGERHEAD... THE ABOMINABLE SNOWMAN. MORE ASSHOLES I USED TO KNOCK HEADS WITH BACK IN THE DAY.
FIGURES THEY SURVIVED.
YOU CAN'T HIDE FROM US, RIGHTEOUS MAKER!
WE'LL BURN DOWN THIS ENTIRE CITY TO GET AT YOU!
C'MON OUT HERE AN' --
A-HA... THERE'S THE PIECE A' SHIT --
YOU THINK YOU'VE GOT A LEGITIMATE GRIPE, SUSHI...
... HERE I FUCKING AM.
RIGHT.
ENOUGH TIME SPENT FEELING SORRY FOR MYSELF. LOOKING DOWN AT THESE POOR BASTARDS... THE INSTINCT THAT KICKS IN... THE PURE ADRENALINE RUSH...
... THIS IS BETTER THAN SEX.

BACK IN THE BADLANDS. THE RUBBER MEETIN' THE ROAD ONCE AGAIN.
IF I WAS A RELIGIOUS TYPE, I'D BE THANKIN' THE LIGHT. BUT I DON'T HAFTA BE. NOT ANYMORE...
ARE YER EARS ON, CONTROL? BECAUSE MY ASS IS IN THE SADDLE --
-- YOU GOT ARNIE B. WILLARD BROADCASTIN' HERE! FIT AS A FIDDLE AND ON THE CASE!
I NEED THE LATEST ON VANITY PLATES, "ELLE BELLE." ANYONE OUT THERE GOT A TWENTY ON THIS SUMBITCH?!
YOUR VERNACULAR HAS A CADENCE I FIND INTRIGUING...
... ARE YOU COMMUNICATING IN SOME FORM OF CODE?
CODE?! SHIT, BOY -- DON'T DISTRACT ME WHILE I'M SNIFFIN' THE TRAIL...!
YOU ARM YOURSELF WITH THE ACCOUTREMENTS OF WAR...
... BUT HOW DOES THIS DEVICE FACTOR INTO YOUR MISSION?
ITS MOLECULAR STRUCTURE IS CURIOUSLY SIMPLE. A PROMISE OF ENLIGHTENMENT, PERHAPS...?

DEPENDS ON WHAT KIND YER LOOKIN' FOR.
I'VE FOUND ME AN OCCASIONAL ANSWER OR TWO AT THE BOTTOM OF A KEG OF COORS.
CURIOUS...
HEY --
-- WUT T'HELL ARE YA' DOIN'?!
THAT WUZ MY LAST ONE, Y'FREAK!
YA DON'T JUST GO AN' WASTE A --
NOTHING HAS BEEN WASTED. OBSERVE WHAT I HAVE WROUGHT FROM THE CHAOS OF MY ACTIONS...
... THIS IS THE SHAPE OF THE UNIVERSE.
YEAH, WHATEVER.
LOOK, AFTER FIXIN' ME UP LIKE YA DID, I AGREED TO LET YA' TAG ALONG --
-- BUT NOW YA' NEED TO SHADDUP AND LEMME DO MY JOB.
BREAKER! BREAKER! I'M REPEATIN' MYSELF! ANYONE WITH A TWENTY ON THAT "ELLE BELLE" RIG, BRING IT TO ME!
COLORS ARE RED, WHITE AND BLUE BUT MAKE NO MISTAKE, HE AIN'T NO --
THE RIDDLE OF CONNECTIVITY...
-- KKKKKKKKK --
-- ZZZZZZZ --

... PLACING MAN AND MESSAGE WITHIN THE SAME SPACE.
-- KKKKKKKKK --
REPORTS OF A SUPERPOWERED MELEE TAKING PLACE IN MIDTOWN --
-- INVOLVING MULTIPLE EXPLOSIONS... CASUALTY COUNT IS STILL UNKNOWN...
LOCAL LAW ENFORCEMENT ESTABLISHING A PERIMETER RIGHT NOW...
... BUT IT'S UNCLEAR HOW THEY PLAN TO QUELL THE --
DID... YOU CHANGE MY CHANNEL--?!
WUT THE HELL IS THIS NOW...?!
LISTEN CAREFULLY TO THE INFORMATION BEING BROADCAST.
WHERE THIS ACTIVITY TAKES PLACE... YOU SHALL FIND YOUR DESIRED TARGET.
DUNNO HOW IN HELL YOU'D KNOW THAT, MISTER -- OR MISSUS -- "ABSOLUTELY", BUT AFTER WHATCHA DID BACK IN MY HOSPITAL ROOM, I'LL TAKE YER WORD FER IT!
HOLD ONTO YER ASS --
-- WE'RE HEADED FER THE CONCRETE JUNGLE!

OH YEAH.
WAY BETTER THAN SEX.
YOU REALLY WANT TO WASTE US?!
YOU'LL HAVE TO STEP UP YOUR GAME!
DHUHHNN--!
FORGOT ABOUT THE SNOWMAN'S BLIZZARD BLASTS...!
GET YOUR SHIT TOGETHER, OLD MAN.
THIS IS JUST THE BEGINNING, BAKER --

-- WE'RE GONNA' MAKE YOU SUFFER!
THE EXECUTIONER'S HOOD IS ON THE OTHER HEAD, ISN'T IT?!
I FORGOT HOW MUCH I MISSED ANGERHEAD'S PARTICULAR BRAND OF TRASH TALKING.
(THAT WAS SARCASM, BY THE WAY)
BUT NOT ONLY IS HE A COMPLETE FUCKING IDIOT...
GUH --
... HE'S GOT GLASS BALLS.
--GYEEAAARRGGHH!!!

SON OF A BITCH CAN BELLOW WHEN HE WANTS TO. LEAST I KNOW HE FELT IT.
MAYBE I CAN FINISH THIS FAST.
THEN AGAIN... NOT TOO FAST.
WE'RE NOT DONE YET --
-- JUST LIKE OLD TIMES, RIGHT?
I CAN'T DENY IT. I'M STARTING TO FEEL LIKE MYSELF AGAIN.
XXX
CRACK AN
ANAL
MAYBE I NEEDED THIS MORE THAN I --
UP HERE, RIGHTEOUS MAKER --
OH SHIT.

-- THIS BELONG TO YOU?!
SNOWMAN!
DON'T EVEN THINK ABOUT IT!
WHOOPS.
TOO LATE.
YOU CAN'T IMAGINE THE SOUND OF A FROZEN HUMAN BREAKING IN HALF.
AND YOU WOULDN'T WANT TO.
AAAWWW YEAH--!
I HOPE YOU FUCKIN' LOVED HER!
WANNA MAKE YOU CRY ABOUT IT--!
FAT CHANCE. I'VE NEVER BEEN IN "LOVE"... WHATEVER THAT IS.
BUT SHE WAS A GOOD FUCK. AND I'M PISSED OFF NOW.

YOU THINK YOU HURT ME, EL SUSHI?
TURN AROUND --
-- SAY "GRILLED CHEESE".
THERE IT IS. THE SMELL OF BACON GREASE IN THE AIR.
GRRAAAAAA--
I USED TO WORRY ABOUT COLLATERAL DAMAGE. BACK WHEN I WAS A PROPER SUPERHERO.
NOW I COULD GIVE A SHIT.
THIS IS A LITTLE MORE PERSONAL, THOUGH.
SYLVIA DESERVED BETTER THAN THIS. SHE ALWAYS KNEW THE RISKS, BUT GODDAMN...!
YO, FUCKFACE --

--I'M STILL HERE!
YOU THOUGHT YOU COULD WALTZ IN AN' END US?! JUST LIKE THAT?!
I WANT MY RESPECT!
RESPECT... THAT'S AN AGE OLD SUPER-VILLAIN OBSESSION.
WE ALWAYS WANT THE THINGS WE'LL NEVER GET.
KOFF!
KAFF!
H-HOLD ON... ANGERHEAD...
...I WANNA... PIECE OF HIM, TOO...

HEY -- ASSHOLE! WHAT'RE YOU DOING?!
WHAT DOES IT LOOK LIKE I'M DOING?! I'M MURDERING THIS FUCK!
QUIT HOGGING THE HERO! THIS IS SUPPOSED TO BE A TEAM-UP--!
WE ALL AGREED --
AND YOU THINK THAT'S ALL I GET --
BACK OFF, SNOWMAN! YOU PUT HIS BITCH INTO DEEP FREEZE--!
-- FUCK YOU!
WHOA!
WHAT DA FUCK, MAN?!
I NEVER LIKED HIM... OR YOU! SO DON'T THINK THAT I WON'T --
JEEZUS FUCKIN' CHRIST --
-- YOU TWO ARE TOO STUPID TO LIVE!

THE VIOLENCE. THE BANTER. THE PATHOS. ALL THE NECESSARY ELEMENTS ARE BACK.
GUESS SOME THINGS NEVER GET OLD.
YOU PUT YOUR FUCKING HANDS ON ME?!
JUST SHUT UP AND GET HIM!
YOU GUYS BETTER KISS AND MAKE UP QUICK. BECAUSE IN ABOUT TWO SECONDS, I'M GONNA --
ATTENTION, ALL SUPERPOWERED COMBATANTS --
-- YOU ARE ORDERED TO STAND DOWN IMMEDIATELY!
WE HAVE YOU SURROUNDED AND WE ARE FEDERALLY AUTHORIZED TO USE LETHAL FORCE!
WHAT THE HOLY CHRIST--?!
THOSE ASSHOLES PROMISED I HAD THEIR "FULL SUPPORT" ON THIS MISSION -- IS THIS WHAT THEY MEANT?!
THE FIRST SIGN OF TROUBLE... THEY TURN THEIR GUNS ON ME, TOO?!
GUESS I'M THE ASSHOLE. I ACTUALLY TOOK 'EM AT THEIR WORD...!
BUT IT NEVER FAILS. THE WHITE MEN IN THEIR BLACK SUITS... THEY WANT WHAT THEY WANT.
AND I'M EXPENDABLE.
FUCK ME.

NO BACKGROUND (MAYBE A FADED COLOR... RED?
PART FIVE
LOGO HERE
...T SURE HOW ...PULL THAT ...F, ARTISTICALLY, ...T I HAVE A ...ELING YOU'LL ...IGURE IT OUT... ...MEH
KNEE PADS
ROUND 1

NOTHING LIKE A LONG DISTANCE REVENGE FUCK, IS THERE...?
IT'S CLASSIC PUPPET MASTER BEHAVIOR...
COME WITH ME!
GODDAMMIT--!
WHAT'RE YOU SO WORKED UP ABOUT, DICK?
REPORTS ARE COMING IN... A GODDAMN WAR ZONE IN TIMES SQUARE! OUR BOY VERSUS A GAGGLE OF FREAKS HE MISSED AT BERTRAND!
YOU'D BETTER SCHEDULE A REPEAT -- WE'RE GOING TO WASHINGTON TO COVER OUR ASSES RIGHT-FUCKING-NOW!
HEY! NOT FOR NOTHING... BUT I'VE GOT A SHOW TO DO HERE --
IT NEVER FAILS. FIGURES I'M TOO OLD TO HAVE THIS MANY BALLS IN THE AIR...
OH, FOR CHRIST'S SAKE! NOBODY CARES ABOUT YOUR PISSANT TALK SHOW ANYMORE!
MEANWHILE, OUR INDEPENDENT CONTRACTOR HAS SCREWED THE POOCH!
... SHOULD'VE EXPECTED I'D END UP GETTING KICKED IN 'EM.
THINK ABOUT WHAT YOU'RE DOING.
FUCK YOU

REPEAT -- ANY AND ALL SUPERPOWERED INDIVIDUALS ARE HEARBY ORDERED TO CEASE ALL COMBAT ACTIVITY!

CONSIDER YOURSELVES UNDER ARREST!

I CAN HEAR THE *QUIVER* IN HIS VOICE.

ALMOST *IMPERCEPTIBLE,* BUT IT'S THERE. THESE BOYS HAVE *NO IDEA* WHAT THEY'VE STEPPED INTO.

AS LONG AS THEY DON'T TRY TO BE *HEROES,* MAYBE THERE'S A CLEAN WAY *OUT* OF THIS.

SHIT.
WE'VE SET A PERIMETER AND AIR SUPPORT IS ON THE WAY. SO DON'T EVEN *THINK* ABOUT...
... HOLY SHIT, IT'S REALLY YOU.
HOW YOUNG ARE THEY *MAKIN'* 'EM THESE DAYS?! NOT TO MENTION *NAÏVE*...!

THEY HONESTLY THINK THAT *ANYONE'S* WILLING TO BE TAKEN *PRISONER* HERE...?!

WE HAVE OUR *ORDERS.* I NEED YOU DOWN ON THE GROUND --

YOU'RE HERE TO RESTORE *LAW* AND *ORDER* --

-- TWO OF MY LEAST FAVORITE THINGS!

AND THERE IT IS -- THE *INCITING INCIDENT*.

IN *THIS* CASE... ONE OF THE ABOMINABLE SNOWMAN'S PATENTED *BLIZZARD BLASTS*.

CUE *ALL HELL* BREAKING LOOSE...

Y'KNOW, I COULDN'T PASS THE *ARMY PHYSICAL* --

-- THEY WOULDN'T LET ME *ENLIST* --

-- AND I NEVER GOT OVER IT!

DIDN'T FORGET ABOUT *ME*, DIDJA, PRICK?!
ANGERHEAD. THIS ONE'S DEFINITELY SUFFERING *EMOTIONAL DAMAGE*.
MY HATRED WILL FUCK YOU UP!
HE AIN'T *EXAGGERATING*, EITHER. HIS *POWERS* ARE TIED TO HIS *MOODS* --

-- AND IT AIN'T AN *EXACT SCIENCE*.

STILL GOT A FEW MOVES IN ME.

MINE'S ONLY A *FLESH WOUND*...

... THE BOYS IN UNIFORM DON'T FARE SO WELL.

I CAN HEAR MY OWN HEARTBEAT... THAT FAMILIAR CHUGGING SOUND... TINY PISTONS PUMPING AT A STEADY PACE...
IT'S A GODDAMN FREE-FOR-ALL --
-- AND, THANKS TO SOME TRIGGER HAPPY JARHEADS THAT CAN'T AIM FOR SHIT --
-- EL SUSHI IS THE FIRST CASUALTY.
GOOD RIDDANCE.
ATTICA!
ATTICA!
ATTICA!
YOU REALLY NEED TO STAND DOWN, SIR!
GET YOUR OLD ASS FLAT ON THE PAVEMENT --
-- RIGHT FUCKING NOW!
FUCK ME. THESE KIDS ARE COMMITTED, I'LL GIVE 'EM THAT...
OKAY. NOW I'M PISSED.
LUCKILY, THIS WON'T TAKE LONG...

C'MON, SUSHI... DON'T DIE ON ME, MAN...!
SUSHI--!
I-I... DIDN'T GO OUT... LIKE A BITCH, DID I...?
... T-TELL MY D-DAD...
... "FUCK YOU" ...
...
SHIT.
NO TIME FOR TEARS, DICKHEAD --
-- YOU'RE NEXT IN LINE.
ANOTHER MOTHERFUCKER DOWN.
THAT'S FOR EVERY POLICE ACTION THAT NEVER MADE THE NEWS--!
ONE MORE TO GO.

I THINK ABOUT MY EARLIER SNOWMAN ENCOUNTERS. HE HAD A WAY ABOUT HIM... MORE LIKE AN OLD-FASHIONED SUPER-VILLAIN.
THAT TENDED TO KEEP THINGS LIGHT.
NOT THIS TIME.
THIS IS FOR SYLVIA--!

YOU SONOFABITCH!
NOT THE FUEL TANK --

AND THERE'S THE TRIFECTA...

... MOT TO MENTION, ONE HELLUVA DIVERSIONARY TACTIC.

GROUND SQUAD TO COMMAND! COME IN! REQUEST IMMEDIATE AIR COVER!
WE ARE UNABLE TO CONTAIN THE SITUATION! REPEAT --

THAT COULD'VE GONE BETTER...

... BUT IT'LL BE A FEW MINUTES BEFORE THEY TAKE THEIR HEADS OUT OF THEIR ASSES AND REALIZE THAT I'M *GONE.*
AS *MESSY* AN OP AS I'VE EVER BEEN INVOLVED IN... IT'S GODDAMNED *EMBARRASSING,* IS WHAT IT IS.
MIGHT AS WELL ADMIT TO MYSELF THAT I'LL NEVER BE AS *CLEAN* AS I WAS IN MY PRIME.
JEEZUS, I NEED TO CLEAR MY HEAD. I'M ALL FUCKED UP NOW.
HER *VOICE* ECHOES IN MY BRAIN. THAT TWENTY-THIRD ORGASM...
ANYWAY...
... THE *LAST* THING I NEED IS ANYONE KNOWING WHERE I AM. SO I FALL BACK ON MY TRAINING.
FIRST THINGS FIRST... COVER YOUR TRACKS. DESTROY THE EVIDENCE.
ALWAYS HAVE ENOUGH SCRATCH TO BUY THE RIGHT KIND OF *SILENCE.*
YOU DON'T WANT THEM EVEN REMEMBERING YOUR *NAME.*
I KNOW THE RIGHT PEOPLE. I KNOW HOW TO *DISAPPEAR.*
IT'S AN ODD FEELING. I'VE NEVER REALLY HAD TO *DO* THIS BEFORE.
NEVER FELT THE NEED TO *HIDE OUT...*
GUESS YOU CAN FIND YOURSELF TRYING *EVERYTHING...*

... IF YOU END UP LIVING LONG ENOUGH.
EVER THE UNKNOWN VARIABLE...
...TIMING.
NEVER BEEN TO TIMES SQUARE BEFORE...
BUT WUT THE FUCK IS THIS ALL ABOUT?
SNFF
SNFF
WHO PUT THESE FELLAS IN THE DEEP FREEZE?
WHY'D YOU BRING ME HERE?!
I CAN GIVE YOU THE TOOLS BUT I CANNOT PROVIDE THE TALENT.
THE FACE OF THE UNKNOWN WEARS AN INSCRUTABLE EXPRESSION.
RIGHT, RIGHT...
SHITHEAD.
LOOKS LIKE ONE BIG CLUSTERFUCK T'ME... THE SMELL OF DEATH IN THE AIR...
... BUT WUT THE HOLY HELL GOT SLAUGHTERED OUT HERE? SOME KINDA ANIMAL?
PHEEWWW!
AND WUT'S MY BOGEY GOT T'DO WITH ANY OF IT?!

YOU ARE ENTERING A WORLD THAT MUST BE EMBRACED, WILLARD. FULLY AND COMPLETELY.
LET IT SURROUND YOU. ACCEPT ITS ECCENTRICITIES.
WELL, SHIT... HOW'M I GONNA DO THAT? THERE AIN'T NUTHIN' HERE!
WAIT A GODDAMNED SECOND...
... YOU GOTTA' BE SHITTING ME!
AND IT ROLLS RIGHT OVER ME... ALL OVER AGAIN...
... THE HUMILIATION.
IT STILL BURNS... LIKE A HOT POKER SHOVED UP MY ASS.
DON'T TELL ME -- HE GOT FRIED BEFORE I COULD GET MY HANDS ON HIM?!
SONUVA-BITCH!
I COME BACK FROM THE GODDAMNED BRINK --
-- AND I AIN'T GETTIN' NO JUSTICE?!
NO SATISFACTION?!
GWAAAHHHH--!
YOU FREAKY PIECE OF SHIT! YOU SET ME UP, DIDN'T YA?!
GET DOWN HERE -- SO I CAN PULL PORK YER FLOATY FUCKNUTS!
CLEARLY, YOUR PERCEPTIONS ARE CLOUDED.
WE CAN CHANGE THAT.

WHADDA YA THINK YER --
-- UH...?
THERE ARE CONNECTIONS FAR BEYOND THE FIELDS WE KNOW.
IT TAKES GREAT INSIGHT TO MAKE THEM.
SURRENDER... AND LEARN...
... FEEL THE RIVERS OF ENERGY FLOWING THROUGH THE MINDS OF ALL LIVING THINGS.
BEHIND CARBON WALLS BUILT HIGH AND STRONG. LET US SET THE BATTLEMENTS ON FIRE.
THROUGH PATHOGEN PATHWAYS, YOU SHALL ZERO IN ON YOUR INTENDED TARGET. YOU MUST ONLY HAVE THE EYES TO SEE...
THE EYES TO SEE... A WORLD OF SHIT...
FEELS LIKE A HAMSTER RUNNIN'... A WHEEL SPINNIN'...
... HEAD'S STILL SPINNING. CAN'T BELIEVE I'M HERE.

THEY SOLD IT AS PARADISE. SO FAR... THEY WEREN'T FAR OFF.
JUST NEVER THOUGHT I'D EVER END UP IN --
BEAUTIFUL, ISN'T IT, BAKER?
THE VIEW --
-- THEY DON'T MAKE 'EM LIKE THAT BACK IN THE "CIVILIZED" WORLD. TOO MUCH POLLUTION.
FOLKS HAVE BEEN ASKING ABOUT YOU.
LET 'EM ASK. I'M NOT EXACTLY ADVERTISING MY ARRIVAL.
UNDERSTOOD. TRUST ME, YOU WON'T REGRET YOUR DECISION.
GOOD TO SEE YOU, BUTCHER. IT'S BEEN AWHILE, HASN'T IT?
THESE TWO WERE A REAL PAIR OF MOTHERFUCKERS BACK IN THE DAY...
... BLACK KNIGHTMARE AND NIGHTMAIDEN. URBAN VIGILANTE ASS-KICKERS OF THE HIGHEST ORDER.
THEY WERE PARTNERS BEFORE THEY WERE LOVERS. A STRANGE COURTSHIP, NO DOUBT.
NOW THEY'RE LIVING THE QUIET LIFE... HERE IN PARADISE. CALL IT A CLUB MED FOR RETIRED SUPERPEOPLE.
Y'KNOW, WE'D BEEN WONDERING WHAT HAPPENED TO YOU. WE HEARD YOU'D FALLEN OFF THE GRID...
... WE JUST DIDN'T KNOW HOW FAR. HOW THE HELL DID YOU DECIDE TO FINALLY PUT YOUR FEET UP?
LONG STORY, BK. AND, TO BE HONEST, I HAVEN'T COMPLETELY DECIDED.
YOU'LL ASSIMILATE IN DUE TIME. IT DOES TAKE SOME GETTING USED TO.
I CAN'T IMAGINE HOW MANY YEARS IT'S BEEN SINCE YOU ACTUALLY FELT SAFE. WELL, REST ASSURED...
... YOU'RE COMPLETELY SAFE HERE.

"IN DUE TIME". YEAH, RIGHT.
WELL, I FIGURE I SHOULD GIVE IT A *SHOT*. HOW BAD COULD IT BE...?
... SO I CONSOLIDATED MY PATENT EARNINGS AND PLACED THEM IN AN OUTER-DIMENSIONAL ACCOUNT AT ABOUT SEVEN PERCENT.

AND THAT'S SEVEN PERCENT AT A *NON-TERRESTRIAL* VIBRATIONAL FREQUENCY. THAT MAKES ALL THE DIFFERENCE.
I'M TELLING YOU... CRIMEFIGHTING DOESN'T PAY. YOU GOTTA' HAVE A HEAD FOR *BUSINESS*.
I GUESS SO.
ME, I SURVIVED KNOWING WHERE ALL THE PENTAGON *SLUSH FUNDS* WERE BURIED...

... AND I'M SURE AS HELL NOT ABOVE A LITTLE SLAP AND TICKLE WHEN IT COMES TO--
-- ICK?
A *TICKLE* IN MY BRAIN...

... DADDY ISSUES... CHURNING UP.
BUT THEY AIN'T *MINE* --
-- AIN'T GONNA *THINK* ABOUT IT.

CHASIN' THE DRAGON ACROSS A NERVE CELL NIGHTMARE...

... BOBBING FOR *TRAUMA* --
-- THE *SCARS* THAT NEVER SEEM TO *HEAL* --
-- TOO MUCH GODDAMN *BLOOD* --

-- DYSFUNCTIONAL DNA... TOUGH TO ESCAPE --
-- ESCAPE THE MINDFUCK I'M STUCK IN...
... WHOSE GODDAMN THOUGHTS ARE THESE, ANYWAY --
... A LITTLE SLAP AND TICKLE...
UH...?
WUT THE HOLY HELL...?!
HOW THE FUCK DID I GET HERE?!
THE SHORTEST DISTANCE BETWEEN TWO POINTS...
YOU!
YOU BEEN FUCKIN' WITH MY BRAIN?!
YOU GOTTA PAIR O' BALLS ON YA' --
ANATOMY NOTWITHSTANDING, YOU MUST ACCEPT THE INSIGHT I AM OFFERING...
... AN OPPORTUNITY TO LOCATE THAT WHICH YOU SEEK.
THE SEARCH FOR TRUTH IS ULTIMATELY A TEST... A TEST OF PURE FORTITUDE...
... AND YOURS IS JUST BEGINNING, WILLARD.
YOU SHEEP SHANK BITCH! YOU CAN'T --
-- DO THAT...
... TO ME... AFTER ALL I'VE --
-- DONE FOR MY COUNTRY...
... THE RED... THE WHITE... THE BLUE...
ENGINE HEART... BEATING...
... THE GRAND EXPERIMENT...
... FUEL FOR EVERY FIRE THAT EVER BURNED --
-- BURNED MY ASS --
-- BUT I CAN HEAR IT BEATING...

... POUNDING IN MY EARS --
GAH--!
THE FUCK--?!
JEEZUS--!
I THINK I JUST SHIT MYSELF...!
GODDAMMIT... WHAT'RE YOU DOING T'ME?!
LOOK WITHIN YOURSELF. YOU AND YOUR PREY ARE NOW SHARE A UNCONSCIOUS CONNECTION.
YOUR INNERMOST THOUGHTS INTERMINGLE FREELY. A DISTINCT ADVANTAGE IN THE HEAT OF THE HUNT.
WELL, FUCK... I DUNNO WHY IT'S GOTTA BE ME...
... SEEMS LIKE SOME KINDA WEIRD-ASS GAME YER...
... PLAYIN' WITH ME...
... AN' I DON'T LIKE... GAMES...
I'M SO CLOSE --
-- NOT EVEN CLOSE --

I'M A GODDAMN *GIVER*...
-- GIVIN' IT TO HER *HARD* --
-- NOT A CHANCE IN *HELL*, BITCH --
THIS AIN'T THE LIFE I *EXPECTED* --
-- THE KIND OF LIFE WHERE YOU TAKE IT AS IT COMES --
-- YOU FIND YOUR MOMENTS OF *GREATNESS* --
-- OCCASIONALLY DELIVERING SOME *JUSTICE* IN THIS GODFORSAKEN WORLD --
-- SOMETIMES YOU GOTTA' *REACH* FOR 'EM --
-- FEELS SO FUCKIN' *GOOD* --
-- *SUPPOSED* TO FEEL SO FUCKIN' *GOOD* --

-- WHAT THE FUCK AM I *DOING?!*
H-HEY...!
C'MON, BAKER --

-- KEEP YOUR HEAD IN THE GAME AND GIVE IT TO ME!
... WEIRD-ASS IMAGES KNIFING THROUGH MY BRAIN... SOME OF 'EM AIN'T MINE...
NO FUCKIN' WAY I CAN BE DOING THIS...

AHHHH, LISTEN... I'M...
I SHOULD GO...

EVERYTHING'S FINE. YOU HAD A GOOD TIME, SO --
ARE YOU KIDDING ME?!
YOU DON'T JUST DECIDE YOU'RE DONE! YOU NEED TO FINISH WHAT YOU STARTED!

AH DAMN. FIGURES SHE'S ONE OF THOSE WOMEN...
YOU SAID YOU WANTED THIS!
LISTEN, KIDDO... I JUST GOT HERE AND I THOUGHT I NEEDED...
... WELL, WHATEVER. LET'S JUST CALL IT A NIGHT.

WELL, THEN GO ON! GET THE FUCK OUTTA HERE!
GODDAMNED HAS-BEEN--!
YEAH... THERE'S AN EGO BOOST FOR YA.

MAYBE THIS WASN'T SUCH A GOOD IDEA...

... PUT OUT TO STUD LIKE SEABISCUIT AFTER HIS LAST SANTA ANITA. AND I CAN'T EVEN DO *THAT* RIGHT.
SHIT'S TOO *MESSY* TO EXPECT SUCH A CLEAN BREAK WITH YOUR PAST.

I DON'T BELONG *HERE*. BUT I DON'T BELONG *BACK THERE*.
NOW MY *MIND'S* GOING CRACKERS ON ME.
FUCK.

SO WHERE'S THE NEW *GLORY*? WHERE'S THE NEXT *MOUNTAIN* TO CLIMB?
IF I'M NOT A *SUPERHERO* ANYMORE... WHAT *AM* I...?
JUST ANOTHER *ASSHOLE* IN PARADISE... WATCHING THE MAIDS WASH MY SHIT-STAINED SHEETS EVERY DAY?
24

NO DIRECTION HOME.
SO WHAT'S LEFT FOR --
HUUURRRRHHHH-

... UUUHHHTTT....
YOU REALLY ARE SLIPPING...
... AREN'T YOU, BUTCHER?
YOU TRIED TO HIDE. BUT I HAVE EYES EVERYWHERE.
AND IN THE END, I CERTAINLY COULDN'T TRUST MY VILLAINOUS BRETHREN TO CLOSE THE DEAL AND TAKE YOU OUT. NOT TO MENTION, THE PLEASURE I WOULD'VE BEEN DENIED.
LUCKILY, THE FATES HAVE SMILED ON ME...
... AS THEY OFTEN DO ON JIHAD JONES.
I WOULDN'T BLAME THEM FOR BEING SO ANGRY. YOU MANAGED TO SURVIVE THEIR VENGEFUL ATTACKS ON YOU.
OBVIOUSLY, I ALSO SURVIVED YOUR FEEBLE ATTEMPT TO MURDER ME. NOW, FOR MY OWN PEACE OF MIND, I THINK I SHALL TURN THE TABLES. THE ONLY DIFFERENCE BEING...
... THERE WILL BE NO CHANCE OF FAILURE.
YOU PITIFUL BASTARD.

PART SIX
AUM KALIKAYAI NAMAH

DEATH TIME HAS COME.
A CHILD OF KALI DENIES ITSELF ALL EARTHLY DELIGHTS.
WE ARE DRUNK ON THE BLOOD OF OUR VICTIMS.
DARKNESS IS THE ULTIMATE MOTHER.
REMEMBER HOW WE USED TO ARGUE THE LIMITS OF KALI'S INFLUENCE? THE PRINCIPLES OF CONSCIOUSNESS?
IS SHE TRULY THE MISTRESS OF THE UNIVERSE?
HOW COMPLETELY GLORIOUS IT ALL SEEMS IN HINDSIGHT.
WE ARE NOTHING IF NOT OUR CONTRADICTIONS. I EMBRACE THAT.
AND, FOR MY WISDOM... FOR MY CLARITY... I AM BESTOWED A GREAT GIFT...
EVER HAVE ONE OF THOSE DAYS...?
YEAH --

-- THEY'RE REALLY *SHIT* WHEN THEY HAPPEN, AREN'T THEY?

HE'S TAKING HIS *TIME* WITH ME. ENJOYING IT. *SAVORING* IT.

TYPICAL SUPER-VILLAIN BEHAVIOR. SOME THINGS NEVER CHANGE. BUT *JIHAD JONES* WAS NEVER AS UNIQUE AS HE *THINKS* HE IS...

... ALTHOUGH HE DID CATCH *ME* WITH MY DICK HANGING OUT. BUT THAT'S LESS ABOUT *HIM* AND MORE ABOUT *ME*.

AND GODDAMN IF I AIN'T PAYIN' THE *PRICE* FOR NOT BEING AS *SHARP* AS I USED TO BE.

MAYBE THE *ULTIMATE* PRICE. AT THIS POINT, WHO FUCKIN' KNOWS...?

SON OF A BITCH *TALKS* A LOT, TOO...

FEELING A LITTLE *WEAK* THERE, BUTCHER?

THESE *HYPOTHALAMIC DAMPENERS* I'VE GOT SET UP AROUND THE ROOM... THEY KEEP YOU IN A NICE, *DOCILE* STATE.

YEAH... AND YOU *NEED* 'EM, DON'TCHA...?
YOU NEVER *DID* TAKE ME ON... ONE-ON-ONE...
FUCKIN' *PUSSY*...!
WELL, KEEPING YOUR ONE-OF-A-KIND, PROTOTYPE *ENGINE HEART* IN *IDLE* DOES GIVE ME A CERTAIN *ADVANTAGE*.
NOW... LET'S TALK ABOUT EXACTLY WHAT I *NEED*...

... I NEED THAT.
OVER AND OVER AGAIN.
SURELY YOU UNDERSTAND THE CONCEPT OF TORTURE...
THAT'S... WHAT GETS YOU OFF...?!
F-FUCKIN' PERV...
YOU HAVE NO CONCEPT OF WHAT GETS ME OFF.
WE BOTH LIVE IN A WORLD THAT CONTAINS SO MUCH SUFFERING... SO MUCH PAIN...
... IT'S TIME YOU FINALLY EXPERIENCED SOME.
FUCK ME. I SHOULD'VE CHECKED THE DEBRIS AT THE CRAZY KEEP... MADE SURE THERE WERE NO SURVIVORS...
... STUPID, AMATEUR MISTAKE...!
THAT'S WHAT PUT ME HERE.
THE SOUNDS OF VIOLENCE.
A SUBLIME SYMPHONY IN MY EARS.
FIND SOMETHING YOU LOVE, YOU'LL NEVER WORK A DAY IN YOUR LIFE.
THAT'S WHAT I ALWAYS TOLD HIM...

JETBOY!
LET THE GAMES BEGIN!
THIS MOVE IS SO PLAYED OUT.
WHAT DOES HE EXPECT?! WE'VE GOT IDEOLOGICAL GOALS TO ACHIEVE!
A MISSION OF MAYHEM!
FROM THE LATIN VERB, "TERRERE"...!
ASYMMETRIC WARFARE!

HHNNN--!
DAMNED INCONVENIENT ORDINANCE...!
TIME TO SWITCH TACTICS --
I CONCUR...
... I'D LIKE TO EXPERIENCE THIS GROTESQUE SYMBOL UP CLOSE.
MY ORDINANCE IS STILL IN PERFECT WORKING ORDER.
BELOVED SIDEKICK.
YOU ARE MY SUNSHINE.
GO FORTH AND CONQUER!
YA GOT SOME NERVE, KID--!
OH, YOU HAVE NO IDEA --

AN IMPACT FOR THE AGES!
WE ARE THE VERY MODEL OF A MODERN MAJOR MUJAHIDEEN!
THIS IS HOW WE DEAL WITH A GREAT SATAN...!
YOUR BLOOD IS MY OIL--!
DON'T WANNA BE TOO DEPENDANT ON THAT --

I'M ON FIIIIRRREEE--!
NG--!
WAIT --
NO--!
LOOKS LIKE YOU'RE FUCKED, KID...
THE VIRAL ARROGANCE OF AMERICA!
I WILL NOT BE "SAVED" --
-- BY THE LIKES OF YOU!

JETBOY --
-- NO--!
THIS... THIS CANNOT BE...
... NOT NOW...!
I CANNOT...
... IMAGINE LIFE WITHOUT YOU.
WE ALL HAVE OUR REASON TO BELIEVE.
MINE IS PREDICATED ON EXTERMINATING YOU FOR THE CRIMES YOU HAVE COMMITTED...

YOUR FINAL MOMENTS FILL MY HEART LIKE NOTHING ELSE.
AND KNOW THAT MY BELOVED WILL HAVE HIS REVENGE IN THE AFTERLIFE... WHERE HE SURELY AWAITS YOU.
HE'S SAYING SOMETHING. BUT I DON'T HEAR HIM.
I'M A LITTLE BUSY.
IT'S BEEN AWHILE...
... BUT I'M STARTING TO REMEMBER WHAT MATTERS.
I'VE PICKED UP A FEW TECHNIQUES FOR THIS KIND OF SITUATION...
... TECHNIQUES THAT HAVE HELPED ME GET THROUGH WORSE THAN THIS.
BREATH OF FIRE... INTERNAL CHANTING...
YI SHI VI... YI SHI VI...
THE THREE ENERGY CENTERS... THEY CREATE A SAFE HAVEN...
YI SHI VI... YI SHI VI...
... A PLACE I CAN GO...
... THAT EXISTS BEYOND THE PAIN.
SHIT ACTUALLY WORKS.

GAH--!
WH-WHU... WHU...
JEEZUS CHRIST...!
≥PANT!≤
≥PANT!≤
≥PANT!≤
HOW IN THE FUCK DID I END UP --
SURELY YOU'VE GOTTEN USED TO A SLIGHT DEGREE OF DISORIENTATION BY NOW...
MMMM... WHATEVER YOU SAY.
LATELY, I AIN'T SURE WHICH WAY IS UP AN' WHICH WAY IS DOWN...
I THINK YOU'LL FIND, WHEN YOU OPEN THE DOORS WITHIN YOURSELF...
... WE'RE MOVING QUICKLY AND TIME IS OF THE ESSENCE.
"TIME" BEING A RELATIVE TERM.
CLEARLY, I AM LOOKING TO FILL THE EMPTY SPACES IN MY OWN BLACK HOLE HEART.
... THERE IS NO DIFFERENCE.
YA' LIKE FUCKIN' WITH ME, DON'TCHA?
AWWW, NO! NOT THIS...
... SUMBITCH.
WUT THE FUCK IS HAPPENING T'ME...?!
WHY AM I NOT FEELIN' RIGHT?!

ARNIE B. WILLARD.
ARE YOU SO CERTAIN YOU WANT TO FEEL "RIGHT"?
MY DADDY ONCE TOLD ME... A MAN'S BEST FRIENDS ARE HIS BALLS --
WISE WORDS.
--!
MMMFFFLLL...!
... COULD SWEAR I JUST HAD A RED HOT POKER SHOVED UP MY SOUL...
... THE RADIO IN MY HEAD TUNED TO THE GOSPEL CHANNEL...
I... DON'T GET IT...
YOUR MANDATE IS PURSUIT, WILLARD...
... AND I HAVE GIVEN YOU THE MEANS TO PURSUE.
I HAVE MADE A SUBLIME CONNECTION. I HAVE PROVIDED EXACTLY WHAT I PROMISED...
... INSIGHT.
YA DID, HUH?
YER A TREE.

GODDAMMIT... I GOT A MILLION VOICES IN MY HEAD...
... NONE OF 'EM FAMILIAR.

IF I CROAKED AN' YER JUST NOT TELLIN' ME... WE'RE GONNA GO ROUND AND ROUND.
NOW MAYBE YOU CAN SHOW ME THE WAY...

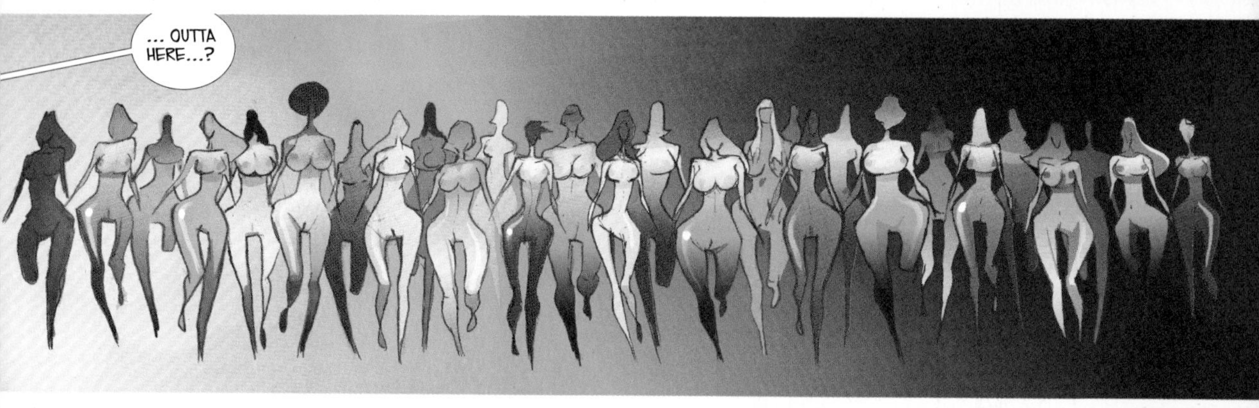
... OUTTA HERE...?

AHHH... NO OFFENSE, NICE LADIES. BUT I AIN'T IN NO MOOD FER AN ORGY RIGHT NOW.
I'M HERE ON OFFICIAL BUSINESS, YA UNDERSTAND...!
GAH.

ALTHOUGH Y'ALL SMELL LIKE PARADISE... I JUST CAN'T --
WAIT A MINUTE.
TAKE A MOMENT AND WONDER EXACTLY WHERE YOU ARE, WILLARD...

... ACCEPT THAT YOU CURRENTLY EXIST WITHIN THE MINDSCAPE OF ANOTHER.
BUT THIS IS NO RANDOM VISIT. THERE IS SOMETHING TO BE FOUND HERE.
LOOK CLOSELY...

SUMBITCH--!
THAT'S HIM, AIN'T IT?!
OUTTA' MY WAY--!
YOUR WORST ENEMY IS YOUR MIND'S OWN RESISTANCE. THAT WHICH YOU CAN IDENTIFY... YOU CAN UTILIZE.
LET ALL THAT IS NATURAL IN THIS WORLD LEAD YOU TOWARD YOUR DESTINY...
... NOT BORNE OUT OF ANGER, BUT OUT OF UNDERSTANDING.
DO NOT DISCOUNT THAT WHICH IS SO OBVIOUS, WILLARD.

NOT SO TOUGH A NUT WHEN YA DON'T GOT YER RIG WRAPPED AROUND YA!
WELL, YA GOT A LOT TO ANSWER FOR!
REMEMBER WUT HAPPENED BACK ON HIGHWAY NINE --
-- YA' FUCKED WITH AN OFFICER OF THE LAW --
-- AN' I DON'T ABIDE THAT!
SO -- ANY LAST WORDS BEFORE I TURN YER ASS INSIDE OUT?!
YI SHI VI.
WHA--?!

EVERYONE NEEDS TO CALM THE FUCK DOWN.
I'VE BEEN IN THIS ROOM ENOUGH TIMES TO KNOW WHEN THINGS HAVE GOTTEN OUT OF HAND...!
HEY, LET'S BREAK THE TENSION HERE, GUYS...
... DIDJA HEAR ABOUT THE PRESIDENT HAVING LUNCH WITH REPUBLICAN LEADERS TODAY? THE ENTIRE MEAL, HE HAD TO EAT WITHOUT SALT, PEPPER AND BUTTER...
WASN'T FOR DIETARY REASONS. THE REPUBLICANS JUST REFUSED TO PASS ANYTHING --
WILL YOU SHUT UP?!
LOOK... OBVIOUSLY, THERE ARE A LOT OF MOVING PARTS INVOLVED HERE --
UNDERSTATEMENT OF THE YEAR, DICK.
TIMES SQUARE! JUST HOW MANY TIMES DOES NEW YORK HAVE TO TAKE IT IN THE ASS?!
I'M NOT SURE WHAT YOU'RE IMPLYING, GENERAL. THIS IS AN APPLES AND ORANGES SITUATION.
LET'S NOT CONNECT ANY DOTS UNNECESSARILY...
FINE...
... THEN LET'S TALK ABOUT THE DESTRUCTION OF THE BERTRAND INSTITUTE.
WE'VE BEEN TALKING ABOUT LEVELING THE CRAZY KEEP FOR YEARS. EVEN THE PREVIOUS ADMINISTRATION FLOATED THE IDEA...
... AS YOU WELL KNOW.

UMMM... OVER TO YOU, DICK.
Y'KNOW, I SAW A HEADLINE ABOUT THE TEA PARTY YESTERDAY --
AGAIN, IF WE'RE GOING TO THROW IMPLICATIONS AROUND THE ROOM --
DON'T. I WILL KILL YOU.
WE ALL KNOW THE GOVERNOR SENT IN THE NATIONAL GUARD TO DEAL WITH TIMES SQUARE. A HARD ASS UNIT, BUT EVEN THEY GOT MORE THAN THEY EXPECTED.
PIECING TOGETHER THE SCATTERED REPORTS THAT WERE COMING IN, ALL SIGNS ARE POINTING...
... TO THIS GENTLEMAN BEING INVOLVED.
I'M ASSUMING EVERYBODY REMEMBERS THE RIGHTEOUS MAKER...?
EFFECTIVE SOLDIER, IN HIS PRIME.
YEAH, UNTIL HE WENT BATSHIT CRAZY --
HE'S STILL ALIVE?!
ARE WE STILL PAYING HIS PENSION...?
WELL, WHY WOULD HE EVEN INVOLVE HIMSELF IN THIS--?!
-- ABSOLUTE LAST THING WE NEED...!
HOLD ON... HOLD ON...!
IF THE RIGHTEOUS MAKER IS RESPONSIBLE FOR ANY OF THIS, OUR COURSE OF ACTION IS CLEAR.
HE'S FAR TOO UNPREDICTABLE TO REMAIN OUT IN THE OPEN...
... SO LET'S JUST CONCENTRATE ON SHUTTING HIM DOWN.

Y'KNOW... SOME THINGS JUST *CHANGE* YA. NOTHIN' YOU CAN *DO* ABOUT IT.

LIKE THE FIRST TIME I HAD A CHEEK FULL OF ***RED MAN*** WHEN I WAS ***TWELVE***...

THIS IS THE PLACE...

... JUST DON'T ASK ME HOW THE HELL I *KNOW* THAT.

IT'S LIKE... I GOT SOME KIND OF *DIVINING ROD* IN MY HEAD... LEADIN' ME PLACES...

LEADING YOU PRECISELY WHERE YOU'RE MEANT TO GO.

WELL, THERE'S JUST SOMETHING ABOUT *BEING* HERE... LIKE I'VE BEEN HERE *BEFORE*...

NOT *YOU,* WILLARD.

YOU SHARE SOMETHING... THE *TWO* OF YOU...

NOW THAT YOUR SUSPICIONS -- BOTH LARGE AND SMALL -- HAVE BEEN ADEQUATELY CONFIRMED, WHAT DO YOU HOPE TO --
ALRIGHT, ENOUGH ALREADY. YOU NEED TO ABSOLUTELY PUT A CORK IN IT.
HE LEFT SOMETHING BEHIND --
-- SOMETHING WE CAN USE.
SHIT.
NEEDS A BIT A' WORK, DON'T IT...?
THIS WILL BRING US CLOSER TO THE TRUTHS THAT WE BOTH SEEK...
... AND SO WE HAVE THE MEANS TO BRING THIS MECHANICAL MONSTROSITY TO FULL TERM.
JUST LIKE HOT RODDING THE CLUNKERS BACK HOME IN BEGGARS' CANYON.
LEMME AT HER.
PART OF ME WANTS TO KILL MYSELF FOR DOING THIS. ANOTHER PART OF ME CAN'T HELP MYSELF.
BUT EITHER WAY...
... WE'RE GONNA FIND THAT LAW-BREAKIN' MOTHERFUCKER ONCE AND FOR ALL.
GODDAMN IT.

PART SEVEN
BLACK FOREST
ALL-AMERICAN

SO I CRASHED INTO MYSELF.
HARD.
NOW I'M HANGING ON BY MY FUCKIN' FINGERNAILS.
DOESN'T FEEL GREAT.
AS A SUPERHERO, I HAD A PRETTY SIMPLE CODE...
... SELF-AWARENESS IS FOR PUSSIES.
I LEARNED HOW TO FAKE IT PRETTY WELL, THOUGH.
HELPED ME IN CERTAIN... SOCIAL SITUATIONS.
NOW I NEED IT FOR REAL.
...
I MAY BE FUCKED.
WITHIN THIS INEBRIATING DARKNESS...
... SOON I WILL DANCE.
THE TIME HAS COME.
SO THE PAIN IS GONE.
BUT I'M STILL STUCK IN THE SHIT.
YOU STINK LIKE OLD ASS LEATHER...
I COULD JUST HANG OUT HERE UNTIL IT'S ALL OVER...
... BUT I'M NOT READY TO LAY DOWN AND DIE.
NOT YET, ANYWAY.
SO I FOLLOW THAT TICKLE IN MY BRAIN...
THE SOUP IS FUCKIN' THICK TONIGHT...

... TAKES A HELLUVA LOTTA FIREPOWER TO CUT THROUGH IT ALL.
BUT I GOT ME SOME COURAGE... I GOT ME SOME CONVICTION...
YER STARTIN' T'SMELL, Y'KNOW THAT...?
... I GOT ME A FUCKED UP CO-PILOT.
YOUR SENSES ARE HYPERACTIVATED, ARNIE B. WILLARD.
REVEL IN YOUR DEEPER PERCEPTIONS.
EASY FER YOU TO SAY --
-- I AIN'T SURE I'M LIKING THIS AS MUCH AS YOU PROMISED ME I WOULD.
WHERE THE FUCK ARE WE GOIN', ANYWAY?!
TO THE END OF EVERYTHING, WILLARD.
STRAIGHT DOWN THE RIVER... INTO THE HEART OF THE ETERNAL ANSWER.

THE "ETERNAL ANSWER", EH? SOUNDS LIKE A LOAD A' HORSESHIT T'ME.
THERE'S YER MOMMA AND YER POPPA AND THE REST IS JUST THE MILEAGE...!
THE ADVANTAGE OF FLESH. A SIMPLE, STRAIGHT LIFELINE.
NOTHIN' STRAIGHT ABOUT MY LIFELINE.
IT'S AS CROOKED AS THEY COME.
LIKE I ACTUALLY KNOW WHAT I'M TALKIN' ABOUT...!
I'M JUST A HEAT-SEEKIN' MISSILE.
FIT TO BURN.
Y'GOT A FEW ISSUES RUMBLIN' AROUND IN THERE, DO YA?
I SEE EVERYTHING ALL AT ONCE...
... AND YET I AM STILL PLAGUED BY THE ODDEST VARIABLES.
QUESTIONS AND ANSWERS... TRUTH AND LIES...
HEY --
-- WHERE YOU GOIN'?!
SUMBITCH DID IT AGAIN...!
CAN'T IMAGINE WHERE HE/SHE RUNS OFF TO...

... GOTTA' BE SOME FUCKED UP, *UNHOLY* PLACE.

... ONLY *PERSPECTIVE* SEPARATES THEM.
AH. OF COURSE.
HERE TO INTERRUPT MY *MOMENT*.

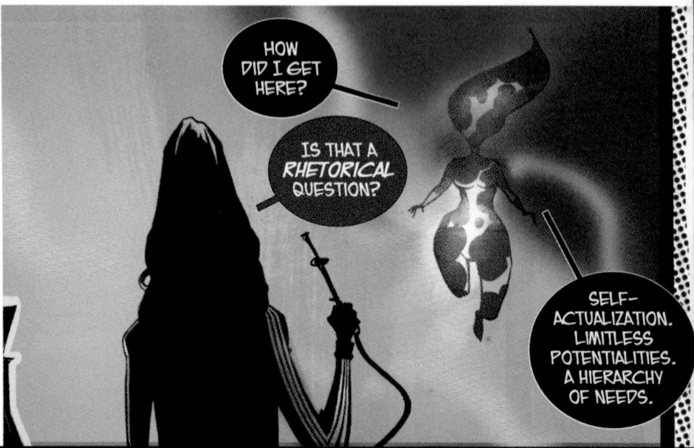
HOW DID I GET HERE?
IS THAT A *RHETORICAL* QUESTION?
SELF-ACTUALIZATION. LIMITLESS POTENTIALITIES. A HIERARCHY OF NEEDS.

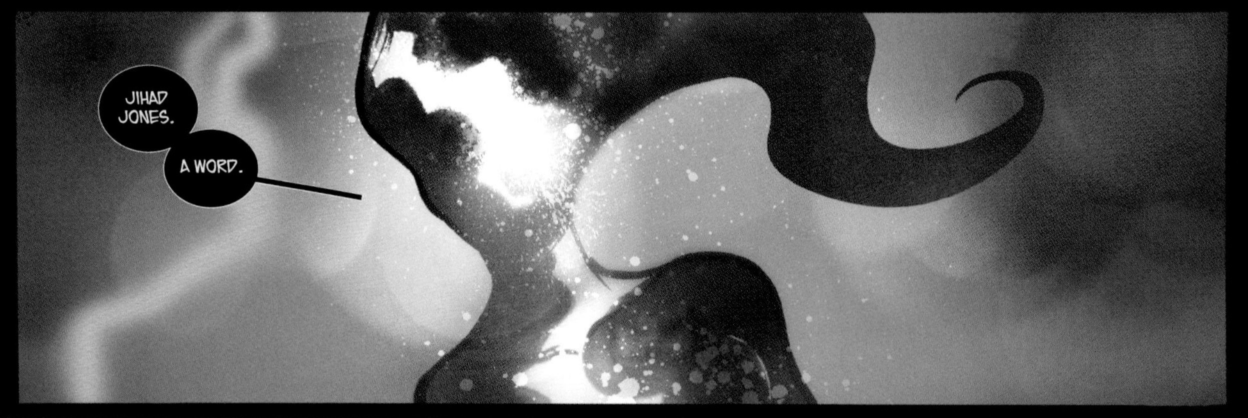
JIHAD JONES.
A WORD.

THANKS FOR KNOCKING.
CAN'T YOU SEE I'M BUSY FINDING *FULFILLMENT?*
TO SEE THINGS ON A *QUANTUM* LEVEL IS TO SEE ALL THINGS *SIMULTANEOUSLY*.
PAST. PRESENT. FUTURE. THERE IS NOTHING *LINEAR* ABOUT IT.

AND YET TIME ROLLS ON.
A PARADOX WORTH *NOTING*, WOULDN'T YOU SAY...?

THERE IS NO PARADOX. THERE ARE ONLY *FACTS.*
I AM MISSING BUT ONE.
AM I MEANT TO *GUESS* WHICH ONE?
I'M NO *VIRGIN* WHEN IT COMES TO *MIND FUCKING,* ABSOLUTELY!
BUT... MY COSMIC HYMEN...
ENOUGH.
I'M THE ONE WHO HAS ACHIEVED VICTORY IN THE PARADIGM THAT FOREVER *TRAPPED* US.
HE BELONGS TO *ME* NOW. I WILL *NOT* GIVE HIM UP.

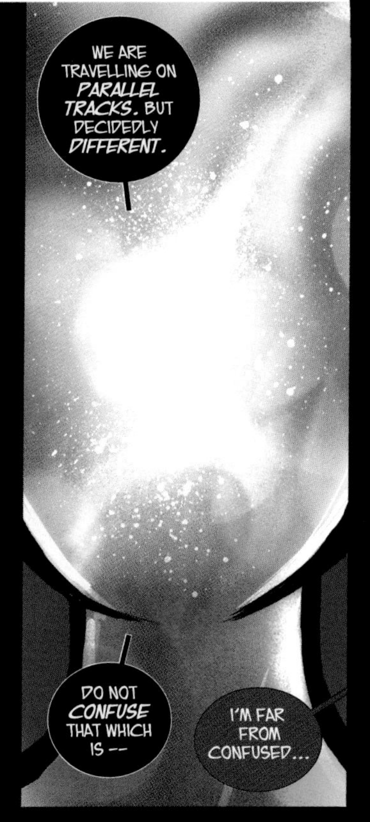

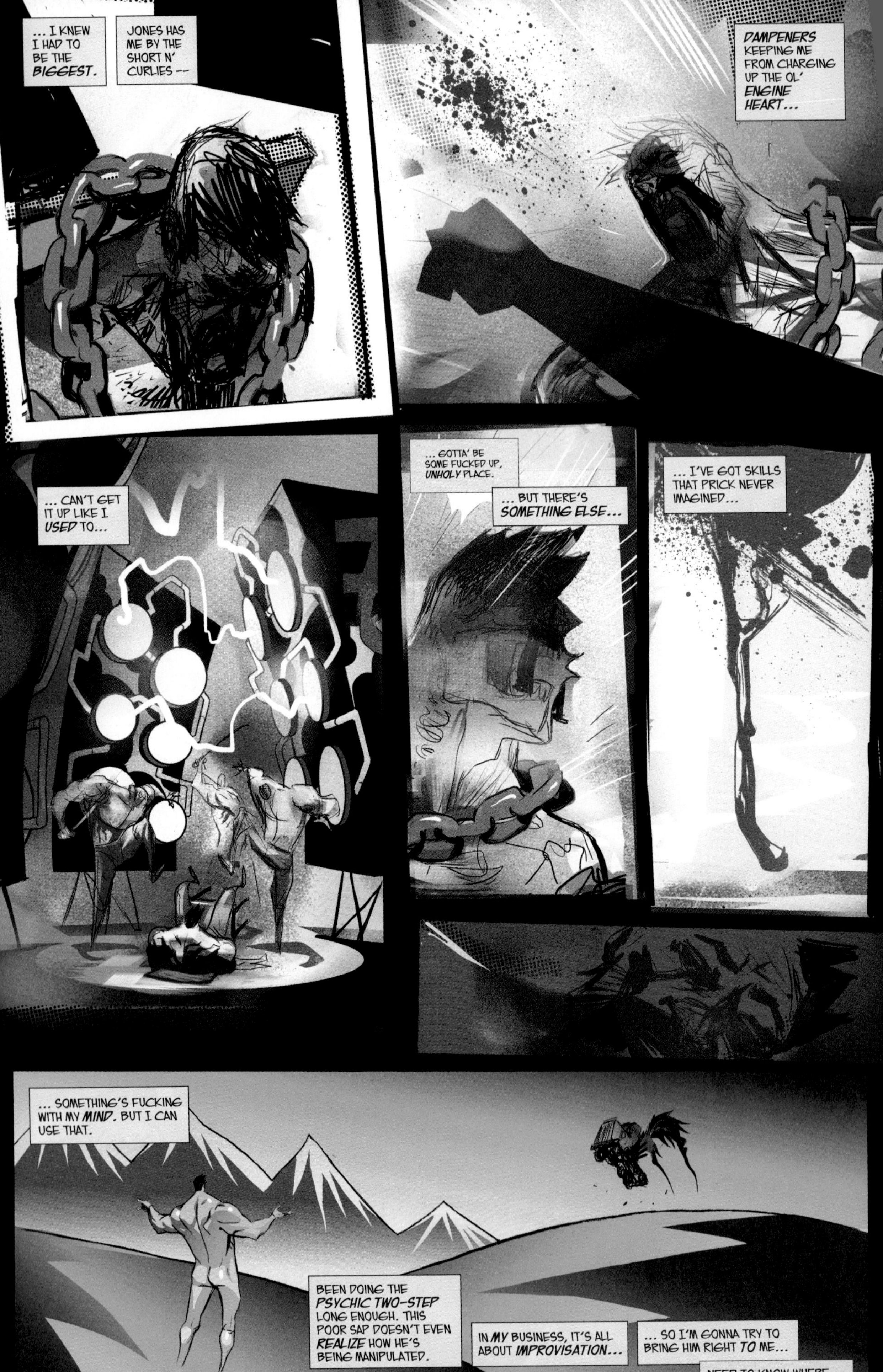
... I KNEW I HAD TO BE THE BIGGEST.
JONES HAS ME BY THE SHORT N' CURLIES --
DAMPENERS KEEPING ME FROM CHARGING UP THE OL' ENGINE HEART...
... CAN'T GET IT UP LIKE I USED TO...
... GOTTA' BE SOME FUCKED UP, UNHOLY PLACE.
... BUT THERE'S SOMETHING ELSE...
... I'VE GOT SKILLS THAT PRICK NEVER IMAGINED...
... SOMETHING'S FUCKING WITH MY MIND. BUT I CAN USE THAT.
BEEN DOING THE PSYCHIC TWO-STEP LONG ENOUGH. THIS POOR SAP DOESN'T EVEN REALIZE HOW HE'S BEING MANIPULATED.
IN MY BUSINESS, IT'S ALL ABOUT IMPROVISATION...
... SO I'M GONNA TRY TO BRING HIM RIGHT TO ME...
NEED TO KNOW WHERE THE FUCK I'M GOIN' --

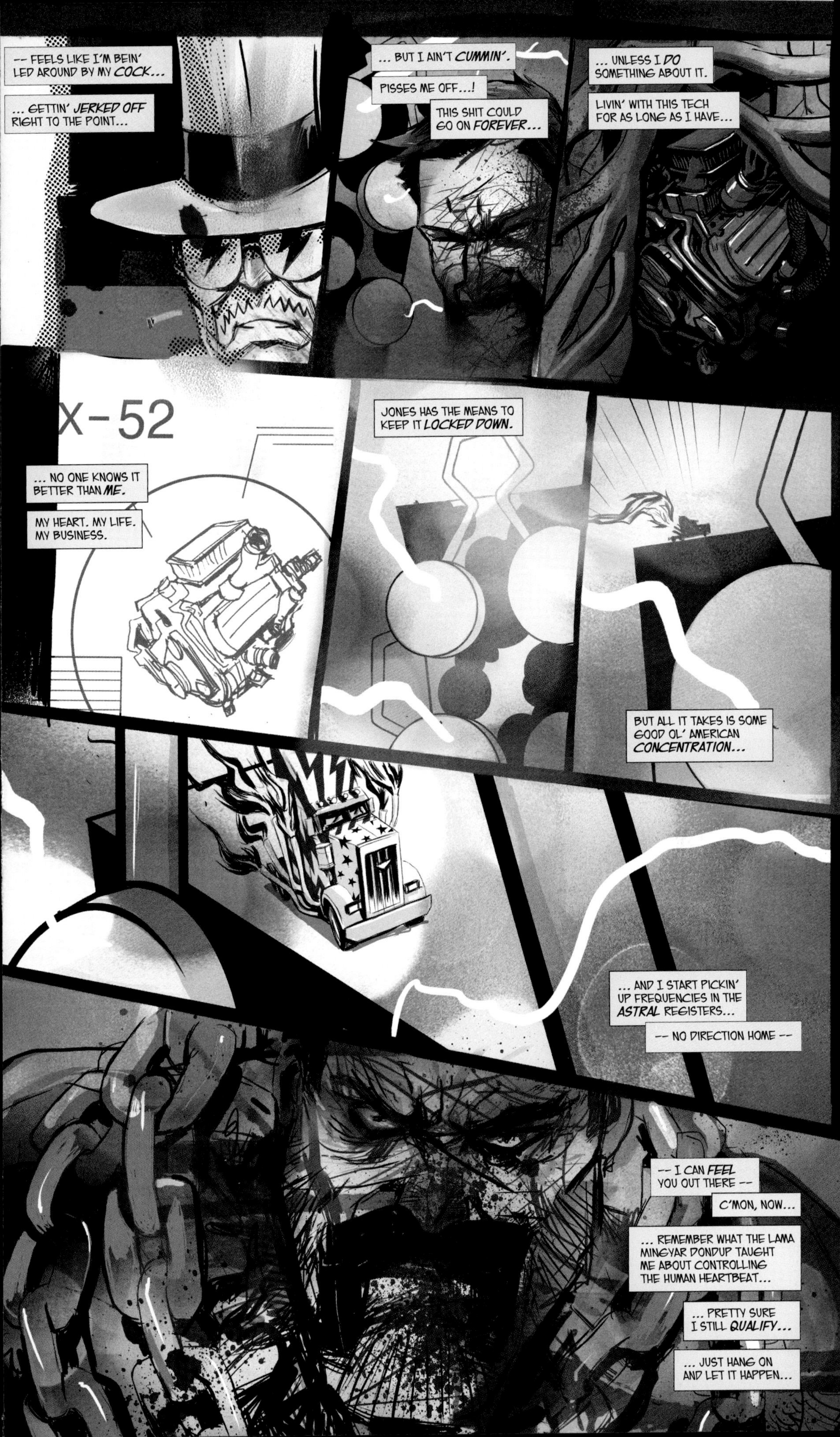

-- FEELS LIKE I'M BEIN' LED AROUND BY MY *COCK*...

... GETTIN' *JERKED OFF* RIGHT TO THE POINT...

... BUT I AIN'T *CUMMIN'*.

PISSES ME OFF...!

THIS SHIT COULD GO ON *FOREVER*...

... UNLESS I *DO* SOMETHING ABOUT IT.

LIVIN' WITH THIS TECH FOR AS LONG AS I HAVE...

X-52

... NO ONE KNOWS IT BETTER THAN *ME*.

MY HEART. MY LIFE. MY BUSINESS.

JONES HAS THE MEANS TO KEEP IT *LOCKED DOWN*.

BUT ALL IT TAKES IS SOME GOOD OL' AMERICAN *CONCENTRATION*...

... AND I START PICKIN' UP FREQUENCIES IN THE *ASTRAL* REGISTERS...

-- NO DIRECTION HOME --

-- I CAN *FEEL* YOU OUT THERE --

C'MON, NOW...

... REMEMBER WHAT THE LAMA MINGYAR DONDUP TAUGHT ME ABOUT CONTROLLING THE HUMAN HEARTBEAT...

... PRETTY SURE I STILL *QUALIFY*...

... JUST HANG ON AND LET IT HAPPEN...

... DON'T FIGHT IT...
-- DON'T FIGHT IT --
-- FEELIN' MY HEART BEATING IN MY CHEST --
-- SLOWING DOWN...
... LIKE A BOMB... COUNTING DOWN TO DETONATION.
FEELIN' LIKE...
... I AIN'T MYSELF... LIKE I USED TO BE...
THE FUCK--?!
... I'M BECOMING SOMETHING ELSE...
... SLOW IT DOWN...
YA' POOTER-POKIN' PUNK-ASS!
I'LL TEAR DAT FACE OFF YER HEAD!
IS THAT... ALL YOU GOT...?
WHAT'S NEXT... GONNA SUCK ME OFF, TOO?!
FUCK YOU, BOY--!

MOTHERFUCKER TRYIN' TO CALL ME OUT --
HOLD ON.
LOOK AT HIM. HE AIN'T MOVIN'.
WHADDYA MEAN? YOU THINK HE'S --
I DUNNO. BUT IF HE IS...
... WE'RE IN DEEP SHIT.
THERE ARE MANY MYSTERIES TO BE FOUND BETWEEN THE MOLECULES OF DARK MATTER...
... BUT NO REAL REFLECTION TO BE FOUND.

THAT'S BECAUSE YOU'RE AN ADVERB.
OR MAYBE YOU'RE TOO CONFUSED TO ACTUALLY RECOGNIZE WHAT YOU'RE SEEING THERE...
NOT ALTOGETHER TRUE.
I SAW MYSELF IN THE ABYSS. COLD EYES STARING BACK AT ME. SOMETHING STIRRED...
... A COMPULSION TO COMMUNICATE.
COMMUNICATE WITH THIS, BITCH.
I HOPE YOU NEVER FIND WHAT YOU'RE LOOKING FOR, YOU SAD, HOPELESS...
... THING.
ANOTHER DISAPPEARING ACT, EH? HMMF...
SOME OF US ARE AT THE CUSP OF ENLIGHTENMENT.
BOSS!
WE GOT A PROBLEM WITH THE RIGHTEOUS MAKER--!

A "PROBLEM"?
WHAT PROBLEM...?

SOMEBODY TALK -- NOW!
...DIDN'T HIT HIM THAT HARD...

BOSS, I DON'T KNOW WHAT HAPPENED...
WE WERE JUST --
I GAVE YOU SPECIFIC INSTRUCTIONS...

...IT'S FAR TOO SOON FOR THIS.

...SLOW IT DOWN...
SPEEDING UP --
-- IT AIN'T ME DOIN' IT!
SUMBITCH BIG RIG --

-- WHOOOAAAAA--!

PICK HIM UP. GET HIM DOWN TO THE MORGUE LOUNGE.
I'M GONNA FILET HIM LIKE A FISH...
... GET THAT TECH OUT OF HIS CHEST AND SELL IT RIGHT BACK TO THE MILITARY INDUSTRIAL COMPLEX THAT *PUT* IT THERE.
ANOTHER DEN OF NATTERING NABOBS... WEAKENED TO THE POINT OF --
-- NOW WHAT--?!

NOW *THAT'S* AN ENTRANCE TO KEEP YER PECKER PLUMP--
-- WHERE*EVER* THE HELL I AM...!
FREEZE, MOTHERFUCKAS--!

I DUNNO WHAT'S *HAPPENING* HERE, BUT I GOT A *FEELIN'* IT AIN'T *LEGAL*--!
YOU! I TOLDJA -- DON'T FUCKIN' MOVE!

!
GODDAMN IT--!

THAT ONE HAD HIS *NAME* ON IT.
NOW LET'S SEE IF I'M HERE TO --
THERE HE IS!
OKAY-DOKEY, YOU *SUUUUM*-BITCH --

-- I'M GONNA HAVE YOU HANGIN' BY YER *BALL SACK!*
THEN I'M GONNA *BUST* YOU OPEN LIKE ONE A' DEM *WETBACK PARTY DECORATIONS!*

I'M ALL OVER YOU LIKE GREASE ON BACON!
WHOSE SHIT DON'T STINK NOW?!
ARNIE B. WILLARD'S, THAT'S WHOSE!
HUH?
WHOZZAT...?
IF THERE'S ONE THING I CANNOT ABIDE...
... IT'S UNINVITED GUESTS.
HERE'S MY INVITATION, ASSHOLE.
HOW QUAINT.
YOUR PLUMAGE SUGGESTS A FORM OF LOCALIZED AUTHORITY. PERHAPS SOME KIND OF OVERNIGHT SECURITY GUARD AT SOME AMERICAN RETAIL OUTLET...?
DON'T MOVE, FUCKO.
I'LL PUT A BULLET RIGHT THROUGH YER THIRD EYE...
ALLOW ME TO RETORT IN A MANNER YOU WILL CLEARLY COMPREHEND --

-- YOU'RE FUCKING WITH A MASTER OF TERROR!
CHRIST ALMIGHTY --
I'M A GOOD SHOT...
... BUT I AIN'T GOOD ENOUGH.
FUCK A TWAT --

I FEEL FRUSTRATIONS WORTH VENTING --

SUMBITCH FIGHTS *DIRTY*.

NOW HE'S *SAYING* SOMETHING...
YOUR TIMING IS, IN A WORD, FORTUITOUS.
I FEEL THINGS HAVE BEEN LEFT... ***UNFINISHED.*** WHAT WITH MY OPPOSITE NUMBER HAVING SHUFFLED LOOSE THE MORTAL COIL FAR ***EARLIER*** THAN EXPECTED.
BUT I STILL NEED SOMETHING TO ***PUMMEL...***

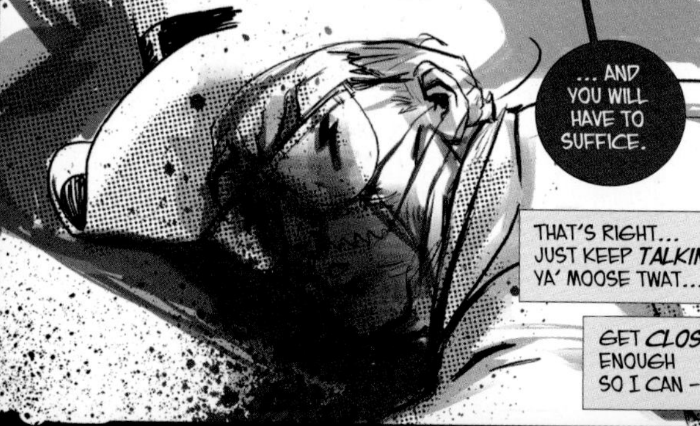

... AND YOU WILL HAVE TO SUFFICE.
THAT'S RIGHT... JUST KEEP *TALKIN'*, YA' MOOSE TWAT...
GET *CLOSE* ENOUGH SO I CAN --

HAH--!
THAT ONE SHOULDA LAID HIM RIGHT THE FUCK OUT --
AH SHIT.
ONE LAST GASP. ONE FINAL GLORY.
A PHYSICAL *EPITAPH,* AS IT WERE.
I'M ACTUALLY IN A *GOOD MOOD* FOR A CHANGE --
-- SO LET'S CELEBRATE VIOLENCE!
YOU LOOK TERRIBLE. ALMOST AS BAD AS THE LATE RIGHTEOUS MAKER.
LET'S MOVE ON. THE SACRIFICE TO *NOTHING* AWAITS.
THIS, BY THE WAY, IS THE MOST *EFFICIENT* MANNER IN WHICH TO SEPARATE THE CERVICAL VERTEBRAE FROM THE SKULL...
HANDS OFF THE FAT LOSER, JONES...

... WE'RE NOT DONE YET.
THAT'S IT... MAKE IT SOUND TOUGH. DON'T GIVE HIM ANY HINT OF HOW FUCKED UP YOU STILL ARE.
STILL TRYING TO GET THE ENGINE HEART BACK UP TO CAPACITY. IT AIN'T HAPPENING FAST ENOUGH...
... BUT I CAN'T WAIT ANYMORE.
I CAN HEAR IT POUNDING IN MY EARDRUMS. MICRO-PISTONS STRAINING TO FIRE. VESICLE VALVES STRUGGLING TO SEND SIGNAL PARTICLES THROUGH WAFER THIN STEEL MEMBRANES.
ALL OF IT SINGING IN UNISON. MY NEW THEME SONG.
THE SOUND OF ALL THOSE YEARS... ALL THOSE DECADES OF DECADENCE... FINALLY CATCHING UP WITH ME.

8-TRACK
PART EIGHT
BASQUIAT ?

I DUNNO, DICK... YOU THINK ALL THIS MIGHT BE JUST A LITTLE --
IT'S EXACTLY WHAT WE NEED...
... AND WHAT THE FUCK DO YOU KNOW ABOUT MOBILIZING A MILITARY ACTION, ANYWAY?!
FAIR ENOUGH. BUT ARE WE INVADING A COUNTRY HERE OR WHAT...?
DEPENDS ON WHETHER OR NOT YOU BELIEVE IN "PROPORTIONAL RESPONSE" OR NOT.
ME? I'M THE KIND OF OLD BASTARD THAT PREFERS BRINGING A GUN TO A KNIFE FIGHT.
YOU PROBABLY COULDA USED SOME OF THAT ATTITUDE IN THE OL' LATE NIGHT COMBAT ZONE, EH?
HEH... YEAH, MAYBE SO.
JUST SEEMS LIKE A LOT OF, Y'KNOW, TAXPAYER DOLLARS AT STAKE WHEN YOU AND I BOTH KNOW WE'RE THE ONES WHO --
WHAT DO YOU CARE?!
BESIDES, THEY SHOULD BE THANKING US.
FOR AN ECONOMY THAT'S GONE STRAIGHT INTO THE SHITTER, WE'RE GIVING IT THE GREATEST ENEMA OF ALL...
... WAR.
MOMENTS LIKE THESE, CLARITY'S A TOUGH ONE TO COME BY...
BUT WHEN YOU REALLY THINK ABOUT IT, IT ALL COMES DOWN TO ONE, SIMPLE THING --

-- WHEN YOU GOTTA' HIT SOMETHING...
... HIT IT FUCKING HARD.
THEN THERE'S KNOWING HOW TO TAKE A HIT...
DIE, VAINGLORIOUS PRICK--!
MAYBE SOMEDAY, JONES --
-- BUT NOT TODAY.
YOU OWE ME BUCKETS OF BLOOD!
AND I WILL NOT BE DENIED!
WHU...?
JEEZUS PALOMINO... GUESS I GOT TATERED...!

... WUT THE FUCK IS GOIN' ON HERE?!
SOME KINDA... BITCH-SLAPPIN' SQUARE DANCE...?
I'LL STOMP YOUR IDEOLOGY INTO MULCH!
I DON'T... GET IT...
... THE BOB-TAIL DRIVER'S... FIGHTIN' FER ME...?
BITCH--!
YOUR BRAIN JUICE IS MY STEAK SAUCE --
YEAH, YEAH, YEAH...
HE'S OUT OF HIS FUCKIN' MIND. MORE SO THAN USUAL.
BUT I'M TRYING TO ENJOY THIS...
... JUST IN CASE THIS IS THE LAST HURRAH.

THIS IS ABOUT YER PANSY SIDEKICK, AIN'T IT?!
I KNEW YOU SWUNG THAT WAY!
TYPICAL AMERICAN HOMOPHOBIA --
-- NO WONDER YOU TRIED TO KILL ME WITH SUCH FERVOR!
BUT WHAT I AM... CANNOT BE EXTINGUISHED!
I AM THE EVERLASTING SUN --
-- I AM THE FUTURE!
JUST SPOUTIN' MORE APE SHIT...
I LET THIS FREAK KICK MY ASS...?!
HANDS OFF, RIGHTEOUS MAKER --
-- YOU HAVE TO BUY ME DINNER FIRST!
YOU HAVE NEVER UNDERSTOOD ME! I POSSESS PROPHECY OF THE MIND!
SO FIERCELY BEAUTIFUL!
I AM BEYOND RAGE!

MY *STRENGTH* IS THE *PAIN* OF A THOUSAND DYING DREAMS...!

RIGHT. HE'S OFF ON A *RANT* NOW...

... THAT GIVES ME THE CHANCE TO TRY A LITTLE *END-AROUND*.

I WALK THROUGH THE *BLACK NIGHT* -- I SCREAM THE *SEVEN TONGUES!*

SHE WHO DESTROYS!

I NEVER HAD A BEEF WITH JIHAD JONES' IDEOLOGY... BESIDES THE FACT THAT I NEVER HAD ANY GODDAMN IDEA WHAT HE WAS *TALKING* ABOUT.

I WANNA BE A *LIVE AND LET LIVE* KINDA GUY...

... BUT THIS FUCKNUT IS A TICKIN' *TIME BOMB*.

I PUT MY *DOGS* DOWN WHEN THEY GO RABID.

IF I COULD JUST... FIND MY...

KALI DOES NOT *GIVE* THAT WHICH YOU *DESIRE!*
BUT I WILL *CONSUME* YOUR REALITY, RIGHTEOUS MAKER -- FOR I AM THE *SIXTH TERRIBLE ELEMENT!*

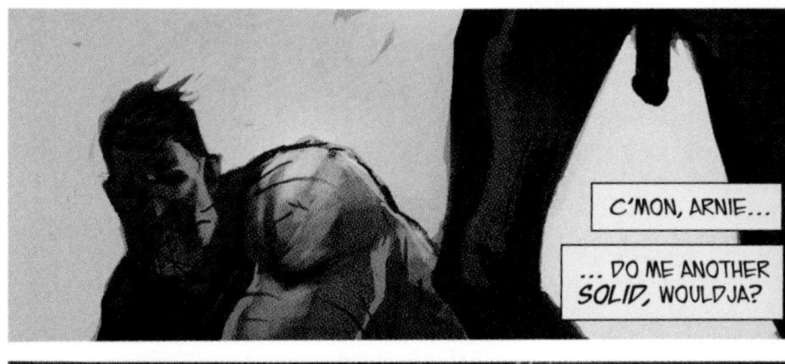

C'MON, ARNIE...
... DO ME ANOTHER *SOLID*, WOULDJA?

I NEED YOU TO GET YOUR *SHIT* TOGETHER...
... GET MY SHIT TOGETHER...
... AND *END* THIS...

THE TIME HAS COME TO ENTER THE FINAL DEMONIC DANCE CONTEST!
JETBOY! YOUR MOUTH FOREVER ON MY DARKHAMMER!
ALL THE TURTLES -- HOPPING AND SCRATCHING!
TUNE HIM OUT. JUST TUNE HIM THE FUCK OUT.
IGNORE THE EXTRASENSORY CROSS-CURRENTS...
... RESIST THE GRAVITY OF HIS PSYCHIC EVENT HORIZON...
... THE SHRAPNEL OF JONES' EXPLODING NIGHTMARES...
... YOU'RE STRONGER THAN THAT, OLD MAN.
ONE MORE TUG ON THE GEAR SHIFT...
... IT AIN'T MIND CONTROL, ALRIGHT?
JUST A LITTLE NUDGE...
THERE WE GO --
-- THERE IT IS...
I KNOW YOU GOT YER ASS KICKED, ARNIE... BUT YOU NEED TO FOCUS...
... CAN'T... HARDLY FOCUS...
... GODDAMMIT...!

C'MON, YA' FAT BASTARD...
ALL YOU GOTTA' DO --
-- IS SQUEEZE --
-- THE TRIGGER --
HNNG--!
FUCKIN' A.
THAT'S ALL I NEEDED --
-- TO MAKE A FINAL, MAD DASH --
-- AND ANOTHER ONE I OWE YA, ARNIE B. --
-- FOR BRINGING ME THE MEANS...
..NNNNN..
... THIS IS... NOTHING...
MY OWN BLOOD... A SWEET ELIXIR OF GLORIOUS --
-- DECADENCE...

NOW *THAT'S* A FUCKIN' GREAT SOUND.
IT'S ALL ABOUT THE *GRILL,* Y'KNOW. ADAMANTIUM AND VIBRANIUM, REINFORCED...
... MAKES ALL THE DIFFERENCE.
IT'S A RARE THING WHEN YOU'RE HAVING A REAL *MOMENT*...
... A GODDAMN *TRANSCENDENT* MOMENT...
... AND YOU'RE COMPLETELY *AWARE* OF IT WHILE YOU'RE *HAVING* IT.
OH YEAH...
... *THIS* ONE'LL KEEP ME GOING FOR AWHILE.
AND THERE IT IS.
FUCK ME.
THEY WANTED 'EM ALL *DEAD*. MIGHT'VE TAKEN ME LONG ENOUGH...
... BUT MISSION ACCOMPLISHED.

MAYBE THIS TIME, I CAN ACTUALLY --
N-NOW HOLD ON, YOU SUMBITCH...
... I HOPE YOU AIN'T THINKIN' THIS IS ALL WRAPPED UP NEAT AN' TIDY-LIKE...!
THIS MAY BE THE END OF THE ROAD ALRIGHT...
... BUT NOT IN THE WAY YER PROBABLY THINKIN'.
YOU AIN'T GOTTA HOPE IN HELL OF WALKIN' OUTTA HERE UNTIL YOU SETTLE UP WIT' ME.
SIGH
RIGHT.
NOT ENOUGH THAT I SAVED YOUR MISBEGOTTEN LIFE, IS IT...?
I KNOW, I KNOW... THAT AIN'T THE CODE.
SO... WHERE D'YA WANNA TAKE THIS, ARINE...?
I-I THINK... YER UNDER ARREST, BAKER-MAN...!
I DON'T CARE... WHAT YOU'VE DONE FER ME... OR ANYONE ELSE...
PAR FOR THE COURSE, THESE DAYS.
JUST GET YER STINKIN' HANDS UP AN' --
NIGHT TERRORS HIDING IN THE HEARTS OF MEN...

... SO MANY SECRETS. KEPT EVEN FROM THEMSELVES.
AND YET, ALL THE ANSWERS ARE WITHIN. THEY ONLY REQUIRE THE WILL TO FIND THEM.
THAT... IS WHAT I ENVY MOST.
THEIR FLAWS ARE THEIR SALVATION.
OH SHIT.
I MISSED THIS ONE, TOO...?
THE ABSOLUTELY.
GUESS I WAS REALLY HOPING I'D NEVER HAVE TO DEAL WITH THIS FREAK SHOW EVER AGAIN...
I SENSE A DISTINCT ABSENCE OF RIGHTEOUSNESS...
YOU REALLY KNOW HOW TO HURT A GUY.
IS THIS ANOTHER PROMISE OF THE APOCALYPSE...?
... YER SUCH A TEASE.
MOTHERFUCKER. THEY DO KNOW EACH OTHER...!
I DON'T KNOW WHAT THE GAME IS...
... DON'T EVEN KNOW IF I CAN PLAY...
WHAT AM I DOIN' HERE?!
THE APOCALYPSE YOU FEAR... IS A FANTASY.
ALL THAT REMAINS...
... IS THE SELF.

YER TALKIN' SHIT AGAIN, AIN'T YA...?!
OR IS THIS MORE FUCKIN' WITH MY MIND?! I'M STILL PISSED ABOUT THAT...!
YOUR MIND, ARNIE B. WILLARD... IS MUCH MORE MALLEABLE THAN YOU COULD EVER COMPREHEND.
THE MYSTERY OF THE HUMAN MIND...
... ITS CAPABILITIES... ITS INHERENT DESIRES...
... ITS WILL TO ACHIEVE SELF-ACTUALIZATION.
THE ONLY DRIVE BY WHICH THE LIFE OF AN ORGANISM IS DETERMINED.
YOU KNOW WHERE YOU CAME FROM... AND THUS HAVE THE TOOLS TO DISCOVER YOUR INTENDED DESTINATION.
I THINK I'M STARTING TO GET IT...
... IT'S A MATTER OF INFORMATION.
THE REST OF US... WE'RE THE SUM OF OUR EXPERIENCES, RIGHT? BUT WE GOT A SENSE OF A STARTING POINT.
ALL THIS TIME... ALL THESE YEARS...
... AND YOU STILL DON'T KNOW YER OWN ORIGIN?
AN EXPANDING UNIVERSE OF PAIN... AND I REMAIN SO EMPTY...
... MY BLACK HOLE HEART... ACHES FOR IT...
-- TELL ME WHAT I AM--!

HEY, ALL YOU HADDA DO WAS ASK...!
LUCKILY, YOU FUCKED WITH THE RIGHT HERO. YOU KNOW I'M ONE OF THE FEW WHO KNOWS WHERE ALL THE BODIES ARE BURIED.
I'M A GODDAMN FOUNT OF KNOWLEDGE...
... EVEN WHERE YOU'RE CONCERNED.
TELL ME.
FINE. JUST REMEMBER THAT YOU WANTED TO KNOW.
DON'T BLAME ME IF YOU END UP DISAPPOINTED...
"... THE THING IS, YOU'RE NOT EXACTLY THE PRODUCT OF SOME GRAND, COSMIC DESTINY. YOUR BEGINNINGS ARE MUCH MORE... HUMBLE.
"YOU STARTED OUT AS A SINGLE, SIMPLE IDEA BURIED IN THE BRAIN OF AN AUTISTIC FIVE-YEAR OLD IN MONTANA SUFFERING FROM A FORM OF LESCH-NYHAN, A MILD CASE OF ALS AND A BIZARRE TYPE OF HYPERPLASIA...
"... BUT SAID IDEA WAS OF GREAT INTEREST TO A GROUP OF BLACK SCIENCE DOCTORS THAT HAD THE TECHNOLOGY TO EXTRACT THAT IDEA AND PUT IT INTO PRACTICE.
"YOU'D LOVE THESE GUYS. TO CALL THEM 'ALTERNATIVE' WOULD BE A GROSS UNDERSTATEMENT. THESE GUYS LIVED OUTSIDE THE BOX.
"THEY HAD THE PASSION TO MAKE THIS SHIT REAL...
"... BUT IT SURE AS HELL WASN'T EASY.
"THERE WERE DIVORCES... THERE WERE DISFIGUREMENTS... THERE WERE DEATHS... ALL IN THE NAME OF GETTING THAT GOD MACHINE UP AND RUNNING.
"AN IMPRESSIVE PIECE OF TECH, NO DOUBT ABOUT IT..."
... A GODDAMN MECHA-WOMB, PRIMED AND PREPPED TO INCUBATE A SPECIFIC KIND OF LIFE FORM.
AND THAT'S EXACTLY WHAT THEY DID.

"THEY TOOK THE IDEA AND THEY GAVE IT FORM. GAVE IT SUBSTANCE. GAVE IT SEX ORGANS. BUILT ACCORDING TO THEIR TWISTED TASTES.
"THEY DIDN'T EVEN BOTHER TO NAME YOU.
"THEY GREW YOU QUICK. THEY NEEDED YOU SUBMISSIVE. WHADDA LIFE YA' LED THERE...
"... SURVIVING ON NOTHING BUT BUCKETS OF ORIGINAL RECIPE THEY'D TOSS IN TO YA'... JUST ENOUGH TO KEEP YER STRENGTH UP FOR YER REAL PURPOSE...
"... TO BE AN OBJECT OF HUMILIATION.
"EVERY FETISH THESE ASSHOLES EVER DREAMED OF... THEY USED YOU TO INDULGE IN THEM. FROM THE ABSURD TO THE UNSPEAKABLE... THEY DID IT ALL.
"YOU WERE THE BISCUIT, BABY.
"YOU WERE THEIR SEX SLAVE."
"IT TOOK A FEW DECADES BEFORE YOU FIGURED OUT HOW TO BLOW THAT PARTICULAR POP STAND.
"BY THEN, YOU WERE PISSED AT ALL OF REALITY..."
... AND IT WAS UP TO GUYS LIKE ME TO MAKE SURE YOU DIDN'T GET TOO BUNCHED UP ABOUT IT.
LAST THING ANYONE NEEDS IS A FREAK LIKE YOU ACTING OUT.
FRANKLY, I'M NOT SURPRISED YOU BLOCKED IT ALL OUT...
... THAT KINDA MEMORY IS A FUCKIN' HEAVY LOAD TO CARRY AROUND.
BUT... I STILL CAN'T...
... REMEMBER...
... I AM...
... LESS THAN NOTHING...

CHECK THIS OUT.
THIS IS ANOTHER BLACK MARKET SPECIAL. AN ENTROPATHIC FIREARM.
PROTOTYPE DESIGN. PLASMA PROTEIN MIX. BIT OF ANTI-MATTER. A ONE SHOT DEAL. MY OWN PERSONAL INSURANCE POLICY...
... AND IT ONLY WORKS ON YOU.
WHAT THE FUCK D'YA THINK YER DOIN' --
STAY OUT OF THIS, JACKASS.
Y'KNOW, AFTER I LOCKED YOU UP AT BERTRAND, I FIGURED I'D NEVER HAVE TO USE IT --
ALL THIS TIME...
... YOU POSSESSED THE FINAL SOLUTION. I ALWAYS SUSPECTED MY OMNIPOTENCE WAS MERELY IMAGINED.
GIVE IT TO ME.
FIGURED YA' MIGHT ASK.
YA' GOT THE ANSWERS YOU WERE LOOKIN' FOR, KID. THE ONLY THING I HAVE LEFT TO GIVE YA'...
... IS YER DIGNITY BACK.
KNOWING THIS... IS TOO MUCH TO BEAR.
MY PATH TO DIVINITY IS NO MORE.
HEY...
... NONE OF US ARE AS DIVINE AS WE'D LIKE TO BE.
ANOTHER DIFFICULT TRUTH...
... MY BLACK HOLE HEART IS AN EMPTY VESSEL.
THERE IS NO CHOICE LEFT BUT ONE...
... AND MUST SET MYSELF FREE --

I ALWAYS WONDERED WHAT WOULD HAPPEN IF THE ABSOLUTELY RUPTURED ITS OWN SOUL SINGULARITY.
WOULD THE GODDAMN WORLD END...?
THERE'S A MOMENT WHERE IT FEELS LIKE IT MIGHT.
JEEZUS FUCK! SOMETHING'S GOIN' RIGHT INTO MY --
M-MOMMA..?
I THINK... I JUST DROPPED A LOG...

HUH.
WELL, THAT FUCKIN' WORKED, DIDN'T IT...?
H-HE... SHE... IT KILLED ITSELF?! WITH YER ENTRO-WHATEVER PEA SHOOTER...?!
NOT EXACTLY, ARNIE...
... IT IS A PROTOTYPE, BUT A TOY PROTOTYPE.
MATTEL TOOK A SHOT AT MERCHANDISING ME BACK IN THE LATE EIGHTIES. Y'KNOW, DOLLS AN' SHIT.
DIDN'T QUITE WORK OUT, BUT I KEPT A FEW SOUVENIRS.
LIKE THIS ONE...
... GUESS THE ABSOLUTELY BOUGHT MY BULLSHIT. HOOK, LINE AN' SINKER.
YOU... FUCKIN' TRICKED IT...
... MADE IT THINK IT WUZ --
NEVER UNDERESTIMATE THE POWER OF SUGGESTION.
BESIDES, I'M SURE DEATH WAS ITS MOST INTERESTING OPTION. IT JUST WOULDN'T ADMIT IT ON ITS OWN. IT NEEDED AN EXCUSE.
ALTHOUGH, JUST FER THE RECORD, ALL THAT SHIT ABOUT ITS ORIGIN... THE KID, THE GANGBANGING, THE CHICKEN DINNERS...
... I MADE ALL THAT UP, TOO.

SO... IF NONE OF YER STORY WUZ TRUE...
... WHERE THE HELL DID IT COME FROM?!
HONESTLY... I HAVE NO FUCKIN' CLUE.
SOME THINGS ARE PROBABLY BETTER LEFT UNKNOWN ANYWAY, DON'TCHA THINK?
WHATEVER IT WAS... IT'S GONE NOW. THE GOOD GUYS WON.
BY THE SKIN OF OUR GODDAMN TEETH, ACTUALLY.
WHO KNEW I'D SCORE WITH A HAIL MARY MIND GAME?
MENTAL CHESS WAS NEVER A SKILL I WAS PARTICULARLY KNOWN FOR.
WHERE...
... WHERE YOU GOIN'?
WUT THE HELL... AM I SUPPOSED TO DO NOW...?
SHIT.
FIGURE I OWED THIS FAT FUCK...
... SO I GAVE HIM THE FULL-ON, PRICE IS RIGHT SHOWCASE PACKAGE.
ALL EXPENSES PAID...

...LET HIM SPEND SOME TIME IN "PARADISE" FOR AWHILE. LET HIM PROCESS THE EXPERIENCE.
SET HIM UP WITH SOME FALSE SUPERPERSON I.D. AND LET HIM BASK IN THE GLORY OF ADVENTURES HE NEVER HAD. LET HIM SIT IN THE SUN AND IMPRESS THE REST OF THE CLIENTELE WITH HIS MOONSHINE WISDOM AND BACKWOODS BANTER.
A LITTLE HEDONISM CAN GO A LONG WAY. I SHOULD KNOW. BUT, HELL...
...I'M SURE HE'LL MAKE OUT BETTER THAN I DID THERE...!
MEANWHILE, I GOT MY OWN GODDAMN DÉNOUEMENT WAITING FER ME...
BREAKER ONE! ALL YOU GEAR JAMMERS OUT THERE -- I HOPE YA GOT YER EARS ON!
CHECK MY TWENTY: I'M TEARING STRAIGHT UP WHAT'LL EVENTUALLY BECOME THE THIRTY-FIVE IN MY NEWLY-MINTED LIBERTY BELLE SEQUEL!
SHE'S JUICED UP WITH METAL FLAKE UPHOLSTERY AN' EVERYTHING ELSE YOU CAN SCAM UNDER A TEQUILA MOON!
THE RIGHTEOUS MAKER IS BACK ON THE ASPHALT AIRWAVES AN' READY T'MAKE A LITTLE TROUBLE IN THE TWENTY-FIRST CENTURY!
SEEMS I'VE GAINED A CUNT HAIR'S WORTH OF PERSPECTIVE SINCE I LAST BROADCAST ON THIS HERE FREQUENCY --
-- YOU LUCKY FUCKS, YOU!
BROADCASTING ON AN OPEN CHANNEL. NOT EXACTLY COVERT...

... BUT THAT'S KINDA THE IDEA.
ALL UNITS! RADIO SIGNAL ACQUIRED!
TARGET CURRENTLY APPROACHING AT ONE HUNDRED AND NINE MILES PER HOUR --
-- ALL UNITS MOVE INTO POSITION! PREPARE TO ENGAGE!
THIS IS... SOME SET UP, DICK.
BET YER BLOATED ASS IT IS, FUNNY MAN.
AND RIGHT ON SCHEDULE, TOO...
... WE'LL BLOW THIS OL' BASTARD SKY HIGH BEFORE HE CAN EVEN SQUEEZE OUT A SINGLE SHIT.
NOBODY FUCKS ME AND GETS AWAY WITH IT...!
THESE TWO...
... SITTIN' FAT AND HAPPY WITH THE ENTIRE MILITARY-INDUSTRIAL COMPLEX SUPPORTING THEIR BIG LIE.
LIKE DUCKS ON THE POND.
STARING DOWN THE FORCES OF AUTHORITY...
BREAKER-BREAKER! THIS IS A CALL TO ALL MY PAST RESIGNATIONS! IT'S BEEN TOO LONG!
DOES THE TERM "BLAZE OF GLORY" MEAN ANYTHING TO YOU FUCKERS?!

AS A ONE-TIME WORKER BEE MYSELF, I LEARNED A LONG TIME AGO:
ALL GOOD WORK IS DONE IN DEFIANCE OF MANAGEMENT.
SOMETHING ELSE I'VE LEARNED THE HARD WAY...
... NEVER TRUST A POLITICIAN.
DO IT HOWEVER YOU PREFER. WITH OUR FULL SUPPORT.
SURE, SURE...
THEY HAD THEIR GREAT IDEA TO PULL ME OUT OF THE MOTHBALLS. AND THEN THEY CUT ME LOOSE.
TIME TO SHOW THESE COCKSUCKERS JUST HOW "EXPENDABLE" I REALLY AM...!
MAYBE THIS IS THE MOMENT I WAS MISSING ALL ALONG...
... A FINAL ACT OF PURE RIGHTEOUSNESS...?
NAH, PROBABLY NOT.
THERE'S SOMETHING MUCH BIGGER AT STAKE HERE.
AN ENTIRE BATTALION'S WORTH OF LASER SIGHTS WASH OVER ME -- AS RED AS THE BLOOD THEY WANT ME TO SPILL ALL OVER MY BRAND NEW UPHOLSTERY -- AND SUDDENLY I'M BAPTIZED...
... BORN AGAIN ...
I DON'T GIVE A GODDAMN. I'M A MOTHERFUCKING SUPERHERO.
MAYBE I'M THE ONLY ONE LEFT WHO REALLY KNOWS WHAT THAT MEANS --
WHOA...
... I JUST CAME.
FINALLY.
FELT GOOD.
FUCKIN' A.

THE END

BUTCHER BAKER™
THE RIGHTEOUS MAKER

A TON OF X-TRA SHIT

THIS IS THE SHAPE OF THE UNIVERSE

Here we go. "Abridged", baby! Everyone present and accounted for, comfy and cozy, I hope... nestled within the warm embrace of the greatest storytelling medium on God's green Earth: the comicbook. I think some of you would have to agree that it's the perfect diamond bullet delivery system for your entertainment-hungry lizard brain. Maybe *most* of you would agree. But, yeah, I'm one of *those* guys... I believe these things can actually change your world. Why? Because they fucking changed *mine* in a big, bad way. Without comicbooks, I wouldn't be living anything close to this life. They saved me from a life of washing dishes, flipping

burgers, digging ditches and other tedious occupations that can be inflicted on directionless Twentysomethings worldwide. So, hell yes, I've got a *personal* stake in this art form, in this medium, in this delivery system. Forget the obvious "modern mythology" bullshit. Forget the Hollywood R&D/collective ass raping that we've been saddled with more intensely for the past decade plus. It's the *power* of the medium that interests me. But, even when I can set aside the dark shit of my own subconscious and look more objectively at what comicbooks mean to the culture, both realistically and potentially… even *that* blows my fucking mind. Comicbooks have that unique ability to force open a window into our very souls and reflect something back to us that can enlighten us even as they thrill us. And besides the visceral aspects of the medium, there's the not-so-obvious social aspects. Want to get a glimpse into mainstream pop culture in

2022? Read a comicbook in 2012. It's like a set of crystal balls hanging perfectly between your hairy thighs. Comicbooks as Lo-Fi Futureshit.

Hardcover format notwithstanding, that's what they're *supposed* to be.

True story: One night, in a goddamned Mel's Diner (of all places!), I ran into "Sturdy" Steve Ditko. Or maybe it was someone *claiming* to be Sturdy Steve. Since there are no recent photos of the man known to exist, I couldn't be certain. He sure as hell spoke with the hard boiled authority of a grand master artist who'd been at Ground Zero for the creation of the Marvel Universe. He talked at length about growing up in Johnstown and designing Spider-Man's costume and kicking ass on the Destructor with the late, great "Artful" Archie Goodwin and examining John Galt and Objectivism... so I was more than convinced. Granted, I'd just run a blistering mind-marathon of my own that day (polishing the chrome hubcaps on several animated television series designed to subvert impressionable young minds worldwide) and was probably still reeling from merely contemplating an anti-Clinton inhale of uncharacteristically massive proportions (to celebrate another day of survival in the Entertainment Industry™), so what I was experiencing in that moment could certainly be up for interpretation. I did my damnedest to hold up my end of the conversation, first by talking in detail about Burt Reynolds' cinematic glory days, back when he was runnin' moonshine and/or bootleggin' beer across the humid, tree-lined byways of my youth. Secondly, by talking about my own history of debunking the Horatio Alger myth, despite the occasional rainbow that I've found myself lucky enough to trip over. I finally asked him about the power and the simplicity of the nine-panel grid... and the next three hours were a complete blur. I'll admit, it wasn't exactly a Kathmandu-level moment, but I could've sworn I saw the eternally dignified ghost of Steve "Baby" Gerber in the corner, eavesdropping on our conversation. At first, I was slightly unnerved by his ethereal presence but when he gave me the thumbs up, I breathed a little easier.

Whether real or imagined, it was an inspired encounter. It was the kind of experience that instantly reinvigorated my love of comicbooks and made me want to dive headfirst into the four-color ocean that was lovingly beckoning me back again. It was like the Power of the Pussy... times a thousand. The last time I'd felt anything close to this kind of electric jolt to my pleasure centers, it was the moment, two weeks prior, when I'd discovered that the one, the only, "Free-Wheelin'" Frank Robbins -- in addition to writing several Batman stories back in the early 70's -- actually *illustrated* a handful of issues, much to the dismay of the average comicbook fan (with his or her average comicbook sensibility). How did I not know this already?! Fucking hell. But, y'know, that just made me love him all the more. Jump on the Internet and do your own Google Image Search. You won't be sorry. If nothing else, this admission should adequately illustrate that, when I want that pure hit of uncut, comicbook goodness, I go to them as a *reader* first. I want to mainline those four fucking colors just like I did when I was a young scrub scrambling my skinny white ass to the nearest drug store or

7-11 to ascend the rickety spinner racks stuffed unceremoniously in the corner. It's the kind of golden memory that can never be tarnished, no matter what kind of nightmares are inflicted upon us with the onset of adulthood.

"C" IS FOR CREATIVITY

So there came a day, a day unlike any other, when I drunkenly stumbled into a local comicbook emporium -- which, here in Hollywood, can be the kind of bitchin', psychedelic wonderland I dared not even dream of as a kid -- and, almost instantly, the miasmic stench of death permeated the air to an almost suffocating degree. It wasn't the environment; it was the goods on display there, primarily those located in the so-called "mainstream" section of said store. I looked around at the racks and shelves and more racks and more shelves of four-color, superhero "entertainment" and in my subsequent dizziness I realized I was *bored as fuck*! How the holy hell did that happen?! I mean... c'mon! I love superhero comicbooks. Superhero comicbooks are life. Superhero comicbooks are sex. Superhero comicbooks make my dick hard. Superhero comicbooks are everything good in this world, aren't they?

(*... and for anyone wondering why I'm sticking to my one-word, "comicbook" moniker for the beloved art form... let it be known that I lifted it from the legendary Stan "The Man" Lee himself, from an interview he gave where he lamented the perception of his chosen profession because the separated "comic book" nomenclature tended to diminish the power contained within. That it was an outdated term. That it suggested frivolity and nothing more. His alternative choice was the term I choose to meme the fuck out of through my own paltry efforts in the press circles I travel within. Hence, the single, all encompassing word, "comicbook". ALL HAIL THE MIGHTY COMICBOOK! And thank you, Stan.*)

I've been a professional in this backwards business for 15 fucking years. I've seen so much, read so much, written so much in that time alone... but I never thought I'd reach my own, personal threshold. So, to survey the current state of the superhero comicbook and find it extremely lacking was like a slap in the face to me. Where are the endless amounts of Lo-Fi Futureshit I've been craving? Honestly, it felt like a piece of my soul was getting stomped on incessantly by countless pairs of tiny feet wearing Gene Simmons' demon boots. Immediately, I reverted to the age-old, "It's not you, it's me"-excuse for my feelings of emptiness. It was difficult to outright blame superhero comicbooks for sucking so hard. I didn't want to admit how much the atrophy had set it. But then I reconsidered, thought to myself, "Fuck all that. Things *are* boring right now. It happens. But what can you do to change it? How much power do you have to spice things up again?"

Confessing my sins to Tom Spurgeon simply wasn't enough, nor was yet another revamp of some Corporate Trademark Franchise Character was going to tickle my brain stem in the manner I was (obviously) hungering for. The fact is, the big Work-For-Hire Publishers are currently mired in a swirling stew of strange continuity and gutless editorial control and all the daring experimentation that occurred there in the early 2000's seems like a distant memory. So to look for that pure hit of unbridled inspiration and enthusiasm at either publishing juggernaut is, at this particular moment, a horribly futile endeavor that would test *any* reader's patience to its limit. And, goddammit, it's not just me. You can

reboot your universe and you can have your big franchises knock the shit out of each other all you want. It just doesn't matter. Movies and TV have finally adopted -- or co-opted -- our secrets and are currently doing them better for a much bigger audience. Personally, I never thought I'd see the day where *any* other storytelling medium would out-pace *us*...!

And, in my despair, I ended up tripping over my own seething creativity and, fuck me, there was the salvation I was looking for all along. The "joyful disdain" (thank you, Greil Marcus) I was feeling for the sleeping pill superhero comicbooks I was seeing all around me actually pushed me to some new peak of Making Shit Up. It's what I've done all along to combat the apathy that's always threatening to creep into the spookiest corridors of my mind... I create things. I Bring Into Existence That Which Would Not Exist Otherwise. That's my job. To get down into the mind mud, motherfuckers. That's what I do. The endless presentation of the New.

To be shamefully honest, once I thought about it... I realized my creativity had been there all along. In *GØDLAND*. In *NIXON'S PALS*. In *CODEFLESH*. In *CHARLATAN BALL*. In *KRASH BASTARDS*. In *ROCK BOTTOM*. In *OFFICER DOWNE*. In *FULL MOON FEVER*. In *DOC BIZARRE, M.D.* In *THE MILKMAN MURDERS*. In *HIT PARADE*. In *SEX*. In *THE BOUNCE*. It just so happens that the prevailing winds were blowing me toward a place that was even deeper... a place that had much more spiritual meaning... a place that was going to deliver me from all evil.

Welcome to Sounding Like A Pretentious Fuckhead 101, right? Well, damn straight (and fuck you, btw). I would happily encourage anyone who has the ability -- the blessed gift -- to tap into their own creativity in a meaningful, productive way to 1) engage it, 2) indulge it and 3) go forth and act like a Pretentious Fuckhead. Life can be a lot more fun when you do those three things and do them to their absolute limit. Okay, maybe not the third one. Sometimes society wants you to reign in your Pretentious Fuckhead tendencies. Sometimes you do. But sometimes you don't. Welcome to this comicbook.

Anyway, back to my epiphany. My moment. The moment that led to the big, fat comicbook you're holding in your hot little hands (and that's what it is, y'know... price point and format be damned). Admittedly, it wasn't exactly a profound one. But it was a potent one. A few disparate ideas scribbled and scattered over years' worth of personal notebooks somehow coming together under a name that I just couldn't get away from, no matter how I tried... BUTCHER BAKER THE RIGHTEOUS MAKER. Kinda rolls off the tongue, doesn't it? But there it was. From the title alone, I knew it had to be a comicbook with *charisma*, goddammit! A comicbook that, as Lester Bangs would put it, flexed its Cheerios. Fuck yes.

CUT TO: I'm making rare panel appearance at an even rarer convention appearance, preaching to a crowd of hopefuls asking about "submission guidelines" and how to "break in" to the so-called "business" of making comicbooks, desperately seeking that magic key that will open the door to actually doing this for a living. I listen politely to the insights of my fellow panelists, lucid thinkers who deliver sobering facts about what to do and how to do it. Meanwhile, I'm the evangelical sumbitch that has no interest in providing "practical" advice. Pick up a guitar and just play. I see the look in their eyes. I've been there. I've been where they are. Before I know it, I find myself standing on the table and demystifying the entire process, proudly proclaiming that they don't need a motherfucking thing to make their own comicbooks other than the imagination and the willpower. Because that *is* all you need...!

GONZO BACKMATTER

Of course, this entire discourse is its own brand of bullshit. I do have a feeling that, on some imperceptible level, it fits the tone of the comicbook that it's backmattering up. You've read it, you can tell me. Is this the kind of backmatter that befits a comicbook called BUTCHER BAKER THE RIGHTEOUS MAKER?

Once more we turn our lazy gaze toward the Bigger Questions: If you ask me what I'm on about while I'm actually writing a comicbook... I'm not sure I could tell you with any absolute certainty. But, y'know, writing is partially about the act of the discovery. If I knew what it all meant beforehand, why would I bother actually writing the goddamn thing? Even this piece that you're reading right now is more mega-mental vomit that probably won't make any real sense -- to me, at least -- until years after the fact. That is, if I ever bother to reread it at all. Another orphan of power.

THE SHORTEST DISTANCE...

There are certain things you simply cannot write while under the influence of NyQuil. However, *this* is not one of those things. Already coming down nice and easy from the buzz of reading Julian Darius' thoroughly cogent essay on Keith Giffen's "Five Years Later" *Legion of Super-Heroes* run -- in a book *full* of Legion-related musings called *Teenagers From The Future* -- ingesting a tiny cupful of nighttime cold medicine only adds to that feeling of complete... *connectedness* that I feel with the universe... and with Julian in particular. I mean, how can someone else have possibly put as much thought into Giffen's dystopian LOSH work as *I* have over the years? It truly boggles the mind (or, in this case, the hivemind). Kent Shakespeare would be proud... in whatever parallel DC Universe he exists in now.

What does this have to do with BUTCHER BAKER you might ask? Well, the truth of the matter is... not a goddamn thing. But now that you've ingested this entire madcap romp of a comicbook, I could only hope that, by your very presence here, you've already demonstrated a firm commitment to this particular work and whatever virtues it happens to possess (*which are still questionable, even now*). And I'm nothing if not a fan of Commitment to Art. It's the kind of commitment that can sustain you for a lifetime. You don't get it with actual *people*, that's for sure.

My love of Giffen's *Legion* is an unconditional one, unchanged by time and perspective. This is what can happen with Art.

You'll notice I don't qualify what I perceive as Art. There is no "Good Art" or "Bad Art". Art exists as an absolute. After all, you can't grade personal expression, can you? How could you possibly judge it? To me, that's all that Art is... personal expression. In fact, that's what the dictionary *should* say, instead of American Heritage's trite definition: "the activity of creating beautiful things." Why the adjective? Why "beautiful"? Who's to say what's beautiful and what isn't? And, even more importantly, why waste time even putting thought towards it? Ladies and gentlemen of the jury, I put it to you... you cannot define Art.

Simply put... Art *is*.

Art is a cosmic hermaphrodite. Art is a patriotic big rig. Art is a 30-day teaser campaign. Art is the way the words "sheep" and "shank" go together to form an expletive. Art is anything you've created out of thin-fucking-air. And anyone can make Art. And everyone *should* make Art.

So that's kinda the Macro of it all. But what about the Micro? Well, maybe that's where comicbooks come into play. Specifically, *creator-owned* comicbooks, just like the one you're holding in your hot, little hands. We've come a long way, comicbooks and I, over the last fifteen years I've been doing this "professionally" (shit, let's not get into professional vs. amateur now... that's a discussion for another cold medicine)... and I doubt that I could say anything *too* profound about what I've learned, the experiences I've had, the highs, the lows, blah, blah, blah. I just know that I've been in the trenches long enough to have some vague sense of what it's all about. For me, anyway. And having done my multiple tours of duty during the "We-Can't-Win-It-War" that is Work-For-Hire Comics, I think I have at least *some* relevant insights on where we can go from here. Now, before you toss this away like it just caught fire in your grip, please hear me out. Give me a chance to put it all into some kind of perspective. Let me at least try and convince you of What Really Matters.

I love me some superheroes. LOVE 'em. Marvel and DC superheroes, I grew up on a healthy diet of both of 'em. I read *Avengers*, *Iron Man*, *Daredevil*, *Thor*, *Fantastic Four*, *Captain America*, *X-Men*, *New Teen Titans*, *JLA*, *Batman*, *Superman*, *Flash*, *Green Lantern*... I was definitely a hardcore reader. These characters got me hooked into the medium and, for that, I'm forever grateful. But, in hindsight, I consider them the gateway to something much larger... the Art of comicbooks. In becoming a professional in the field I loved so much, I've been able to write most -- if not all -- of these characters I grew up reading. I've been able to plug myself into the Big Song and sing along with reckless fucking abandon, sometimes out of key *and* out of time. And each time, it's a pleasure and a privilege.

But here's the thing... they don't really need me. They don't need any of us. Superman would still be here if I'd never spent the three years that I did writing his adventures. Batman would still be here whether or not Grant Morrison had spent the past five years making his series the thrill ride it was. Believe it or not, Daredevil would still exist whether or not Frank Miller ever got his hands on the book. Listen, you can connect with a few readers and you can make a few bones, but ultimately you're not necessarily *creating*... you're merely *contributing*. Now, this is a worthwhile endeavor, in and of itself. There is a fair bit of Art involved, but it's not Something From Nothing. And, for some writers and artists, it's all they've ever wanted out of their creative life. To them, I say... more power to you, brothers and sisters. I feel ya' big time. But, for me, as I moved into my teenage years as a comicbook reader, some other influences started showing up in my weekly haul...

Nexus. *Badger*. *Captain Victory*. *Starslayer*. *Ronin*. *Thriller*. *American Flagg*. *Jon Sable*. *Love & Rockets*. *Journey*. *Cerebus*. *Mage*. *Grendel*.

Void Indigo. The Rocketeer. American Splendor. Big Numbers. Lloyd Llewellyn. Stig's Inferno. Concrete. Mister X. Bacchus. Maus. Strange Days. Marshal Law. The Jam.

... in other words, comicbooks that wouldn't exist without their creators' initiative, their passion, their inexplicable compulsion to *create something new*. C'mon, motherfuckers! This is important stuff! This is God saying, "Let there be Light -- *and there was Light*"-level stuff! Tell you what, go back and read over that list again. The rest of us can wait until you're finished...

Y'know, those comicbooks gave me something far beyond their entertainment value (which was *considerable*, no doubt about it). They laid down tracks, pointed me in a direction, unleashed the beast inside of my dark, black soul... the will to create. The will to make Art. And there are moments when nothing else matters. Now that's a goddamn fucking *gift*, isn't it?

THE DANCE OF A THOUSAND TINY DEATHS

The character of Butcher Baker was designed to be something of an archetype. Or was it designed to be a comment on an archetype? At this point, it's tough to distinguish between the two. I mean, when am I *not* commenting on archetypes? The notion of a patriotic superhero in the "Captain America" mold was something I had a keen interest in, seeing as I live in America. I'd done a few variations on this archetype in previous work... see the Constitution of the United States of America in *Automatic Kafka* and Crashman in *GØDLAND*. For some reason, I found them very affecting to write, each in their own way. I finally got a chance to write Captain America in his purest "Man Out of Time"-incarnation in the first *Avengers: Earth's Mightiest Heroes* mini-series and, even then, I felt like I tapped into something beyond what I'd expected.

The notion of wearing your nation's flag as a superhero costume is certainly a curious one. So tell me, why does the American flag seem to work best as a fashion statement? We've seen British superheroes sporting the Union Jack, we'd seen Soviet heroes wrapped in the red-with-yellow-hammer-and-sickle flag. Hell, remember Vindicator/Guardian from Alpha Flight and, before that, Captain Canuck? But something about those characters always seemed more like a bit of a pose, more obtrusively deliberate as a vague political statement. Superheroes proudly wearing the red, white and blue seemed to operate on another level. Shit, is it really because *I'm* American that I feel that way? Am I that fucking shallow?

Or am I just that fucking fashion conscious? Did the Founding Fathers have some sense that we'd be a nation obsessed with looking good? Was Betsy Ross the Versace of her day? Or was

it George Washington himself, who (legend has it) gave ol' Betsy a pencil sketch of the flag for her to sew? Was there some precognizant shit at work where someone, somewhere knew that Jack Kirby and Joe Simon would appropriate this flag design to create their iconic hero?

(*then again, it doesn't take much research to dig up the fact that the American flag had its antecedents in other, similarly-designed flags. Most notably the British East India Company flag... if you're a fan of Sir Charles Fawcett, that is*)

Okay, okay... enough with the fucking history lesson. The real meat of the matter is... what does dressing in America's colors mean *today*, in the second decade of the Twenty-First Century? Does it mean *anything*? When the *Captain America* film needs to change its title for release in other countries... what does that say about the global perception of the good ol' red, white and blue? I think there's something to be said for any modern superhero who decides -- or, more specifically, its *creators* decide for them -- to wear the American flag in any capacity? Maybe it's something of a *dare*... a bit of attitude display where you're announcing something akin to, "I know a lot of people hate this, and *that's* why I'm doing it!" You're inviting controversy. You're asking for trouble.

Sounds like Butcher Baker in his prime to me...

IF YOU GUYS WERE THE INVENTORS OF FACEBOOK, YOU'D HAVE INVENTED FACEBOOK

An interview excerpt containing extreme self-examination:

JOE CASEY: So, Joe, what's the book about? I mean, what's it *really* about...?

JOE CASEY: Oh, fuck off.

JOE CASEY: Come on, Joe... don't be that way. This isn't the time for your usual interview answers where you try to stir up shit and piss people off. Let's really crack you open and see what's inside...

JOE CASEY: Are you kidding me? You actually think I'm going to be "real" in one of these goddamn things?!

JOE CASEY: Well, that's the idea, isn't it? Readers might *want* to gain some actual insight from you. After all, you're one of the creators and the writer of this comicbook. Presumably, they're reading it right now and here you are... why not provide more in-depth analysis of what it is they're reading?

JOE CASEY: Why *should* I? They've bought the thing, they've read it, it's all right there in the comicbook. I'm not holding anything back, am I?

JOE CASEY: That's a good question, Joe. *Are* you holding something back? Or is everything you are to be found in the panels of the comicbook?

JOE CASEY: I say again... fuck off.

JOE CASEY: Why the hostility?

JOE CASEY: I think to anyone paying attention to this exchange, it should be obvious why I'm hostile in this circumstance. You're no Tom Spurgeon, y'know...

JOE CASEY: Harsh.

JOE CASEY: You think so? I thought I was holding back...

JOE CASEY: So you don't want to talk about your personal feelings about BUTCHER BAKER THE RIGHTEOUS MAKER?

JOE CASEY: My "personal feelings"?! We're not trying to win a Nobel Peace Prize here... it's a motherfucking comicbook where shit blows up and a bunch of freaks try to beat the shit out of each other! What kind of personal feelings is *anyone* gonna have about that? Either they're into it or they're not...!

JOE CASEY: So you're not trying to make any sort of political statement here? No manner of meta-commentary to be found? There's no deeper message that you're trying to convey...?

JOE CASEY: Okay, *now* you're just trying to piss me off, aren't you?

SHE'S A BEAUTY

"Maybe there's something wrong with me. Sometimes I really think I have some sort of deep genetic defect or something. Some kind of mutation. I didn't turn out normal. That's why I have all this resentment and contempt and everything like that. But self-hatred is a strong motivating force in my work." -- Robert Crumb, from the documentary, *The Confessions of Robert Crumb*.

I remember once, not too many years ago, I was soaking in my hot tub in the porn-invested San Fernando Valley of California. I was reading an old *Iron Man* comicbook from the late 70's. Issue #126, "The Hammer Strikes", by the powerhouse creative team of David Michelinie, Bob Layton and John Romita Jr. The golden age of the Golden Avenger, without a doubt. I'd first bought this issue when it was brand new on the rack at the Jim Dandy convenience store on Franklin Road back in Tennessee. As I was soaking, sweating and leisurely flipping through the pages, I felt this bizarre urge... something I'd never experienced before... and the next thing I know, I had my *nose* pressed against the badly colored newsprint, taking in the exotic fragrance that is an authentic newsprint comicbook.

That unmistakable smell took me right back to childhood, like it was reconnecting an umbilical cord to some sort of tangible innocence that I'd been convinced was long gone. I can't really convey how strong the sensation was, but I can tell you it was indeed profound. It made me realize that comicbooks are more than a story, more than appreciating the drawing, more than following your favorite characters or creators. Comicbooks are an *experience*. And a unique one, at that.

For me, the best experiences *I've* had not only reading, but *making* comicbooks, have not simply transported me to a brave, new world of possibilities... they've actually *created* them. They've momentarily saved me from whatever tedium my life was mired in... whether I was nine years old and not knowing what the fuck my

life was going to be... or whether I was fifteen years old and grappling with the utter confusion of adolescence and the constant search for pussy... or whether I was twenty-seven years old and dipping my toe into the waters of a career as a professional writer, a metamorphosis that completely fucked me up and convinced me I was dying... or even now, as a fully-functioning "adult", still wondering if things will ever feel truly authentic (the truth of *that* most likely being: sometimes they do and sometimes they don't. Kind of like those old Mounds/Almond Joy candy bar commercials...). Clearly, I owe comicbooks a fuckton.

Creating Art is a life preserver. Life in general certainly has the power to knock you around and turn you inside out in every conceivable way (hell, that's what it's *for*, isn't it?). Art is what we use to combat that. Art is what saves us.

Like I said... Art *is*.

PLAY IN THE SUNSHINE

Years ago, I was shooting the shit with a prominent and talented comicbook writer who also happens to be a good pal, and he was relating his experiences being part of a four-man writing team on a well-received weekly superhero series ("weekly" being somewhat unique in the mainstream, especially back then). You could debate the overall artistic quality of this particular weekly series, depending on your tastes, but this writer knew damn well that they weren't exactly creating a literary masterpiece for the ages. And that admission was *not* accompanied by regret or shame or *any* negative feelings whatsoever. But something he said did

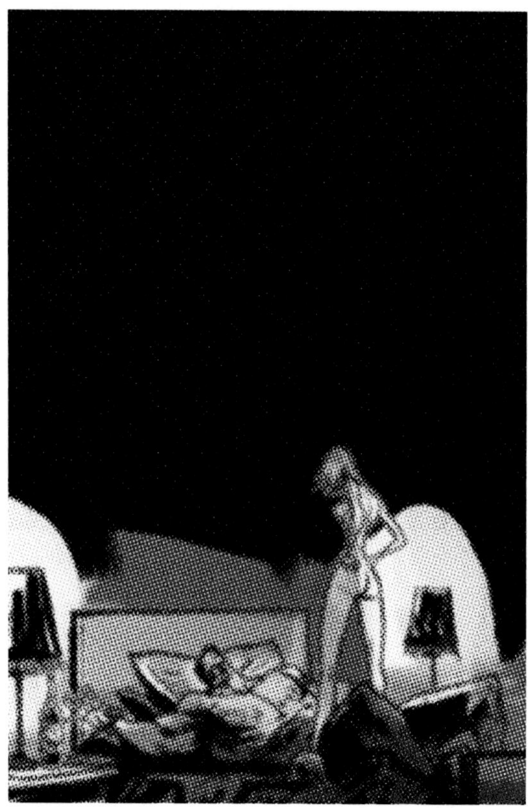

strike me as an obvious truism, something that perhaps none of us want to admit to ourselves... referring to the (relative) sales success of the series, he attributed it mostly to the following: "People just like getting their crappy superhero comics." When he said that, I knew exactly what he meant. He wasn't pronouncing judgment on the readability of the series or the merits of the ideas contained within, he was simply stating that the current readership of mainstream superhero comicbooks are, to a degree, an insatiable lot -- not too terribly discriminating -- and they simply want to be fed on a regular basis. Quality is beside the point. Regular delivery of said "crappy" content is where it's at. Given a choice between a mediocre superhero comicbook delivered at an endless, steady clip and a single, unpredictable shot of supreme artistic achievement... his theory suggests that most readers would choose the mediocre comicbook. And I think, in general, I agree with him.

My own goofball theory on this is a fairly simple one, and it relates to a human being's relationship with food. Would you rather have one great, gourmet meal a year (and nothing else) or three squares a day -- every day -- of obvious lesser quality? Before you answer, let's simply cut to what's realistic: there's really no choice in the matter. The one great meal might be an experience for the ages... *but you need three squares a day to live*. In your mind, even though you may be able to rationalize that the one, great, gourmet meal is obviously the better choice... you know you'd ultimately choose life. Same with superhero comicbooks. Generally, comicbook readers who have grown up on the art form -- and let's assume they've been raised on a steady diet of Marvel and DC superhero comicbooks -- are simply conditioned to survive on that steady diet of, to keep up the metaphor, junk food. That's what those serialized, never-ending (save for the occasional reboot and renumbering) superhero comicbooks are... they're junk food.

Now, don't get me wrong. I like junk food. But, let's try to be real here, people... there's good junk food and bad junk food. Like there's American chocolate and there's British chocolate, right? There's a difference. And while junk-for-junk's-sake certainly exists... there's also that rare junk that somehow, through some strange inner-workings of the universe, elevates itself into something *greater*. Maybe not high art, but who gives a shit about high art? Frank Miller's original *Daredevil* run is a violent orgy of junk food goodness. Alan Moore's writing on *Saga of the Swamp Thing* is purple prose gobbledygook of a high caliber, but gobbledygook all the same. Kirby in the 1970's? Beautiful, nonsensical noize that occasionally -- albeit effectively -- siphons collective mythology much like one might siphon gasoline from a parked car's gas tank by sucking on a rubber hose. And so on... and so on... and so on...

What the fuck am I *talking* about here...!?

SNOT-LICKIN' SOCK MUNCHERS

I think I'm seeing a change on the horizon. A shift in general perceptions. Having been on the campaign trail to pimp many a comicbook series, I've had my ear to the ground much more intensely than I ever had before. I'm plugging into the wider comicbook conversation with more than a passing interest as I wave my hands in twisted semaphore signals trying to encourage folks to buy my shit and what I get out of the experience is a real sense that we're all on the precipice of... something different.

First of all, I'm starting to see the fatigue when it comes to having to talk about the latest issue of Insert-Top-Ten-Superhero-Comicbook-Issue-here... the "been there, done that"-attitude when it comes to the latest line-wide events... the forced anticipation of upcoming releases that feel like the same old stuff we've been fed for the past few years. Even a line-wide reboot is generally greeted with an exhausted chorus of "Oh, yet another line-wide reboot..." On the Internet and in the Direct Market shops, we've constructed a culture completely and irrevocably dependent on these things... things that seem to be testing our resolve on a weekly basis. The real problem seems to be, we're stuck in this culture like it's turned into quicksand. A lot of us still kinda want to have our crappy comics, but there's not much else to grab onto and think about the website or the store or the blogger (or the creator, for that matter) that depends on genuine enthusiasm for mainstream comicbook content when that enthusiasm might be waning. The junk food is starting to make us a little nauseous.

But, y'know, that happens every once in a while. If there's one thing you certainly can count on in this industry, it's that it's cyclical as a motherfucker. You may not be able to set your watch by it, but if you take a few steps back, it's actually possible to see the bigger picture.

I'm no alarmist, okay? It ain't my gig to try and freak people out with predictions of doom. Especially when I actually feel fairly positive about the whole thing. Look at a Diamond sales chart from, oh, let's pick a month in 1996. November 1996, to be more precise. Look at the top ten. X-books and Spawn titles and classic Marvel heroes by Image creators. The #1 book that month? Superman: The Wedding Album Collector's Edition. Crappy junk food, no doubt about it. Obviously, every comicbook is somebody's favorite, no matter how misbegotten that opinion might seem to be. But I don't know if history has been very kind to these particular comicbooks and the quality of content found within. And, goddammit, if I didn't break into the business just one year later...!

A quick aside about November 1996... the superhero comicbook that, in my humble opinion, changed everything debuted that month. JLA #1 by Grant Morrison and Howard Porter. The comicbook that reminded the rest of us what good junk food really tasted like. It was a mere #24 on the sales chart and sold just above 100K. Meanwhile, that Superman wedding album catastrophe sold almost 230K. I dunno exactly what that says about this Unified Oddball Theory I'm trying to spout here... but it says something.

If you ever have a few hours to kill, check out John Jackson Miller's "Comic Chronicles" at *www.comichron.com*. The amount of sales data he's accumulated is both exhilarating and depressing, all at once.

JUNK IS PUNK

My foray into chart history might actually have a purpose. Speaking from actually being there, I can tell you that the late 90's was also a time when creators, readers, retailers, etc. knew that a change was going to happen. It had to. We had no other choice. Of course, the notion that an industry where even during what is still widely referred to as a "crash" period gave us monthly superhero comicbooks that regularly sold 150K and higher sometimes makes me wonder why anyone still bothers. But we're going to stop talking about sales and start talking about content. We knew the content had to change. We knew the approaches that had worked in the early 1990's were no longer cutting it. And so we changed. There was Morrison's JLA and all that it inspired. There was the Warren Ellis Forum. There was Wildstorm. There was Jemas & Quesada's Nu Marvel. There was Bryan Singer and Sam Raimi. There were less specialty event books. The junk food was starting to go down, dare I say, with a hint of the gourmet. In terms of quality, the measures we all seemed to take... actually worked. For awhile, anyway.

When no one was looking (or buying), superhero comicbooks actually got kinda hip again. But, as cycles go, it's never long before the rot sets in again. The ever-so-slight uptick in sales tends to necessitate a way to perpetuate it, to turn that "slight uptick" into a bona fide upward trend that you wave in the faces of stockholders and board

members to justify God-knows-what. That's where the return of event books comes from. And here we are, on the tail end of yet another "event cycle" (hopefully). Sales are low enough now that we can all claim for real that not a huge number of people are looking (or buying). So, if we're still following the cycles... where does that put us right now...?

My opinion? It puts us all -- creator, publisher, reader, retailer -- in the best possible place.

Because we have nothing to lose. Because we have no other choice. And that's fuckin' freedom, bitches. That's what we wanted all along, wasn't it? Well, spark a fat one and raise it to the sky, 'cause we finally got it.

Fuckin' A, I'm psyched to be in this business...!

THE SIZZLE

Have you ever heard Neal Adams' insights into the origins of the universe, otherwise known as his "Growing Earth Theory"? Fascinating shit. I first heard about it on a VHS tape containing raw video footage of an interview that Mister Adams did with a few friends of mine who had a great little local TV show about comicbooks and comicbook culture (way before it was fashionable... we're talking about the late 90's, folks). Mister Adams graciously talked on camera about Batman and the X-Men (two of many titles where this particular artist made history) for about five minutes before launching into more than a half-hour's worth of monologue on how the Earth was formed, debunking the commonly held theory about how continental land masses exist and evolved. You've heard the name, "Pangea", right? Adams calls it nonsense. And in the interview footage I saw, he's such a good communicator, knowing his audience was primarily a comicbook reading audience. He kept his explanations relatively simple, he didn't let himself get bogged down by too many scientific terms like "subduction" or "neutral matter". He spoke primarily in layman's terms, wanting to be clearly understood, and you can see in his face how fucking into it he is.

Now, Adams wasn't the first wild man to suggest this theory. From Australian geologist, Samuel Warren Carey, to German physicist, Pascual Jordan, quite a few big brains have put thought to the idea of an expanding universe. But I'd never heard of these guys at the time. As far as I was concerned, Neal Adams served it up first. And sometimes you just never get over your first time, do you?

Little did I know that I had already read about Adams' theory in a couple of issues of Fantastic Four -- issues #263 and #264, to be exact -- written and drawn by 80's mainstream powerhouse, John Byrne. In that two-parter,

Byrne created an Adams stand-in curiously named, "Alden Maas", who espoused a similar theory of planetary creation, but used it as a jumping off point for a villainous scheme to use the Human Torch to re-ignite the Earth's core. Go figure. But, goddammit, I love the fact that I read it in a comicbook when I was too young to even comprehend exactly what I was reading.

Luckily, I don't have to waste time explaining this shit -- or *trying* to explain it -- to you. These days, you can hop over to www.nealadams.com and read about it, watch videos about it, listen to the man himself narrate his thoughts and ideas on the basic nature of our universe. Believe me when I tell you, it's compelling as hell. Great musical accompaniment, too.

Whether or not you or I *believe* Adams' theories is completely beside the point. Catch me on the right day, and I might be completely on board... while, on another day, I might consider myself a skeptic. That's just how it goes. But, like I said, that's beside the point. The man is having *ideas*. Big ideas. Cosmic thoughts. And this is a *Batman* artist...!

ALL THE PUNK ROCKERS AND THE MOON STOMPERS

It occurred to me recently... my own career has been, for the most part, about doing work that allows me to present a particular dichotomy that exists in my chosen means of personal artistic expression. The dichotomy is as follows:

Comicbooks are a disposable medium.

Comicbooks are *not* a disposable medium.

Avengers #161 ("Beware the Ant-Man") cost exactly *thirty cents* off the spinner rack at my local Jim Dandy convenience store... and yet that comicbook meant *everything* to me. *Thor* #337 (Walt Simonson's first issue as writer/artist) cost sixty cents. *Saga of the Swamp Thing* #21 ("The Anatomy Lesson") cost seventy-five cents. *Daredevil* #181 (the death of Elektra) was, at the time, a double-sized issue and cost a grand total of one dollar. All of these classics -- yes, they *are* classics, muthafuckaz -- were formatted, priced and printed to be *extremely* disposable. We're talking about cheap newsprint here. Cheap production values. These were still the comicbooks you were meant to roll up and shove into your back pocket. In other words, *disposable*.

And yet... I never did dispose of them. Instead, I carefully placed them inside individual Mylar bags, in some instances backed with a comicbook-shaped piece of white poster board for added protection. And, looking back, I'm convinced I did that for a specific reason... which I can assure you was *not* to keep them in "mint" condition (whatever *that* means). It was because I was so affected by what was contained in those comicbooks, I knew there was a *permanence* there that was much bigger than its delivery system. Even at such a young age, I had a sense that the creators involved were not at all feeling the limitations of paper stock, printing inadequacies, audience demographics and general social stigma.

There's a part of me -- admittedly, the part that's able to ignore the horrifically low pay and the general disrespect the publishers felt towards creators -- that does feel like I missed out on an era of making comicbooks that was both glorious and can never be replicated. My first professional comicbooks were printed on a type of paper that was *somewhat* newsprint-like. There was maybe a hint of the disposable nature of the periodicals still hanging around in 1997. But I knew it wasn't quite the same. There was a certain... *arrogance* that was slowly creeping into the industry. Into the mainstream, especially. We were no longer approaching the medium with the same attitude as my heroes had. We were becoming dangerously self-important. We were denying the disposable nature of our art form. We were concentrating too much on adjusting our limitations and not spending enough time transcending them. It was something that took me years to reconcile. Most of it was clearly nostalgia. Hey, even *I'm* not immune to a bit of nostalgia now and then. But it wasn't *all* about nostalgia. There was a sense of... I dunno... call it misplaced intent. In hindsight, we *had* to go there. We *had* to try and rise about our own self-image and we had to be loud about it. We *had* to seek out legitimacy. We *had* to obtain mass cultural acceptance.

You know what else has obtained mass cultural acceptance? *Dancing With The Stars*.

Goddammit, they're *comicbooks*. There is certainly true artistry to be found within the medium. But their real, mythical power exists only in the mind. And, to me, that's where it belongs. That power is what is decidedly *not* disposable about them.

On the other hand, I look at my bookshelf and I see permanent, hardcover editions of some of my favorite books. My *Nexus Archives*. *Jack Kirby's Fourth World Omnibus*. My original *Elektra Lives Again*. *The Amazing Screw-On Head and Other Curious Objects*. The *Justice League International* hardcover collections. *Batman: Year One*. *Madman Gargantua!* My *Marvel Masterworks: Black Panther*. *The Mad Archives*. *X'ed Out*. The *Crisis on Infinite Earths Absolute Edition*. *Howard Chaykin's American Flagg!* Why *shouldn't* these works be presented in formats that honor just how fucking great they are (as this one is)? Certainly, they should be in every library across America, available for generations to come. They *should* be discussed in colleges and universities as they would discuss *any* great work of literature. Forget about mass cultural acceptance... we simply deserve some goddamn *respect*, don't we?

Well, don't we...?

Sometimes I have dreams where I'm wide awake. Sometimes I have dreams about *Ben 10* roller coasters being built in the UK. Sometimes I have dreams that all superhero comicbooks are done in Frank Miller's deceptively genius 16-panel grid template made popular in *Dark Knight Returns* (although he first employed it late in his creator-owned *Ronin* series), which would certainly separate the men from the boys, creatively speaking. Sometimes I have dreams where I've actually tapped into that unused percentage of our brain power, just like Deathstroke the Terminator. Sometimes I have dreams where Henry Gyrich picks *me* to be on the Avengers' roster to fulfill some weird government quota. Sometimes I have dreams where I'm hooked up to William Marston's lie detector invention and being asked if seeing Wonder Woman tied up gets my dick hard.

Sometimes I have dreams where there's an actual *soundtrack* that thunders through the air when someone opens up a truly great comicbook... it's the sound of an arena full of Canadians losing their shit on the opening number of Van Halen's 1984 tour stop at the Montreal Forum. When Diamond Dave jumps off that big ass drum riser as "Unchained" kicks in and the stage lights come up in full, it's a moment of rock n' roll glory that may just be the ultimate in orgasmic release. Just go on YouTube, look it up and hear it for yourself. It's Kirby-styled spectacle, live on stage.

KEATON: "I'M BATMAN." CASEY: "FUCK, YES!!!"

Okay... prepare yourself as we enter into some true fanboy minutiae shit, possibly the likes of which you have never experienced. Or maybe you have.

Imagine, if you will, Christmas of 1988. Now... think about that date for a moment. *1988*. Before five hundred cable channels. Before cell phones. Before the Internet. Before Tivo. Before Netflix. Before much of anything other than trickles of information from a fairly spotty fan press (spotty if you lived in the back woods of Tennessee, as

I did at the time). In fact, I don't even remember *how* I learned that the first, fabled teaser trailer for the Tim Burton *Batman* film was playing in front of certain movies in multiplexes across our great nation. But somehow I had.

Much, much later I learned that producer Jon Peters had rushed this teaser trailer out in response to the growing dissent about the film and its casting choices, rumblings that made it all the way to the goddamn *Wall Street Journal*. Hey, kids! Comics! But at the time, I only knew three things: 1) Jack Nicholson was the Joker, 2) Michael Keaton was Batman and 3) the director was the guy who directed *Pee Wee's Big Adventure* and *Beetlejuice*. And now I knew something else... an actual teaser trailer existed and it became my life's mission to see it.

My partner-in-crime for this endeavor, this cinematic scavenger hunt, was future *Stumptown* artist, Matthew Southworth. We'd grown up across the street from each other, bonded as cultural outsiders from an early age, and now we'd heard rumors that this infamous teaser trailer was playing in front of the Oliver Stone film, *Talk Radio*. Not necessarily a film I would've seen otherwise, no matter how much of a Stone fan I might've been. Maybe it was the Eric Bogosian of it all. In any case, it was suddenly the *only* film I could ever conceive of ever buying a ticket for. Now, *Talk Radio* was not a film you would consider as ever being put into "wide release". I mean, it wasn't exactly a blockbuster. As far as we knew, it was playing in a single theatre way across town, a multiplex I'd actually never been to in my life. My recollection is that we'd found out late in the evening, that there was possibly one showing left that night. It didn't matter. Since Matt was as fanatical as I was about seeing this thing, we hopped into my red Toyota pickup and hit the highway. I remember racing out there through the dead of night, wondering if the information we'd received was even accurate. It would've been a helluva bummer to go all the way out there only to find out this goddamn thing *wasn't* showing in front of this movie we had no real interest in seeing. We made it just in time. And, mere moments after we'd entered the theatre, there it was. Ninety seconds long and kinda life-altering. The motherfuckin' *Batman* teaser trailer...

The flames shooting out of the Batmobile exhaust. The car chase with guns blasting. Keaton as a tuxedoed Bruce Wayne. The grappling gun in action. Jack Palance! "Nice outfit." Keaton making post-coital excuses. Batman crashing through a skylight. "Alfred, let's go shopping." Nicholson in his Joker whiteface emerging from the shadows. Batman and Vicki Vale sliding across an escape line. "Wait till they get a load of *me*..."

Sitting in that theatre -- and there were maybe ten people in there with us -- those ninety seconds washed over me like maybe nothing else I'd ever experienced up to that point. And, as I later learned, there was a particular *reason* for that. Remember back when I said that Jon Peters rushed this thing into theaters? Well, even calling it "rushed" is a bit of an understatement. As far as I could tell, principal photography was still taking place over in England. So this cut footage was both fresh and raw. We're talking unmixed production audio. We're talking no Elfman score. No score at all, in fact. Not even temp shit. There was no real polish to this hastily assembled sequence of shots. In that moment, it looked like a Scorsese flick from the mid-Seventies, all dark and demented and seeped in urban decay. It was goddamn *glorious*. It was everything we'd hoped a *Batman* movie would be.

(We didn't stay for *Talk Radio*, by the way. To this day, I still haven't seen it.)

Now, everyone just hold on a second. We're getting to the good stuff now. Y'see, in my blow-by-blow of the teaser above, I left out my favorite moment. Maybe one of my favorite moments in *any* superhero movie, before or since. It's the famous bit where Batman is holding a greasy-ass mugger over a high ledge, the mugger begging like a bitch for his life. Still pissing himself, the mugger shrieks, "What *are* you?!" The answer is simple, but effective: "I'm Batman." It was the moment where I knew, beyond a shadow of a doubt, that Keaton -- and Burton -- was taking this shit seriously. And isn't that all any of us ever wanted from either of them?

And, in a way, it didn't even end up in the finished fucking movie...

Here's the thing: this teaser trailer, put together months before any SFX were done, before any post-production sound mixing was done, before any looping was done -- "looping" being when an actor goes in after filming and, in a controlled studio environment, redubs his or her own dialogue, syncing it up with the film as it plays back on a video monitor in front of them (okay, I feel weird explaining something that I have a feeling *everyone* reading this already knows) -- presented Keaton's performance that occurred on the day, including his original read of the "I'm Batman" line. That original read, the original audio, had so much more attitude, so much more *bite* than the looped line reading that eventually saw release in the finished film (where the now clichéd "whisper voice" was first used... hell, it was ridiculous *then*). If you don't believe me -- or if you've never paid that close attention (*imagine that!*) -- look 'em up on YouTube and compare the "late 1988" teaser trailer with the more widely seen, more polished, "official" trailer that came out three or four months later. Trust me, they're both there. Both contain the "I'm Batman"-moment. One was, "I'm Batman, fuckface!" The other was, "Mmmah'm Baht-Mahn." One has balls, the other doesn't. Hey, don't take *my* word for it. Go see (and hear) for yourself.

In fact, the entire film ended up lacking in the balls department. The Elfman score was distractingly overwrought (and let's not even go *near* the Prince songs), the film itself was overly theatrical, operatic in a weird way, Nicholson's Joker was way too over-the-top, Batman couldn't turn his fucking head, Gotham City looked like a sadly under-populated backlot set, they hit the Phantom Of The Opera thang way too hard (especially in the climax), the SFX looked cheap and Kim Basinger wasn't even close to being jerk-worthy. And don't get me started on the Joker being the one who kills Thomas and Martha Wayne and/or Alfred letting Vicki Vale in the Batcave...!

Ironically, after all the bullshit that got stirred up when he was cast, Keaton was the absolute best thing about the film... despite the misstep of his whisper voice that only *ER's* own George Clooney somehow managed to avoid in *his* abortion of a Batman film. To this day, Keaton remains my favorite cinematic iteration of Bruce Wayne.

Hey, don't get me wrong... I was caught up in that summer's Bat-Mania, just like everyone else was. Saw the flick several times in its opening weekend alone. But, goddamn, this was *not* the film that the teaser trailer promised. The film *I* wanted to see was raw and real and had genuine atmosphere. The film that was released tried way too hard to be polished and professional. Of course, the film went on to be the first modern day blockbuster with box office totals of nearly a half-billion dollars... so what do I know?

Well, I know what I like.

JUST KEEP TALKING... EVENTUALLY YOU'LL SAY SOMETHING

Obviously, if you're reading this now, you're probably aware of the fact that eight issues of BUTCHER BAKER THE RIGHTEOUS MAKER have been individually released into the world previous to this collection. They've been bought, read, reprinted, tweeted and re-tweeted, torrent-ized, occasionally blogified... you name it. One crazy chick actually tore up the first issue on a video podcast (which might be my favorite reader reaction to any comicbook I've ever helped give birth to... if it pissed off *this* sad shut-in so badly that she was provoked to mindless violence,

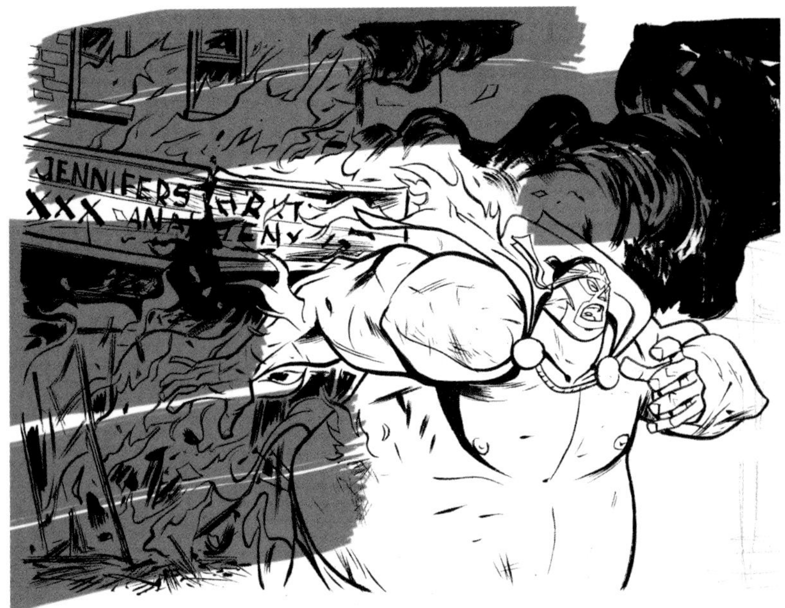

then I *know* I'm doing something right. Thank you, Nameless Weirdo Lady, whoever and wherever you are...!).

So, clearly, the conversation evolved from its original, one-sided argument for personal expression, screaming into a silent void, to an expressly interactive experience where creators and readers are sending psychotropic messages back and forth as the work itself publicly unfolds in front of all of our eyes. It's what I think all comicbooks *should* be... a discussion between creators and readers. Doesn't matter which side you're on. I remember *countless* conversations I had with Steve Englehart, Jim Shooter, Mike Baron, David Michelinie, John Byrne, Alan Moore, Walt Simonson, Howard Chaykin, Frank Miller, Matt Wagner, etc. that occurred simply from reading their work as a kid... they provided me with pages and pages of great material to feed my sponge-like brain, and for my part, I set out on a journey to better understand their craft, to learn the language of comics, and eventually to make them for a living. In other words, they spoke to me through their work and I found a way to say something back. And I'm probably *still* having a conversation with at least some of them. Thank Christ.

But there's the "interactive experience" of comicbooks in a nutshell. It's very simple, very direct, but incredibly potent for me and, I'm assuming, others like me. Thinking back to those bygone days of 1997, when I broke into the business professionally, I honestly think I'd forgotten about that kind of interaction between the work (and its creators) and the readership that consumes it. It took a few years for that fundamental relationship to become an active part of my work life. Now that's *all* there is, and it feels pretty goddamn great. Interesting what a so-called "billion dollar" boys' action franchise can do for your perspective on creating Art...

HELP YOU FEED THE WIRES WHEN YOUR HEAD UNWINDS

I wrote a strange comicbook series a few years ago called *The Intimates*. It was for the now defunct branch of DC Comics known as Wildstorm. In that book, I came up with this weird graphic manner in which to present random information that was maybe -- *occasionally* -- related to the story content. I called it an "info scroll" and it was meant to emulate the ticker scrolls that you'd always see at the bottom of the TV screen on CNN or MSNBC or other all-news stations at that time. Makes perfect sense for a comicbook about teenagers, doesn't it? Hey, I could probably rationalize it more definitively at the time...

Anyway, as the series went on, it got more and more difficult to come up with the bits of random text that were supposed to fill the info scroll. Did I mention these things were on *every single page*? Oy vey! Coupled with the fact that the book was sliding downhill for me due to... well... Wildstorm in general was sliding downhill for me (and for everyone else, too, it seemed). Anyway, I was feeling more and more frustration where this series was concerned, so I started to use the info scrolls as a way to vent that frustration. If I wasn't such a lazy fucker, I'd get up and go dig out and dig out the final issue, #12, to really illustrate my point. But I *am* a lazy fucker so you'll just have to take my word for it... I was directly referencing the sad state of affairs as best I could. Hopefully, they were more funny than they were pointed. Although, if I were being completely honest, I'm sure there was some bitterness that bled through, whether I wanted it

to or not. And if I know *me* -- and sometimes I do -- I probably wanted it to.

But it was definitely a situation where, on the one hand, I'd used a storytelling device to express some more personal content. On the other hand, clearly I'd started running out of legitimate, *story-related* uses for the info scrolls. A little embarrassing, in hindsight, but it is what it is.

A DIRECT RISE IN A YOUNG MAN'S LEVI'S

Let's face facts... these days, it's extremely difficult to enjoy the exquisite sensation of being in the right place at the right time. With the Internet and other modern, weirdo conveniences, you can be in a lot of places at once. But that's not the same thing. I'm talking about *timing*. I'm talking about *destiny*. I'm talking about a moment that can never be duplicated.

What the fuck *am* I talking about...?

There was a time, as an extremely young scrub, where I had to scavenge for comicbooks. Drug stores, convenience stores, the occasional magazine rack in a mom-n-pop bookstore. That's where I found my four-color escapism. And even these discoveries were tacked onto the coincidence of being in the car with a parent when *they* decided a pit stop at the local Jim Dandy was in order (which, if I recall, it rarely was... my folks weren't the type to succumb to sudden cravings for a cherry-flavored Icee). As I grew out of my kindergarten years, my negotiation skills became considerably sharper, and I was able to convince, cajole and ostensibly wrangle a trip to the local Kwik Sak so I could raid their spinner rack on a fairly regular basis. In retrospect, I made out pretty well under that system. I bought a fuckton of comicbooks in that period. And then, somehow... in some manner which I honestly cannot recall... I heard about a store that actually *specialized* in selling comicbooks. By that time, I was comfortably situated in my pre-pubescent years and my negotiating skills were at their peak, so it wasn't long before I'd managed to score a parental coach to visit said store. Upon arrival, I was blown away by the presence of two things: new-to-the-week comics (many that *weren't* published by Marvel and DC) and tables full of back issues. It was the present and the past all in one glorious location. I think my Dad was less impressed.

In any case, the comicbook I remember bringing home from that first trip to the "comicbook store" was *New Teen Titans* #4. You know, the one where they fight the JLA. Again, another significant comicbook, historically speaking, since this Wolfman/Perez classic was the series that single-handedly saved DC Comics... precisely because it was a massive success in the very environment that I had just discovered: the Direct Market.

(*if you really don't know what I'm talking about when I talk about the "Direct Market"... just go look it up, wouldja? Jeezus Christ...!*)

Of course, now that I knew such a store -- such a concept -- existed, my negotiating skills went into overdrive, having to convince a parent (usually Moms) to drive into the city to this so-called "comicbook store" so I could really bring home a fistful of four-color goodness. Longbox Diving became a favorite pastime. This place was my Mecca. My Shangri-La. Each and every precious visit hooked me in more and more to this art form, to this culture. And, being the early days of this Direct Market, we were growing up together, both of us maturing in strange and fantastic ways.

But these trips were still dependent upon the mercy of my parents. They still had to chauffeur my ass around. That alone made these trips random, at best. *My* habit was not *their* habit, and that was the one thing I could never convince them of. No, if I was going to cement my relationship with the Direct Market -- if I was going to fuck this bitch on a regular basis -- there was one, final component that was necessary to remain true to my gal...

... that's right, motherfuckers. A *driver's license*.

FRIDAY IS THE NEW SOMEDAY

Once I got my driver's license... well, all hell broke loose based on the newfound freedom I was experiencing, but let's stick to the topic at hand. Now I could fully and completely dive into the weekly fix of buying comicbooks. And I would buy them specifically on Friday. It was the gateway into my weekend. When I was a junior in high school, I would skip my last class (fuck off... it all worked out for me, didn't it?), hop in my Honda Prelude (again, fuck off) and head into the city, to the comicbook store. Then I'd cruise home, curl up in a chair in my parents' den and read the shit out of that week's haul. There was something... *ritualistic* about it. I really value those memories. I couldn't say for sure if there was any anti-social quality to that ritual. Fuck it, I'm sure there was. But I didn't need anyone or anything else on those endless Friday afternoons in my late teens. For me, at that time in my life, I fuckin' *lived* for Fridays. For me, Friday was New Comic Day. And that lasted a good couple of years, until I realized I had only one way out of the otherwise dead-end existence I was dealing with at the ripe old age of eighteen...

... *college*.

WEDNESDAY IS THE NEW FRIDAY

Okay, I'll admit it right now... for me, college was a complete waste of time. Academically speaking, I mean. For hanging out, sleeping late, chasing girls, playing bars and generally fucking off... it was just what the doctor ordered. One other thing this new lifestyle provided the next step in my lifelong comicbook romance: the ability to go buy comicbooks each and every Wednesday, practically the moment they hit oxygen. Finally, I was a front line consumer. It was the absolute center of my week, the event that most everything else revolved around. Especially my studies. Eventually, even the "college" aspect of college life fell by the wayside. I was free and clear to fully indulge in my passion with reckless abandon. And then, the ultimate irony hit me like a ton of bricks...

... the comicbooks themselves started kinda boring me. It was the early Nineties. It was post-Burton *Batman*. It was the creative giants of the Eighties pretty much conceding the field. It was five covers on *X-Men* #1. It was all kinds of things. But, in hindsight, I can honestly say... I was just burned out. I was falling out of love, to some degree. The relationship had lasted so long, it was only natural that some measure of fatigue was going to set in. It happens to the best of us.

Luckily, it wasn't long before I realized what needed to happen if this love affair was going to continue... instead of simply *reading* comicbooks, I had to start *writing* them. It was the only way forward for me, the only way I could really evolve with this art form. And so I did. Turning pro was the culmination of this journey I'd been taking, begun long ago. It was being in the absolute right place at the absolute right time.

History. Can't live with it. Can't live without it.

WHAT IT IS

Here's something out of left-fucking-field: I own three Mike Baron *Flash* scripts. Not photocopies, mind you, the actual, drawn-on-yellow-legal-pad-paper scripts that Baron gave to editors and artists. The goddamn *originals*. I love these fucking things. Then again, I love Baron's writing. Y'see, for those of you who don't know... in the first decade of his professional comicbook career, Baron never typed out scripts the way the rest of us tend to do. He did thumbnails of every page, stick figure drawings with accompanying script, all done by hand, usually with a ballpoint pen. There was no keyboard involved. No typewriters. No computers. Fuck, yes. I just always got off on the idea that these were what he was sending in to editors at DC and Marvel.

He sent them to me a year or so before I went pro. At the time, I was a loyal recipient of a *Nexus* newsletter that was being distributed (through the mail!), and if I'm remembering correctly, Baron was selling original *Nexus* scripts and I probably contacted him with a mash note via that address. Through our correspondence, eventually we were making trades... I was sending him CD's I could easily purchase locally of LA area pop bands (a longtime obsession of Baron's), he was sending me original *Flash* scripts (a favorite series of mine from the late-80's DC Renaissance). I definitely thought I was getting the better end of the deal, each and every time. I mean, c'mon, a lot of people probably own a copy of *Flash* #2, the finished, printed comicbook. And at least a small cult of people own a Wondermints' album. But only one person on Earth owns the original script to *Flash* #2: Yours Truly. Believe me when I tell you... it's not something I take lightly.

It's things like this -- a couple of Baron manuscripts, several sets of Keith Giffen breakdowns, Alan Moore's thumbnails from the 1st issue of the *Violator Vs. Badrock* mini-series, the *DC One Million* editorial bible, photocopies of Walt Simonson's college *Thor* story, Steve Seagle's original *Primal Force* proposal, uncensored art pages from *The Authority*, the list goes on -- that really make it for me now, that really transport me. It's the benefits of being "in the club", so to speak.

Granted, anyone in their right mind can take a step back and maybe owning something like this -- an original Mike Baron script -- can seem pretty meaningless. I fully admit, it only takes a *tiny* bit of perspective to feel that way. But, step into my myopic world for a goddamned attosecond and it means *everything*. Hell, it's there inherent worthless that I contend *makes* them great. Holding these scripts in my hands... there's an actual *energy* that vibrates off these things, I can feel it in my fingertips. These are the things that should be protected. Artifacts of a bygone era of comicbook Artistry.

Someday, I might even talk about the *Thriller* proposal and scripts I received from another hero of mine from that era, Robert Loren Fleming...

"VETERAN SCRIBE" AT WORK

Lately I've seen myself described by a few folks as a "veteran scribe". Talk about a phrase that can chill a motherfucker to the bone...! But what can you do? You work and you keep working

and eventually you're not a rookie anymore. It's evolution, innit? But, jeezus, there are a lot older writers still vital in the field that are literally generations ahead of me. It's just one of those things, I guess... the mixed emotions you feel when someone tosses a word like "veteran" in your general direction.

Besides, as I was forced at gunpoint to remind ol' Tom Spurgeon, it was several men well into their 40's that created the Marvel Universe, all of them 20-plus year "veterans" in the field by that point.

Ah, fuck it. I guess I should consider the context, too. When someone claims, "The veteran scribe seems to be losing his mind in the backmatter text pieces of his own comicbook"... that ain't so bad, is it?

Is it...?!

THERE'S FEVER IN THE FUNKHOUSE NOW

I feel like I spend a lot of my precious time chasing the dragon. Not quite the dragon *some* of you are probably thinking of when I use that euphemism (shame on you motherfuckers, btw). I've got my *own* dragon, thank you very much. And it's a good one. It's the kind of dragon you *want* to be chasing... if you happen to be into the same shit that I'm into.

It's the buzz that comes from, for lack of a better term, the act of creation. And after spending literally *decades* re-experiencing it over and over and over… I'll admit it, I've become a full-blown addict. I first got a taste of that feeling when I was too young to know better, and I've been on its ass ever since. The feeling itself is tough to accurately describe. You know it when you feel it. It's where the tried and true visual of the cartoon-lightbulb-over-the-head comes from. Never was something so indescribable so perfectly represented.

But, as great as it is, it can also be a fuckin' roller coaster, I can tell you that. Sometimes it feels great, sometimes it feels less great. The "less great" part can be a fuckin' drag… because you're never sure if it's just a hiccup in the program or if you're actually sliding down the back side.

Now, the part about "chasing the dragon" where it ruins your life and you end up in the gutter, not caring about fuck-all and all that gnarly shit… well, I really hope that doesn't happen. But the sheer *purity* of feeling when your mind conjures up something that previously *did not exist*… I tend to think that's a feeling that's worth the risk. Because, when you think about it, it really is a rare thing; how many people in the world actually spend their time thinking up original ideas? Trust me… that number's a lot less than you might guess. Hell, I might not even *be* one of 'em…!

But it definitely does something to your brain… to your perceptions… to the way you look at life… to be able to fully engage in that precious act of creation. It's like having an itch scratched in just the right way. Forget about the merits of the idea itself, since that puts us squarely in subjective territory. I'm simply talking about the actual *birth* of said idea. The tingle in your mind. The realization that, suddenly, something *is*. Something exists. There's an aspect of it that's pretty goddamn miraculous, if you ask me. To put it in more relevant terms, there was a time when BUTCHER BAKER THE RIGHTEOUS MAKER did not exist in any recognizable form. Before anyone could *read* it, we had to *think* of it first. And just the "thinking of it" is truly the most sublime part of the entire process. It also marks the other thrilling part of creating something… it's the beginning of, for lack of a better term, the discovery of an idea. It's the part of the process where, through various ways and means, the idea reveals itself more fully to you, it evolves within your mind, it coalesces, it solidifies, etc. And it *is* a process, in so far as, if creation is an "act", then discovery is a "process".

NOW WATCH HIM DIE

Apropos of practically nothing, here's a little anecdote only tangentially connected to the idea of discovery (and barely, at that): On February 25, 1983 (the actual date, to the best of my limited historical knowledge), I was spending the night at a friend's house. While I was gone, without any real direction from me that I can recall, my Mom videotaped the ABC Friday Night Movie airing that very night. Now, anyone of my generation (the dreaded Generation X… that's right, motherfuckers, that ol' chestnut of a classification) will remember the famous early 80's intro to ABC's network movie premieres, the "star tunnels" forming the marquee graphic, accompanied by the catchy orchestration and classic Ernie Anderson voiceover (father of director, Paul Thomas Anderson, btw), pimping the film about to be shown. You look that shit up on YouTube… it's like opening up a direct connection straight back to your own childhood.

A bizarre aside: some of these films needed "content disclaimers" placed at the front of the broadcast, parental warnings and other info. Looking back now, some of these were absolutely hilarious. One in particular, when ABC broadcast Stanley Kubrick's *The Shining*, of all things, read like this (again, picture the Ernie Anderson voice in your mind):

Tonight's film deals with the supernatural, as a possessed man attempts to destroy his family. Although edited for television, it may not be suitable for young viewers. Parental discretion is advised.

"... as a possessed man attempts to destroy his family"?! Fuckin' A.

Anyway, back to Feb. 25. The disclaimer placed in front of this particular film made claims that what you were about to watch, "deals with street gang warfare and contains scenes of violence". This will be tangentially important later on in this (meaningless) discussion.

Oddly enough, I didn't rush home the next day from my friend's house to watch what my mom had taped. No sir. What I remember happening is that I didn't even recall that *any* movie had been taped. It wasn't until maybe a week or two later, when both my father and I were felled by some sort of flu bug and ended up bumming out in the same room, probably bored out of our fucking skulls, that this VHS cassette tape was unearthed and I said to my Dad, "Hey, let's watch this... whatever it is."

What it was... was *The Warriors*.

I really can't get too much into what this film is, for any of you poor bastards that haven't seen it, because we'd be here all day. It's just that good. Here are the basics: Released in 1979. Based on the novel by Sol Yurick. Directed by Walter Hill. Starring Michael Beck, James Remar and Deborah Van Valkenburgh. A Coney Island street gang, wrongly accused of the murder of a popular gang leader, has to fight its way home across New York where every other gang is out to get them. Like I said, if you haven't seen it... God have mercy on your soul. It's a goddamn cult classic. It's a comicbook movie without the comicbook.

For any of you who have seen this flick, this will probably seem even odder. Imagine watching *The Warriors* for the first time... *with your Dad*. Lemme tell ya'... it definitely adds to the experience.

My Dad and I were poster boys for the so-called Generation Gap. Don't let the current climate of arrested-adolescence-in-adults-who-oughta-know-better fool you... back in the 80's, growing up in *my* household, the Gap existed, big time. What I liked, he didn't understand. And vice versa. And here we were, watching this weirdo "gang movie" together that, as I took it all in during that first viewing, seemed to hit me on about twelve different levels. Some conscious and some unconscious. Two hours later, the movie's over and I'm pretty fuckin' speechless, still trying to process what I had just seen, my young mind sufficiently blown. My Dad's response...?

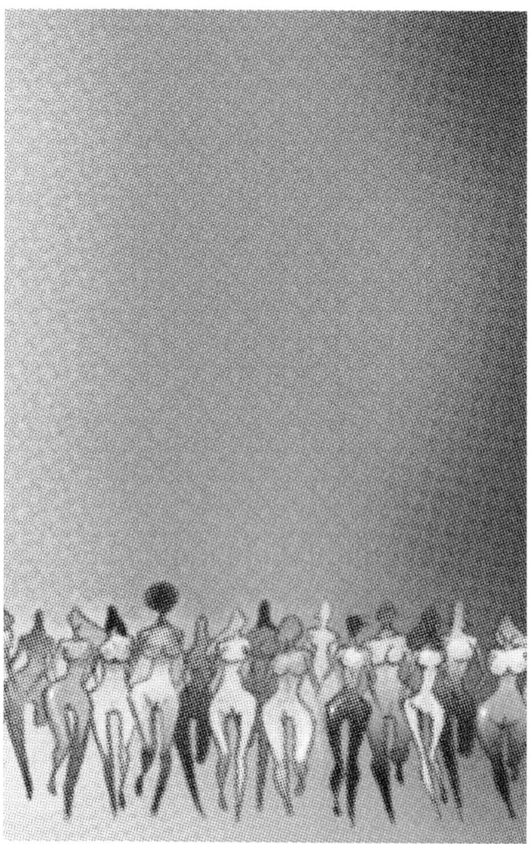

"Not only was that movie too violent, it was completely unrealistic."

Gotta' love him. Okay, so he was half-right. But none of that is the point of this story. Just the set-up.

So I was kinda in love with this fuckin' movie. For all the right reasons, as it turns out. Not that I had any penchant for "gang violence", but certainly the comicbook aspect of this film spoke to me. And, as far as I can tell, it was probably the first exploitation film I'd ever seen (I place *that* particular label on it in hindsight... I doubt the filmmakers felt that way about it when they made it, and it *was* released by a major studio). Not that I could make the genre -- or even artistic -- distinction at the time, but I'm sure I felt like the perceived grittiness of *The Warriors* was on par with films I would later see by hardcore cinematic motherfuckers like De Palma and Scorsese. In other words, to a pre-teenager, *The Warriors* and *Taxi Driver* are practically the same film. I didn't know it was kinda schlocky. At least, not until a bit later in life.

Two sequences stood out for me in this movie. Both of them action scenes. The Baseball Furies chase/fight and the showdown with the Punks in the subway station bathroom. These were the so-called "scenes of violence" the ABC disclaimer had warned me about. But let's break it down: The Furies fight was about twenty seconds long.

The Punks' ass-beating lasted maybe forty-five seconds. All told, the so-called violence of this movie -- the moments where punches are actually thrown between gang members -- lasted *less than two minutes* of screen time. There's also no blood whatsoever. There are a total of two on-camera deaths (possibly four deaths, but I'm not counting Cleon and Luther, since those are more implied than seen). Sorry, but that ain't a lot of violence... certainly not enough to merit any kind of disclaimer.

But then, I started hearing about the urban legends surrounding this film... that its theatrical released was marred with a bit of real-life violence that ultimately got it yanked from theatres (as it turns out, a lot of this was complete bullshit... but this was pre-Information Age, so you tended to accept things as you heard them). I still couldn't understand it. Why was this film -- clearly a pure action/adventure film that, as I later discovered, was based on the Greek epic, *Anabasis*, written by Xenophon (at least, that's what Yurick's novel was based on) -- such a lightning rod for some weird controversy involving violence in film?

Maybe six months or so later, I thought I'd found the answer. This coincided with another important discovery that folks my age can appreciate and almost no one else can... the video rental store. My earliest recollections of these stores were fairly intimate Mom-and-Pop affairs (pre-dating corporate chains like Blockbuster Video by at least a few years) that were a goddamn cinematic smorgasbord. It was in one of these stores that I saw it... the VHS rental copy of *The Warriors*. I also saw the film's MPAA *rating* for the first time: R.

Cue the incessant begging -- by me -- at the feet of my befuddled and bewildered mom to please, please, pleeeeeeaaaseee rent this fuckin' thing for me. Now, being occasionally susceptible to her own child's begging, and given the fact that she knew that, by that point, I'd essentially already seen the film several hundred times (hell, she'd taped it for me off TV), she quickly relented and soon we were on our way home, me with this hot little videocassette cradled in my hot little hands. As soon as we got home, I practically threw the tape into the VCR. I think I hit the play button with a Superball I threw at the machine. And now a movie I had pretty much memorized... was a whole new movie.

There was a lot of swearing. There was a bit more sleaze. There was more tongue in the kiss between Swan and Mercy. The characters came off a little scummier than in the network TV version (edited for television), more like desperate street rats. And then... there were the two action scenes that had originally thrilled me so much: the Baseball Furies fight and the Punks fight. I don't remember being completely aware that the fight scenes in the TV version were cut down from their original theatrical version when I first saw them with my Dad... they were so frenetic to begin with, what pre-teenager was going to know from bad edits? But when the Baseball Furies confrontation came up on the rental copy, I was slack jawed. It was... *longer*! Every single moment seemed to be extended. Where, on TV, Swan threw *one* punch to take out a Fury, here he threw *three*! Plus, they actually *wailed* on each other with those baseball bats! The Punks fight in the subway men's room was way more vicious, with entire moments that were obviously excised from the TV version. To my mind, the amount of material I'd missed watching it on network TV was absolutely *epic*...!

Now, let's go back to the scoreboard, shall we? This is where the discovery capabilities of a pre-teenager loom so large in the moment, but with perspective and the passage of time, you realize just how much you yourself brought to the revelation, as opposed to what was actually *there*. From a pure stopwatch mentality, the facts don't lie...

The Baseball Furies fight (TV version): 20 seconds.

The Baseball Furies fight (original, theatrical version): One minute, 30 seconds.

The Punks fight (TV version): 45 seconds.

The Punks fight (original, theatrical version): One minute, 30 seconds.

Sigh.

So, okay... maybe the theatrical version wasn't quite as epic in reality as it seemed in my mind at the time. But that's not the point, is it? That extra two minutes of screen time scattered between the two fight scenes was all I needed to set my imagination off. Just discovering the mere existence of that extra footage made me feel like something more than just a mere spectator. I felt *involved*. I felt like I had a relationship with this particular piece of art. And if I could have it with *this* piece of art, I could have it with *other* pieces of art. More than anything, it probably made me think there *was* a larger world out there. One that I had to seek out. One that I had to discover. It was a seminal moment in my young life. Another gold bar placed in the Yellow Brick Road.

Or, as the Gramercy Riffs would say (*almost* in unison), "RIFFS! YEAH, RIGHT!"

Okay, even *I* know that went nowhere...

THIS OFFER IS UNREPEATABLE

In the assembly line process that comprises making modern comicbooks (for all of us non-cartoonist types), the relationship between writer and letterer is, to me, a pretty special one. Once I'd entered this business as a true professional, it didn't take me long to realize how important it is to have that relationship, if I really wanted to get my creative intent across as a comicbook writer. They say good lettering should be invisible, that you shouldn't notice it. But, fuck that, I notice when it's good.

Rus Wooton is a name you see in the credits of just about every comicbook I write now. Over the years, we've established a collaborative synergy that's as important to me as any part of the process *can* be in the art of making comicbooks. Since I'm kind of a lettering snob (fonts, point size, balloon shape, tail style, placement... you name it, I've got an opinion on it), I depend on the letterer to help execute my vision -- whatever that may be -- of how the writing looks on every page of my comicbooks. There are some true masters of comicbook lettering out there, and I've worked with a few of them, but Rus has been there -- gone the extra mile, put in the extra effort when necessary, never shied away from experimentation -- every single time. He's a motherfucking master in *my* book. He puts up with my last-minute tweaks and seems to care about the finished product as much as I do. He's insanely good at what he does and I'm both thrilled and relieved that he's agreed to work with me, time after time. As the years roll on and the books we share credits on increases exponentially, his input and his talents are something I continue to value and (hopefully) appreciate more and more with each project we work on.

I hope he's not too embarrassed when he reads this, but... he's a real mensch, that Rus.

I ALMOST HAD A WEAKNESS

Right now, it's much more important to me to make some Art that has a sense of... *completeness* to it. I've done my share of WFH gigs where I sure as shit wasn't able to either 1) keep things going or 2) end things the way I wanted to. Even though serialized, open-ended comicbook series are organic, evolving things and I love that about them, there are some things that aren't *meant* to last forever. Things like *Ronin*. Or *The Death-Ray*. Or *Elektra: Assassin*. Or *The Filth*. Or *Escapo*. Or *Stray Toasters*. Or *Enigma*. Or *Batman: Year One*. Or *Asterios Polyp*. Or *Rogan Gosh*. Or *All-Star Superman*. Or *Watchmen*. Or *Hard Boiled*. Those are just a handful of my favorite books that all have a

genuine power in their finite nature. Whether or not BUTCHER BAKER is one of those things that was better served by having a beginning, a middle and end, only time will tell.

And, of course, there were *other* factors at work...

I'm just gonna own up to it... as we headed into the final issue, our regular monthly schedule had... slipped. Okay, it slipped like a motherfucker. As much as we tried to front load some significant lead time into the building of this beast, once you're on the production treadmill, that lead time gets eaten the fuck up. And, once you slip, it's tough to get it all back on track. Most series *never* do... not without compromising their individuality and their uniqueness. For a series like this, that would've been heartbreaking.

We've got to respect the Art we've created... by making sure it doesn't suck (if such a thing is, in fact, possible). At the same time -- and this is the part where I'm cringing with supreme guilt as I type this -- I'm a big believer in the Regular Delivery Pact of the periodical format. That... specific kind of *promise* that a publisher (or, in this case, the creator) makes to the consumer. If you've committed yourself to showing up on a monthly basis, then you'd damn well better be there on a monthly basis. Simple, right? But, believe me, I speak from experience... a few of my books over the years have dropped that particular ball and I have to live with the consequences. It sucks and I hate it and with each new project, whether it's creator-owned or WFH, I do everything I can to ensure that I live up to my part of the Regular Delivery Pact. Sometimes it works out, sometimes it doesn't. All I can do is own up to the fuck up and to try and do better next time, to keep stepping up to the plate and to keep swinging.

But even *that* wasn't the *real* deciding factor to commit to this as a finite series from the get-go, to do eight issues and be done with it. We knew going into this thing that we wanted to go balls-out with each and every step of the process, from the series development to the teaser campaign to the graphic design to the story content itself... all of it required an intensity that's simply difficult to maintain over a long stretch. And impossible to maintain consistently with no end in sight. Consider this cult favorite movie quote:

"The light that burns twice as bright burns half as long."

- Joe Turkel as Dr. Eldon Tyrell from the film, Blade Runner.

I'd like to think that's somewhat applicable here (*c'mon, I said "somewhat"*). We wanted to burn like the Sun but we knew going in that we'd never be able to avoid the inevitable burnout. So we had a built-in solution to make sure that didn't happen. And I think the solution worked. Eight issues of this kind of content was its own kind of mountain. Embarrassing lateness aside, I guess we climbed the fucker, planted our flag at the top and now we can all appreciate the view and keep an eye out for the next mountain to conquer.

Wow. That sounded impressive, didn't it? All highfalutin' an' shit...

Ah, fuck it. I feel like I'm probably just making excuses here. Look, we had a story to tell, and we told it. What's left to say, really?

THE SUNSHINE BORES THE DAYLIGHTS OUT OF ME

From the very beginning, I entered into this project with one specific creative ethos: **Audacity as a virtue**. My favorite definition of the word, *audacity*, is Merriam-Webster's: "bold or arrogant disregard of normal restraints"... which I'd like to think describes this particular series, on *some* level, at least. Now, certain folks might be more inclined to use the word in a more pejorative sense. Your parents, for instance. I get that. But, y'know... fuck 'em. Being deliberately audacious in a culture like this one -- meaning, the mainstream/superhero comicbook culture -- is nothing to be shy about. A lot of my favorite comicbooks over the years could be described as audacious (among other things). And more

power to 'em. It was probably what drew me to them in the first place. So to embrace audacity -- to put it forth as, like I said, a *virtue* as opposed to a hindrance -- is something worth exploring. Especially in this day and age, right? Anyway, I think it certainly worked on *this* book.

Actually, it's how I've personally been approaching *all* of my comicbook work for the past couple of years, simply as an overriding principle. It's the kind of attitude that makes Art interesting.

5IVE GEARS IN REVERSE

I've had this sense lately, as I've kept a toe or two in the water of WFH comicbooks, that there is a class of creator that is inevitably *misunderstood* by editors and publishers, regarding our skill sets. In the past, when I've been hired by Marvel or DC... I've been hired as a writer. In a lot of ways, that's a very limiting job, especially when it comes to making comicbooks. As a writer, I'm expected to put some thought into the story I'm writing, I'm expected to type up a script and turn it in on time and then, generally, I'm probably expected to collect my check and move along. Nothing to see here, folks. Let the professional comicbook makers actually *make* the comicbook. But, from an early age, I was interested in the medium to such a degree that just writing was never going to be enough. When I would sprawl out on the floor of my bedroom, drawing my own comicbooks, I tried to duplicate everything I saw in the books I was buying at the Kwik-Sak and Jim Dandy's. I remember drawing the 70's "Marvel Comics Group" banner across the top of my covers. I remember drawing the Comics Code Authority stamp. I remember drawing in the UPC code box. I drew the logos. I wanted to create the complete package. I simply didn't see creating comicbooks in that strict assembly line manner that generally occurs at the big WFH publishers. I saw the whole thing -- the whole package -- as something I wanted to have a hand in. Why? Because it's fun. It's fun to help design a logo. It's fun to consider packaging. It's fun to put your eyeballs on lettering proofs and make those final adjustments that actually improve the narrative flow. It's fun to have that control. Even when it drives my WFH editors completely insane.

That's right... creating comicbooks from scratch, being involved in every part of the process, is motherfucking fun.

And I don't think I'm the only one who feels this way. Sure, there are writers out there who just type up the script and turn it in. *Good* writers, as a matter of fact. But I think the reason I ultimately ended up at Image Comics... is because I wanted to make comicbooks. And I feel like I'm part of a generation of creators who, like me, weren't content to simply type scripts and collect checks. I kinda liken it to the independent film movement of the late 80's/early 90's. Soderbergh, Tarantino, Rodriguez, etc.

were filmmakers who did it all. They could write, they could shoot, they could edit, they could score their own films, much to the confusion of an industry where each job is compartmentalized (and unionized). They were *much* more the "auteurs" than the previous "Movie Brat"-generation of filmmakers were marketed as. And that's what a lot of modern comicbook creators have become. We're not just "writers". We're not just "artists". We're not "just" *anything*. We make comicbooks. And I think the next generation of comicbook makers is going to follow *our* lead. And the editors and publishers in the WFH space are going to be just as confused.

Hell, maybe all this hot air is me just trying to compensate because I'm not a full-on cartoonist. But if you're *not* a Frank Miller or a Paul Pope or a Jeff Smith, don't give up hope. You can still indulge in your megalomaniac tendencies and make some goddamn comicbooks. I know *I* have. How else would this book even *exist*?

THE BLUE BUS IS CALLING US...

So that's it. End of line. I don't know if I should feel proud or embarrassed. Probably a bit of both. Hopefully, we all got out before this whole thing went completely off the rails.

In any case, for however many of you stuck around, I hope it was a fun ride. And I really hope that -- for all the apeshit I was spouting, for all the so-called "shock value" contained in the comicbook itself -- that the overriding feeling that you might come away from this experience with is one of great *optimism*. There's no better medium than comicbooks and what BUTCHER BAKER tried to do, more than anything else, was to help support that opinion, in some small way. I don't imagine you're going to see this book optioned by a Hollywood production company or turned into a major motion picture any time soon (not if I can help it... and I fucking can). And I think that's probably a good thing. It's become some kind of stupid, unspoken validation when a creator-owned comicbook turns up in *Variety* or the *Hollywood Reporter*. Trust me, it's not. It's *that* kind of thinking that can sap you of your optimism. Luckily, I don't think that way. *My* fucking optimism remains gloriously intact. The experience of making this book has fueled me in ways I couldn't even describe to you. Needless to say, I'm gonna live for a good, long while on *this* buzz.

Of course, it's not enough. It never is. So, if you'll excuse me, I'm gonna go make some more motherfuckin' Art.

AND NOW... THE DREADED ADDENDUM

Okay, fuckers... here's the real deal. The preceding, interminable ramble was, in its original form, serialized in the back of the individual issues of BUTCHER BAKER. As those issues were hitting the stands, there was maybe just as much talk about the crap I was spewing in the back of each issue as there was about the comicbook itself. When it came to the notion of funding this book myself (along with the fine folks at Image Comics, who graciously front a share of the production costs... but I paid Huddleston a page rate in addition to cutting him in on a piece of the IP ownership), I decided early on that, for mainly budgetary reasons, there would only be eighteen pages of story and art per issue. That's a bit low by modern standards... *by two fucking pages*. These days, a typical Marvel or DC Comic is a whopping *twenty* pages of story. And they charge about four bucks for them. BUTCHER BAKER -- in its original, periodical comicbook form -- cost a penny under three bucks. For whatever reason, I just felt a little skeevy charging that amount for only eighteen pages of material. So, I figured, I would fill

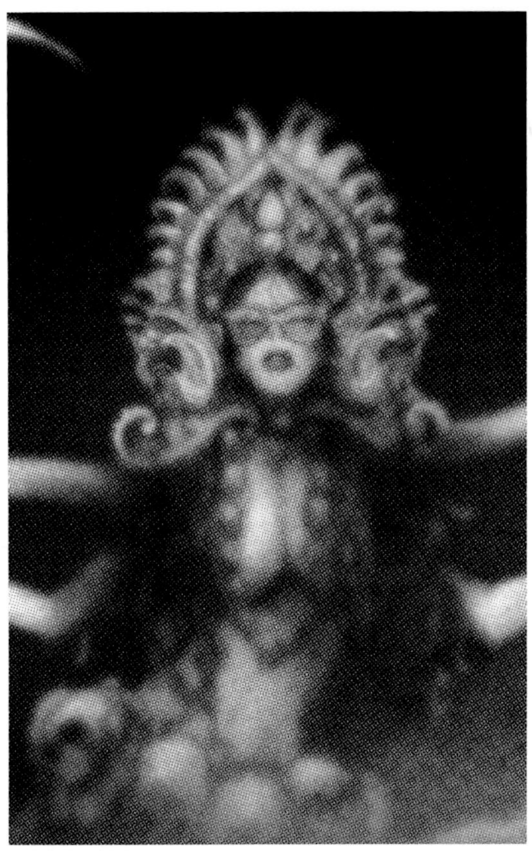

out the rest of each issue with, essentially, essay material and some random Huddleston development sketches. In the industry they call it "backmatter". Whatever. Since I was already working for free anyway (as I do on every single one of my creator-owned books), I might as well put in the extra effort to make sure that no one was feeling ripped off in any way. It felt right, it seemed like a workable model for periodical publishing (and one that I'll probably do again)... but I honestly didn't know if I'd have that much to say.

Yeah, right. Anyway...

What was interesting about the inclusion of the essays was the kind of feedback I got on them as each issue was released. Most readers seemed to dig 'em. Some reviewers jumped up my ass about them, as though I was trying to rewrite the U.S. Constitution (and if you get *that* joke, then God bless you), but I honestly feel that if you really read what I was spouting off about, you pretty much knew the score. I've got no problem getting my poor man's Lester Bangs on and, as it turns out, writing in the essay form is actually an enjoyable kind of writing. Under certain circumstances, it can even be somewhat cathartic.

But, for the record, I never promised *coherence*, did I...?

Now, lemme also say this: anyone who thinks they actually *know* me from reading these things... well, that's debatable. It's an honest conversation, I'll give you that much. But just because a writer occasionally comes out from behind his (or her) fiction and talks directly to their readers doesn't mean he's (or she's) actually bared his (or her) soul in any significant way. For a writer, even non-fiction turns out to be fiction.

The other interesting side effect of this essay material was that some people felt like my commentary was some strange attempt to elevate the material to some higher plane of literary existence, as though anyone in their right mind would mistake BUTCHER BAKER THE RIGHTEOUS MAKER for, say, *War and Peace*. I really don't think so. But there were certainly those who somehow felt as though the comicbook itself never measured up to the ambition on display in the backmatter. To those people... I call bullshit. Maybe it was all the "Art" talk. But did I ever claim or even suggest that Art equals Importance (or, even worse, Self-Importance)? Fuck, no! Art exists way beyond any sort of classification, and its perceived importance -- or perceived *lack* of it, for that matter -- is not a part of the equation.

So I never looked at BUTCHER BAKER as anything more than what it was... a drive-in, exploitation, sex-n-violence comicbook. Sexploitation, if you will. Nothing less, but certainly nothing more. No matter how hard you look inside of it, I don't think you're going to find any Grand Statement On The State Of Comicbook Storytelling, nor is there very much pontificating on the Idea Of The Superhero. This was all about simply telling a story with some style and some balls and giving readers a psycho-sexual thrill ride that might distract them from their otherwise miserable lives for a few minutes (or at least two good shits... I do my best to write something a little more substantial than a one-shit comicbook).

Granted, I have written some relatively heavy shit in my day. Things that are intensely personal to me. Things that attempt to explore something deeper. But all of my heroes in the field were able to swing in several directions and simultaneously stand with their feet planted within different worlds. Alan Moore was writing *From Hell* at the same time he was writing *Violator Vs. Badrock*. One was an intricate study of a heinous human event (based on real events) and the other was a grindhouse orgy of pseudo-Satanic weirdness. And, as a fan, I dig on both books equally. But even more than that, I really dig that he wrote both, that he didn't completely disregard one simply because he was writing the other. Granted, one he did for love and one... well, he almost certainly did for money (you can guess which was which). But, for chrissakes, Alan Moore wasn't going to waste his precious time on something he didn't *want* to write, no matter how much money was involved. And what I learned from that was… it's okay to write something for the sheer fun of it.

That's what BUTCHER BAKER always was for me… a bit of fun. But then some of the reader response suggested that it was something else, and then the interminable delay between issue #7 and the final issue, #8, threatened to give the book even *more* import while, at the same time, exposed its obvious vapidity by its drop off the radar. During that delay, I don't recall seeing a lot of people clamoring for whatever they thought was going to happen next in the adventures of ol' Butcher. Issue #7 ended on a pretty powerful cliffhanger, exploitatively speaking, and I just don't think the majority of the series' readers much cared how the actual *story* was going to continue. If anything, they were more invested in the comicbook actually existing on some level *other* than a story one. Oddly enough, I seem to recall readers -- myself included -- feeling that way about *Elektra: Assassin* (which was obviously a huge inspiration for this book) when *that* motherfucker of a series was first appearing on the stands in periodical form. So, what the fuck, maybe we're in good company…

I'm glad this one is out of my head and out in the world, especially in this form. It wasn't the easiest birth, that's for sure. But there were levels of this particular creative process that were as rewarding as anything I've ever done in this business... levels that are *so* personal, even a loudmouth like *me* wouldn't devalue them by writing about them here. So, yeah... BUTCHER BAKER THE RIGHTEOUS MAKER made it through that wet, slimy canal of creation and, lo and behold, here it is. It exists. It lives. It breathes. It pees on your fucking rug.

ROLLING AROUND IN THE DEVELOPMENT PIT

This is how shit starts. The Secret Origin of a pure, comicbook orgy of four color madness. The transference of something obscenely intangible from the deepest depths of the mind... to the endless expanse of the page... from idea to execution an' all that fucked up stuff...

Okay, fuck all that supreme wankery for just a second. Indulge me. In reality, the origins of the idea date back to another series I wrote years earlier, for another company that, on many occasions, didn't know what the fuck they were doing with themselves (*let's see just how cryptic I can be without putting a legal action target on my back... play at home!*). I had come up with a sequel of sorts, taking a supporting character from the previous work and promoting him to a starring role. A No-Prize shall be awarded to anyone who can figure out which earlier series and which character I'm talking about here. Shouldn't be too hard to figure out, really.

In any case, I soon came to my senses. Besides, the company in question was disintegrating right before my eyes, on every conceivable level. So I had an After-School Special-style epiphany and realized what I could do. What I *needed* to do. It was just a matter of taking something that was corporately-owned and morphing it into something creator-owned. This is a process that I highly and enthusiastically recommend to any creator out there who thinks they've got the perfect story for some dusty old character languishing at some dusty old publisher. It's taking something good and making it better. If you've already got the chops as a creative motherfucker, it doesn't take much to turn something unoriginal into something original.

So if you're a patented. pathological Process Junkie like I am, you might find some of this shit vaguely interesting. If not... well, it's an easy section to skip over, isn't it...?

Subj: **Butcher Baker**
Date: 8/16/2008 12:20:49 PM Pacific Daylight Time
From: JoeCasey
To: mhuddl
CC: JoeCasey

Hey Mike –

Okay, as promised, here's a few beginning notes on the BUTCHER BAKER idea. Please think of this as a very open process. I'll throw some general ideas at you, some character ideas, names, etc. but if anything sparks any ideas from you – beyond the visual, I mean – then definitely hit me back.

The idea, in a way, is to tell (on the surface, at least) a pretty straightforward action/superhero... but then pack it with asides, ideas, concepts, moments, etc. that really give it our individual stamp. A lot of my work tends to be that way, where if you strip away all the "wackiness" that I have so much fun doing, it's really a very simple story with really simple characters. Same thing here.

So, onto the few notes that I have...

Butcher Baker is a patriotic superhero, but he doesn't dress like Capt. America or wear a flag-based uniform. He wears a white outfit (S&M gear meets sci-fi uniform) and wears a modified hockey goalie mask (think Jason from Friday the 13th, but a little sleeker, and more original in design than just a "typical" hockey mask). There should be a "soldier" quality to Butcher, in both his personality and his visual (my idea for him is that he used to work for the government but has gone freelance... that's what makes him a "Righteous Maker"). Without the mask, he's got a full mustache and beard stubble (very porn star, I know, but it'll be cool, I think). As I said before, he drives a big 18-wheeler (without the trailer, though). This thing IS decorated in the stars n' stripes, very patriotic. In fact, its name is "Liberty Belle" and when it's going, big plumes of fire should shoot out of the exhaust pipes.

Which brings me to another overall point... a vibe we should try and inject into this series is the whole muscle car culture, any vehicles or tech is individually modified to reflect the personality of its owner (hero OR villain). This is why I asked you about Smokey and the Bandit... that whole redneck, moonshine, mid-70's car chase movie-vibe. The GONE IN SIXTY SECONDS, VANISHING POINT, DUKES OF HAZZARD (on the cheesy side) kind of feeling. That bad taste, anything-goes kind of vibe...

In terms of story, here's what I've got... Butcher Baker is recruited for a covert superhero operation. The Powers That Be are sick and tired of paying for the incarceration of most of the super-villains in this Arkham Asylum-type institution called THE CRAZY KEEP, so they want Butcher to go in and blow it up, with all the villains inside of it. He will not be acting in any "official" capacity, so if he's caught, it's his ass (since, technically, what he's doing is an illegal act of mass murder). But Butcher takes on the gig (both out of ego... and out of the fact that he's tangled with most of these villains in the past and he's eager for the world to be completely rid of them).

The only resistence he runs into is a renegade highway patrolman who, in his own way, is a crazy fuck. His uniform should be a cross between a highway partolman and a black Nazi uniform. Even his helmet should be reminiscent of the Nazis, with the spike on top. I don't have a name for this guy yet, but he's after Butcher at first for a simple speeding violation, but a true rivalry grows as Butcher starts to "play" with this guy, enjoying the cat-and-mouse aspect as a nice diversion from his mission of murder.

So, ~~after a small series of kooky misadventures getting there,~~ Butcher reaches the Crazy Keep and actually succeeds in his mission, setting explosives and blowing the fucker into powder.

The initial e-mail from writer to artist, laying down the basic concepts and the goals of the series. Handwritten margin notes occurred after the fact, as more ideas were formed.

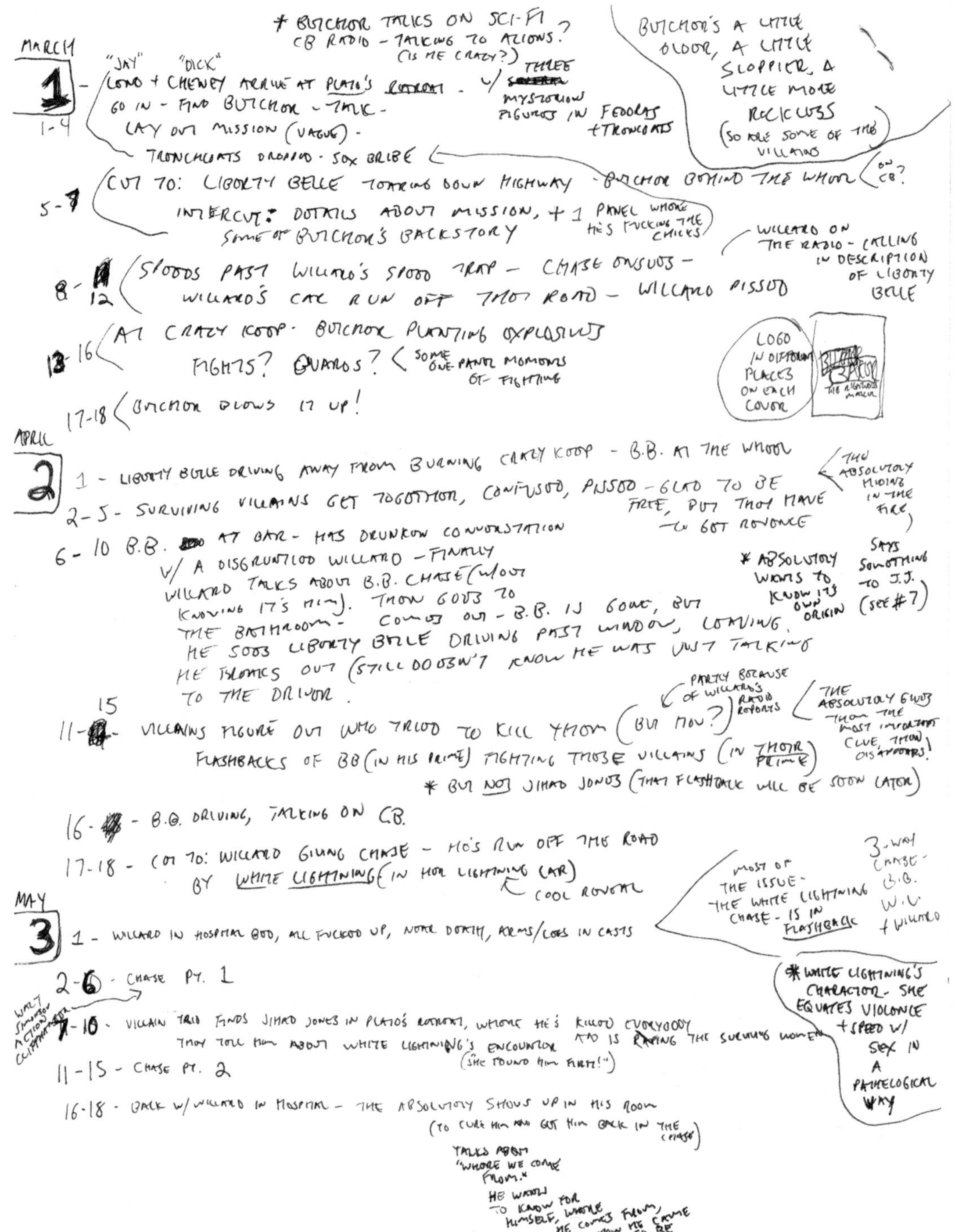

* BUTCHER TALKS ON SCI-FI CB RADIO - TALKING TO ALIENS? (IS HE CRAZY?)

MARCH

1 - "JAY" "DICK" LENO + CHENEY ARRIVE AT PLATO'S RETREAT - W/ THREE MYSTERIOUS FIGURES IN FEDORAS + TRENCHCOATS
1-4 GO IN - FIND BUTCHER - TALK -
LAY OUT MISSION (VAGUE) -
TRENCHCOATS DROPPED - SEX BRIBE

BUTCHER'S A LITTLE OLDER, A LITTLE SLOPPIER, A LITTLE MORE RECKLESS (SO ARE SOME OF THE VILLAINS)

5-7 CUT TO: LIBERTY BELLE TEARING DOWN HIGHWAY - BUTCHER BEHIND THE WHEEL (ON CB?)
INTERCUT: DETAILS ABOUT MISSION, + 1 PANEL WHERE HE'S FUCKING THE CHICKS
SOME OF BUTCHER'S BACKSTORY

8-12 SPEEDS PAST WILLARD'S SPEED TRAP - CHASE ENSUES -
WILLARD'S CAR RUN OFF THE ROAD - WILLARD PISSED
WILLARD ON THE RADIO - CALLING IN DESCRIPTION OF LIBERTY BELLE

13-16 AT CRAZY KOOP - BUTCHER PLANTING EXPLOSIVES
FIGHTS? GUARDS? < SOME ONE-PANEL MOMENTS OF FIGHTING

LOGO IN DIFFERENT PLACES ON EACH COVER

17-18 BUTCHER BLOWS IT UP!

APRIL

2 1 - LIBERTY BELLE DRIVING AWAY FROM BURNING CRAZY KOOP - B.B. AT THE WHEEL
(THE ABSOLUTELY HIDING IN THE FIRE)
2-5 - SURVIVING VILLAINS GET TOGETHER, CONFUSED, PISSED - GLAD TO BE FREE, BUT THEY HAVE TO GET REVENGE
6-10 B.B. AT BAR - HAS DRUNKEN CONVERSATION W/ A DISGRUNTLED WILLARD - FINALLY WILLARD TALKS ABOUT B.B. CHASE (W/OUT KNOWING IT'S HIM). THEN GOES TO THE BATHROOM - COMES OUT - B.B. IS GONE, BUT HE SEES LIBERTY BELLE DRIVING PAST WINDOW, LEAVING. HE FREAKS OUT (STILL DOESN'T KNOW HE WAS JUST TALKING TO THE DRIVER.

* ABSOLUTELY WANTS TO KNOW ITS OWN ORIGIN
SAYS SOMETHING TO J.J. (SEE #7)

11-15 - VILLAINS FIGURE OUT WHO TRIED TO KILL THEM (BUT HOW?) PARTLY BECAUSE OF WILLARD'S RADIO REPORTS
FLASHBACKS OF BB (IN HIS PRIME) FIGHTING THOSE VILLAINS (IN THEIR PRIME)
THE ABSOLUTELY GIVES THEM THE MOST IMPORTANT CLUE, THEN DISAPPEARS!
* BUT NOT JIHAD JONES (THAT FLASHBACK WILL BE SOON LATER)
16 - B.B. DRIVING, TALKING ON CB.
17-18 - CUT TO: WILLARD GIVING CHASE - HE'S RUN OFF THE ROAD BY WHITE LIGHTNING (IN HER LIGHTNING CAR) < COOL REVEAL

MOST OF THE ISSUE - THE WHITE LIGHTNING CHASE - IS IN FLASHBACK
3-WAY CHASE - B.B. W.L. + WILLARD

MAY

3 1 - WILLARD IN HOSPITAL BED, ALL FUCKED UP, NEAR DEATH, ARMS/LEGS IN CASTS
2-6 - CHASE PT. 1
7-10 - VILLAIN TRIO FINDS JIHAD JONES IN PLATO'S RETREAT, WHERE HE'S KILLED EVERYBODY AND IS RAPING THE SURVIVING WOMEN
THEY TELL HIM ABOUT WHITE LIGHTNING'S ENCOUNTER ("SHE FOUND HIM FIRST!")

* WHITE LIGHTNING'S CHARACTER - SHE EQUATES VIOLENCE + SPEED W/ SEX IN A PATHOLOGICAL WAY

11-15 - CHASE PT. 2
16-18 - BACK W/ WILLARD IN HOSPITAL - THE ABSOLUTELY SHOWS UP IN HIS ROOM (TO CURE HIM AND GET HIM BACK IN THE CHASE)
TALKS ABOUT "WHERE WE COME FROM." HE WANTS TO KNOW FOR HIMSELF, WHERE HE COMES FROM, HOW HE CAME TO BE

On this page and the next, the handwritten outline laying out the basic beats of all eight issues of the series. Good luck reading the chicken scrawl...

4 JUNE

1-3 – FLASHBACK – B.B. IN MID-80'S – BOSNIA? (CENTRAL AMERICA) LEADING U.S. TROOPS – COVERT OP!

4-5 BACK TO PRESENT – B.B. ~~DRINKING – RELAXING~~ IN BED W/ FORMER SUPERHEROINE, HAVING SEX WHILE HE TELLS HER THIS STORY – IN TIMES SQUARE

6 – OUTSIDE, LIBERTY BELLE (PARKED) – EXPLODES

7 – B.B. RUSHES OUTSIDE – TOTAL CHAOS – ANGERMOTO, EL SUSHI + ABOMINABLE SNOWMAN READY TO FIGHT ← DRIVING MOTORCYCLE

8-10 – WILLARD/ABSOLUTELY – AT END OF SCENE, THEY HEAR ABOUT BATTLE RAGING IN TIMES SQUARE → (TALKS ABOUT "WHERE HE CAME FROM")

11-17 – BIG FIGHT – LOTS OF DAMAGE – THE SUPERHEROINE IS TAKEN HOSTAGE + KILLED A MOMENT LATER

18 – THE MILITARY MOVES IN TO "CONTAIN" SITUATION – B.B. PISSED (HE KNEW HIS MISSION WAS SECRET – THAT HE WAS EXPENDABLE, BUT THIS CROSSED THE LINE)

5 JULY

1-9 (BIG FIGHT IN TIMES SQUARE – B.B. IS ABLE TO GET THE VILLAINS AND THE MILITARY TO FIGHT EACH OTHER WHILE HE ESCAPES – B.B. STEALS ARMY JEEP

10-16 (WILLARD + ABSOLUTELY SCENE – THE ABSOLUTELY DOES SOME COSMIC HOCUS POCUS (THAT INVOLVES GAY SEX) THAT LINKS WILLARD'S MIND W/ B.B.'S. IT'S AN ABSTRACT THING, BUT IT ALLOWS WILLARD TO BE MORE INTUITIVE WHEN LOCATING HIM. — CROSS-POLLINATION OF THEIR "ORIGINS"

WHILE B.B. IS CONVALESCING AT A CLUB MED-TYPE RESORT FOR RETIRED SUPER-HEROES (A FEW OF THEM WERE B.B.'S CONTEMPORARIES, BACK IN THE DAY)

17-18 (B.B. GOES BACK TO HIS BUNGALOW – JIHAD JONES IS WAITING FOR HIM

6 AUG

1-3 B.B. PRISONER OF JIHAD JONES – TORTURED, BEATEN – A SERIES OF "NEURAL DAGGERS" SENT INTO B.B.'S BRAIN, KEEPING HIM DOCILE, IMMOBILE (LIKE HEAT LAMPS SURROUNDING HIM)

4-7 FLASHBACK TO EARLIER B.B./J.J. CONFRONTATION – B.B. KILLS J.J.'S GAY LOVER/PARTNER/EVIL SIDEKICK, SNAKESKIN

8-10 BACK TO PRESENT, MORE BEATING/TORTURE – B.B. GOES INTO MEDITATIVE TECHNIQUES TO ESCAPE THE PAIN →

11-14 – WILLARD + ABSOLUTELY – THEY'RE INSIDE THE MEDITATION

15-16 – "JAY" + "DICK" TALKING TO MILITARY GENERALS – THEY SELL B.B. UP THE RIVER, DENY THEIR * INVOLVEMENT, ETC.

17-18 – ~~[illegible]~~ WILLARD SHOWS UP AT SAFEHOUSE – UNCOVERS LIBERTY BELLE II – NEW TRUCK! (DIRECTED SUBLIMINALLY BY B.B.)

7 SEPT.

(16-PANEL GRID)

1 – B.B. STILL GETTING BEATEN BY J.J., BUT HE'S STILL HOLDING ON...

2-3 – LIBERTY BELLE II SCREAMING DOWN HIGHWAY – WILLARD + ABSOLUTELY IN CAB – WILLARD IS SLIGHTLY CONFUSED – ALTERNATELY THINKING HE'S EITHER GOING TO ARREST OR RESCUE B.B.

4-5 – J.J. IN ANOTHER PART OF THE COMPOUND – ABSOLUTELY APPEARS AND THEY TALK (A FEW PHRASES SAID BY THE ABSOLUTELY – HE SAID TO J.J. IN #2) – THE ABSOLUTELY DISAPPEARS

6-10 – WHAT B.B., TIED UP, BEATEN, BLOODY – HE'S REASSESSING THINGS, SLOWING HIS HEARTRATE DOWN TO 1 BEAT PER MINUTE – KIND OF A QUANTUM THING, DR. MANHATTAN – INTERCUT W/ WILLARD DRIVING

11 – J.J. + ABSOLUTELY, J.J. WAVES HIM AWAY – ABSOLUTELY DISAPPEARS – HIS MINIONS COME IN, "HE'S DEAD, BOSS!"

12 – IN ROOM W/ B.B., THE MINIONS UNTYING HIM, TURNING OFF NEURAL DAGGERS – LAYING HIM OUT – SUDDENLY –

13-14 – TRUCK CRASHES IN – EVERYONE GOES FLYING (OVER B.B.'S BODY) – WILLARD GETS OUT, GUN DRAWN

15 – FINDS B.B.'S BODY, TRIES TO "ARREST" HIM, BUT B.B. IS STILL OUT OF IT – THEN W. TURNS TO SEE J.J. – RECOGNIZES HIM, AIMS GUN AT HIM

16-17 J.J. ATTACKS, THROWS WILLARD ACROSS THE ROOM, BEATS THE SHIT OUT OF HIM, POUNCES, KNIFE AT HIS THROAT, VOICE FROM OFF –

18 – B.B. UP AND READY TO FIGHT (SPLASH)?

8 OCT.

1 – JAY + DICK + MILITARY MOVEMENT GEARING UP – MOBILIZATION

2-6 – B.B. VS J.J. – WILLARD, GROGGY, FINDS GUN, WINGS J.J.

7-8 – B.B. JUMPS INTO TRUCK – HEADLIGHTS ON – RUNS OVER/SLAMS INTO/CRUSHES J.J., KILLS HIM

9 – WILLARD HAS GUN ON TRUCK, B.B. GETS OUT – "GUESS IT'S ONLY FAIR... YOU DID HELP ME OUT." WILLARD CONFUSED AND PISSED.

10 – ABSOLUTELY APPEARS. B.B. RECOGNIZES HIM AS AN OLD ENEMY. WILLARD STILL CONFUSED/PISSED

11 – ABSOLUTELY SPEECH – "WHO AM I?" IS WHAT HE WANTS TO KNOW – B.B. CAN ANSWER

12-13 * – ABSOLUTELY'S ORIGIN – MIND-BLOWING – ABSOLUTELY CAN TAKE IT, CAN'T ACCEPT IT –

14 – HE OPENS UP HIS BLACK HOLE HEART – COLLAPSES IN ON HIMSELF – B.B./WILLARD HANGING ON, SO THEY DON'T GET SUCKED IN, TOO

15-16 – B.B. ADMITS HE MADE UP ~~[illegible]~~ ORIGIN STORY TO FUCK W/ ABSOLUTELY, LEAVES WILLARD ALONE

17 – WILLARD EPILOGUE

18-20 B.B. IN NEW LIBERTY BELLE – DRIVING – COMES UP ON MILITARY ROADBLOCK – B.B. SEES JAY + DICK – SMILES – PRESSES GAS PEDAL DOWN

ENDS W/ B.B. SQUARING OFF AGAINST THE MILITARY, AND HE LOVES IT.

* ABSOLUTELY ORIGIN – IT BEGAN AS A SINGLE IDEA IN THE BRAIN OF AN AUTISTIC CHILD BEING EXPERIMENTED ON BY BLACK SCIENCE DOCTORS

ESTABLISH HIS "BLACK HOLE HEART"

4-7 We then FLASHBACK to an earlier Butcher/Jihad Jones confrontation (seeing both of them in their prime) and we learn the reason for Jihad's hatred of Butcher… in this flashback we see that Butcher killed Jihad's super-villain partner/sidekick (and gay lover), ~~SNAKESKIN~~. JET BOY

8-10 Back to the present. More beating and torture. Butcher goes into intense, guided meditation techniques to escape the intense pain. (LOGAN? MEETS ALADIN)

11-14 But then we CUT TO a scene with WILLARD and THE ABSOLUTELY. Due to the vague, psychic link that Butcher and Willard share, both Willard and the Absolutely (who can pretty much do anything on a quantum level) find themselves INSIDE the guided meditation (like an astral plane-type environment, but more surreal). But this encounter allows Willard to more precisely "locate" where Butcher is in the real world. ABSOLUTELY GIVES FULL EXPLANATION OF PSYCHIC LINK BETWEEN THEM

15-16 Meanwhile, "Jay" and "Dick" meet with the Joint Chiefs. The disastrous op in Times Square (with so much collateral damage and many civilian casualties) has put them on the spot… but naturally they not only deny any knowledge of Butcher's activities (or his original mission), they suggest an all-out manhunt to bring the "rogue hero" in. In other words, they completely sell Butcher out to save their own asses. START TO LAY IN A MORE SYMPATHETIC CONNECTION THAT WILLARD HAS W/ BUTCHER

17-18 Finally, WILLARD and THE ABSOLUTELY arrive at one of Butcher's SAFEHOUSES (which Willard now has intimate knowledge of, due to the psychic connection he shares with Butcher). He pulls off a big tarp to reveal… the LIBERTY BELLE II, bigger and badder than the first one!!!

STAY CLOSE FROM #2?

ISSUE SEVEN

16-PANEL GRID

1 We pick up with BUTCHER still getting beaten and tortured. But he's not dead yet, and he's definitely got a plan…

2-3 Meanwhile, the LB II is screaming down the highway… with WILLARD behind the wheel! THE ABSOLUTELY rides shotgun. Willard is displaying confused behavior… alternatively thinking that he's going to arrest Butcher and/or rescue him (the psychic link is clouding his brain to some degree… or is Butcher somehow bringing him to his aid?). But the Absolutely dematerializes out of the cab…

4-5 … and shows up in JIHAD JONES' secret h.q. to talk privately with Jihad. A FEW THINGS THE ABSOLUTELY SAYS ARE THE SAME THINGS HE SAID IN ISH #2 - A DR. MANHATTAN QUANTUM MOMENT

6-9 Meanwhile, Butcher is left alone, still bound and his brain dampened. He's also experiencing a few random "mind flashes" of Willard driving in his truck. Again, is he using their psychic link to bring him closer? The connection is so vague (the dampeners really work), he has no choice but to try an alternate plan involving a new trick… slowing his heartbeat down to once per minute.

10 Back with Jihad and the Absolutely, still talking. It's clear these two don't get along, and when Jihad waves him away, the Absolutely disappears in a pique. Then Jihad's minions rush in, "He's dead, boss!"

11 They all rush into the other room, where it does seem like Butcher is dead. They lay him out on the ground, turn off the neural dampeners, etc. when suddenly…

12-14 … the LB II crashes in through the wall, sending everyone (including Butcher's "lifeless" body) flying in every direction. WILLARD jumps out of the truck, gun drawn. He finds Butcher's body, tries to arrest him (but, of course, Butcher is still out cold). Willard turns to see JIHAD, ~~recognizes him~~, and aims his gun (he's gonna arrest *someone* today!).

15-17 JIHAD attacks, throws Willard across the room, beats the shit out of him, pounces on him and puts a knife at his throat. And then, a voice from off…

18 … it's BUTCHER, awake and ready to kick ass!

Excerpted from the final, more detailed outlines typed up for each issue, with more handwritten margin notes scribbled in as each full script was being prepped and new details were being birthed. Seek out the unused bits of dialogue and revel in the wonder of what could have been...

"year jammers"

ISSUE EIGHT

1 We open with "Jay" and "Dick" taking an active role in the military mobilization, ready to go out and find BUTCHER and bring him in.

2-8 We CUT BACK to the full on fight between BUTCHER and JIHAD JONES. Two mortal enemies going at it. As they fight, WILLARD comes to and groggily fires his gun, winging Jihad and temporarily wounding him. As Jihad staggers, Butcher jumps into the LB II, guns it and runs over Jihad, killing him.

9 Now WILLARD trains his gun on the truck, intent on finally (!) arresting Butcher. Butcher gets out of the truck, "I guess it's only fair… you did help me out." Willard is both confused and pissed off.

10 Then THE ABSOLUTELY reappears. Butcher recognizes him as another old enemy that should've been killed when he blew up the Keep. Willard is still confused as to what's happening here.

11 Then the Absolutely spells it out. All he wants to know about himself is where he comes from. A total "Who am I?" speech. Butcher offers up, "Hell, I can tell you that."

12-14 He then relates the Absolutely's origin (which, at the moment, consists of the following idea… he began as a single idea in the brain of an autistic child being experimented on by black science doctors, the idea being to create what is essentially a cosmic sex slave). The notion is so depraved and demeaning that the Absolutely (who honestly thought he was some kind of higher order of god-being with some sort of divine origin) can't accept it, he can't handle the truth. So he basically opens up his own "black hole heart" and commits cosmic suicide, imploding in on himself. Butcher and Willard have to hang on, in order to not get sucked into the temporary singularity (which dissipates as soon as the Absolutely disappears).

15-16 With only Butcher and Willard left, Butcher admits that he totally made up the Absolutely's origin to fuck with him. He admits, "He may be a god after all, but I sure as hell don't need *him* knowing that. This way is better." At this point, Willard decides to let Butcher go free…

17 So, we finish with a pair of epilogues: the first being WILLARD. We'll have some one-page scene with the character, showing him in a better place or whatever…

18-20 Then we have the final epilogue with BUTCHER, who is once again tearing down the highway in the LB II. As he barks into his CB radio, this whole adventure has given him a new perspective on life, "I may be older, but I'm better." At that point, he comes over the hill and sees a MASSIVE military roadblock up ahead. When Butcher sees that "Jay" and "Dick" -- the assholes who got him into this mess and have clearly sold him out -- are among the military officials present, he smiles. He presses the gas pedal down even further… ready to kick some REAL ass!

MAYBE I'LL RUN FOR PRESIDENT.

WHY THE FUCK NOT?

THE END

BB GIVES HIM THE GUN THAT WILL ALLOW HIM TO END HIMSELF W/ DIGNITY

shoots himself w/ ENTROPATHIC PISTOL (ACTUALLY A PROTOTYPE FOR A BUTCHER BAKER KID'S TOY GUN THAT NEVER MADE IT TO MARKET)

TOWARD MEXICAN/TEXAS BORDER (HE'S GOING HOME)

WHAT THE FUCK IS THIS SHIT?!

Now, *this* is how you announce a fuckin' comicbook series, right? Anyone who might've been online in November of 2010 might actually remember these teasers popping out, one a day, for the entire month.

The very concept of doing teasers for comicbooks is relatively recent. Back in the day, you'd just do ads. No big deal. More white noise. But the idea of "announcing" a new project *without specifically announcing it* became more prevalent as the industry in general was becoming more media savvy in its practices. And by now, everyone's done everything under the Sun to "tease" something that's "coming soon", from silhouetted images to cryptic bits of text to abstract visuals... personally, I feel like I've seen it all.

But I'd never seen it done like *this*.

I had help. Graphic design guru, Sonia Harris, did a lot of the heavy lifting here. She took my weird ideas and corralled them into a great-looking, focused information campaign that, for the most part, actually held most people's attention for the month these things were trickling out. That takes talent, y'know. Betsy Gomez (at the time, Image Comics' PR & Marketing Coordinator... whatever *that* job title means) did her part, setting it all up and making sure these things got out, each and every day, like clockwork. Articles were written about this campaign, debating its perceived merits and its perceived faults. It got folks talking. It fucked with their heads. It did exactly what it was supposed to do, which was to create some awareness for this... *thing* called BUTCHER BAKER THE RIGHTEOUS MAKER.

I have no idea how these will play, presented in this format. But they look so great, they have such a power on their own, there's no fuckin' way I wasn't gonna run these bad boys in this book. Looking back, they were an intrinsic part of the project. They were Performance Art on a grand scale. Even now, I'm not 100% certain that the actual comicbook lived up to the promise of these teasers. Guess you can be the judge.

And I'm *still* waiting for some other teaser campaign to top it...

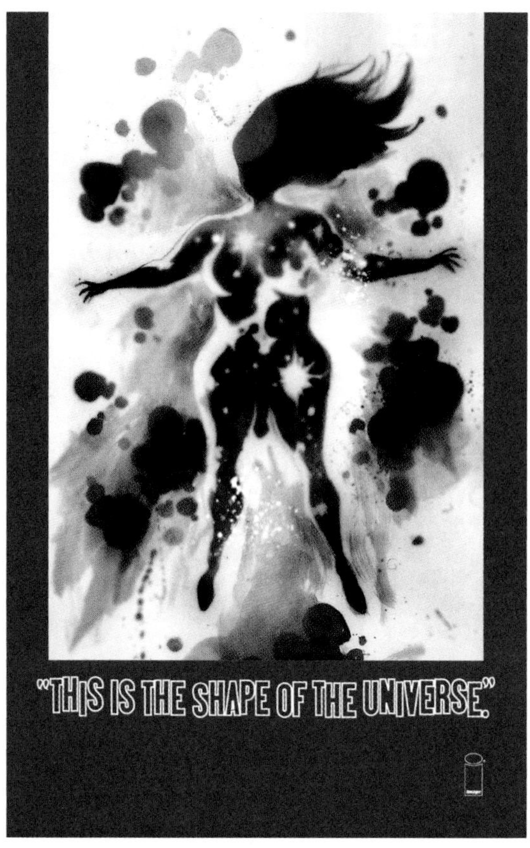

"THIS IS THE SHAPE OF THE UNIVERSE."

November 1st, 2011

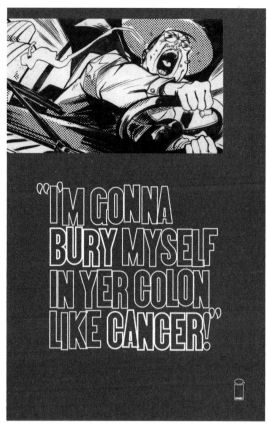

"I'M GONNA BURY MYSELF IN YER COLON LIKE CANCER!"

November 2nd, 2011

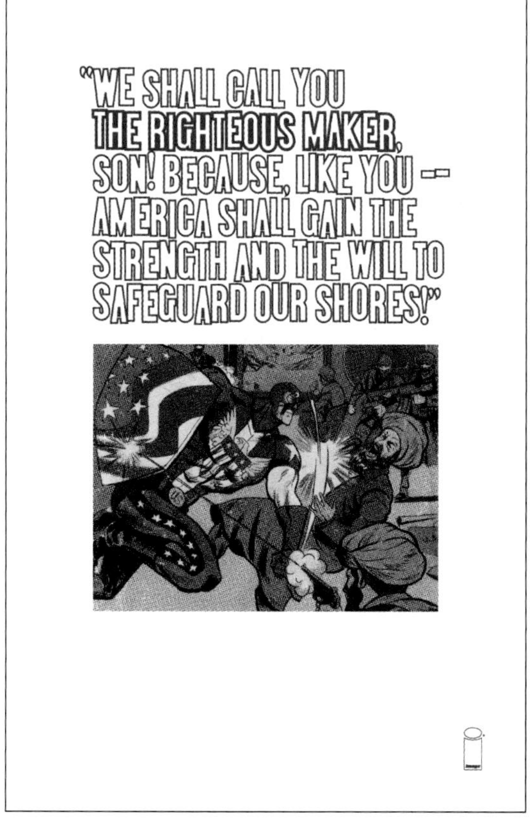

"WE SHALL CALL YOU
THE RIGHTEOUS MAKER,
SON! BECAUSE, LIKE YOU —
AMERICA SHALL GAIN THE
STRENGTH AND THE WILL TO
SAFEGUARD OUR SHORES!"

November 3rd, 2011

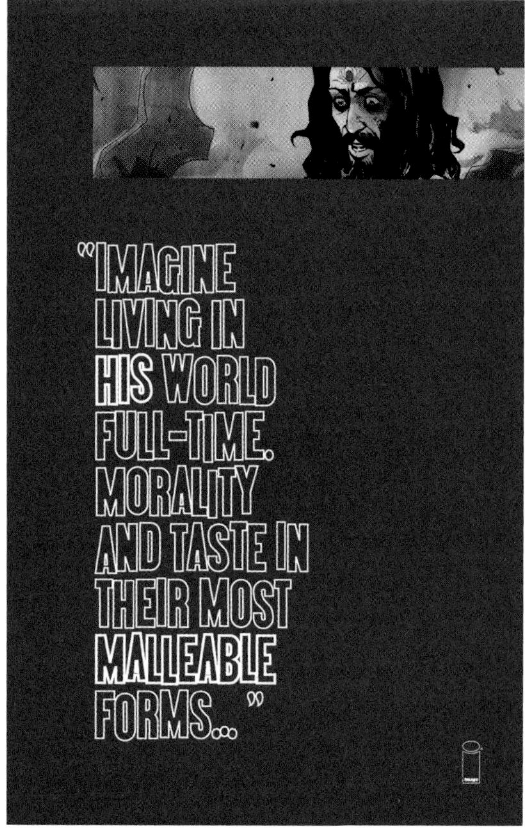

FULL-TIME.
MORALITY
AND TASTE IN
THEIR MOST

November 4th, 2011

November 5th, 2011

November 8th, 2011

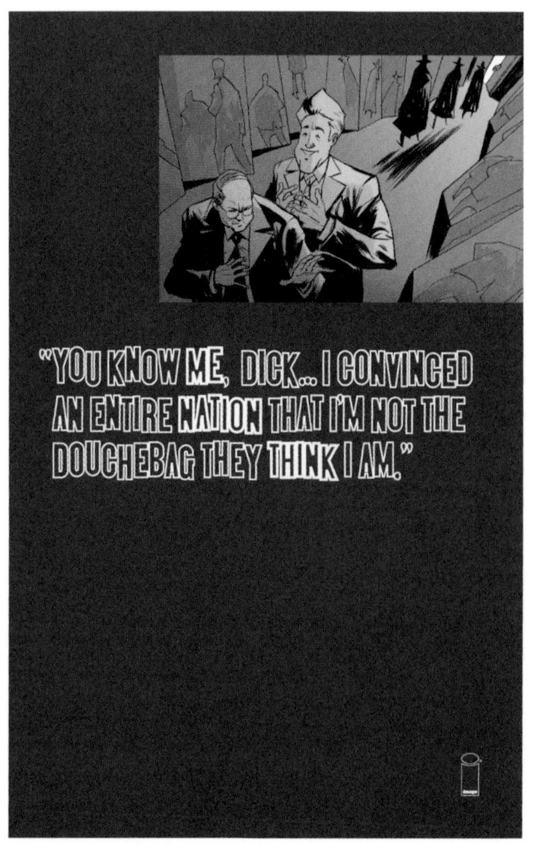

November 9th, 2011

November 10th, 2011

November 11th, 2011

"YEAH, FOR A SUPERHERO, HE WAS A SADISTIC SON OF A BITCH."

November 12th, 2011

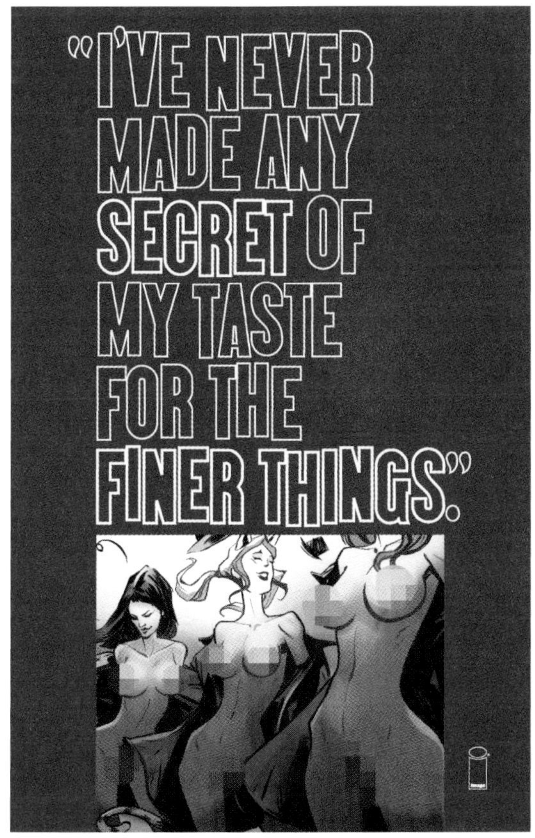

November 15th, 2011

November 16th, 2011

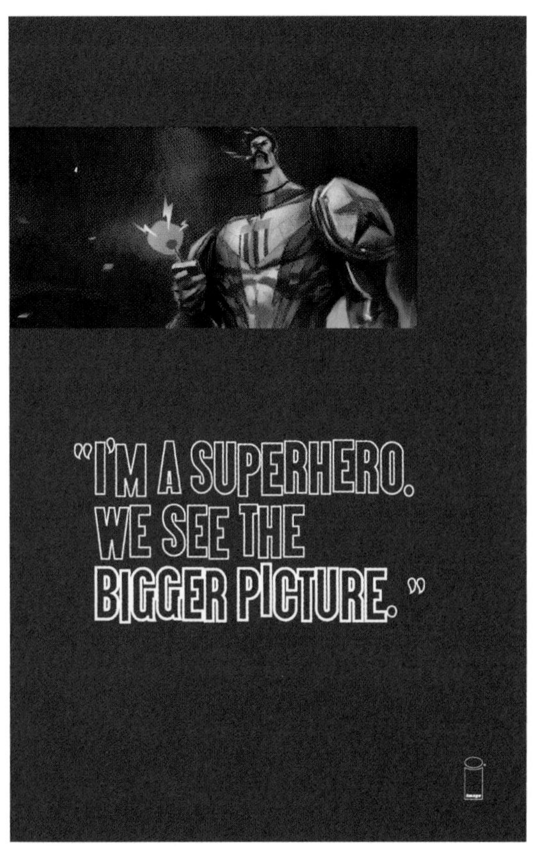

"I'M A SUPERHERO. WE SEE THE BIGGER PICTURE."

November 17th, 2011

"SO WHO ELSE MADE IT OUT OF THE CRAZY KEEP ALIVE?"

"WHO ELSE IS GUNNING FOR ME?"

November 18th, 2011

"LOOKS LIKE THIS BULLDOG'S GOT AN ITCH OF HIS OWN..."

November 19th, 2011

"WHAT'S THAT SMELL?"

November 22nd, 2011

November 23rd, 2011

November 24th, 2011

November 25th, 2011

November 26th, 2011

JOURNEY OF A LOGO DESIGN

Great logos aren't born, they're torn. Torn, that is, from the brains of creative and talented artists working their asses off. Here's a bit of insight into the wild and wacky world of logo design, from terrible sketch to finished product. What you see on these pages tells its own kind of story. It's all about thinking out loud, graphically, until you find that sweet spot where the ethereal suddenly becomes the inevitable. That's when you know you've got it.

In this case, designer Sonia Harris wrapped her sticky-ass fingers around an admittedly vague idea, wrestled that shit to the ground and made it beg for mercy. She shared the notion that this kind of logo -- adorning this kind of comicbook -- had to have its own pair of balls and they had to be swingin' hard. We're talking about balls that can knock down skyscrapers. She wanted to lean into the harsh tradition of the pulp action roots this series reveled in and then blow it out of the water with a proverbial Talent Torpedo.

When it's all said and done, there's a brashness to the BUTCHER BAKER logo that cannot be denied, an attempt to be completely reflective of the content found within the pages of the comicbook itself. And when you see how fucking amazing it looks on the final covers, it's hard to take any issue with the process and any strife that might come with it. Maybe that's just part of the dinner. Fuck it, this ended up being a great goddamn logo.

My own strange, hand-drawn sketch that kicked things off for Sonia...

The base font came first. Plenty to choose from, but when you find the one to go with, it just feels right. →

And once chosen, different angles were tried, tested and tossed around... →

... followed by experiments into arching the logo to get closer to that swashbuckling vibe. →

Once things were in the correct neighborhood, it was time to say hello to the requisite multiple outlines and drop-shadowing.

At this point, a few issues reared their ugly head... outlining on the inside wasn't working as well as it should've. The kerning was a little too wide for comfort. A few additional curving options still didn't quite nail it 100%.

Finally, an all-new, all-different font choice sent things down a more comfortable road, and the angles it provided lent themselves much better to the angling and the arching involved. Finally, logo nirvana was achieved!

COVER GLORY

Issue #1

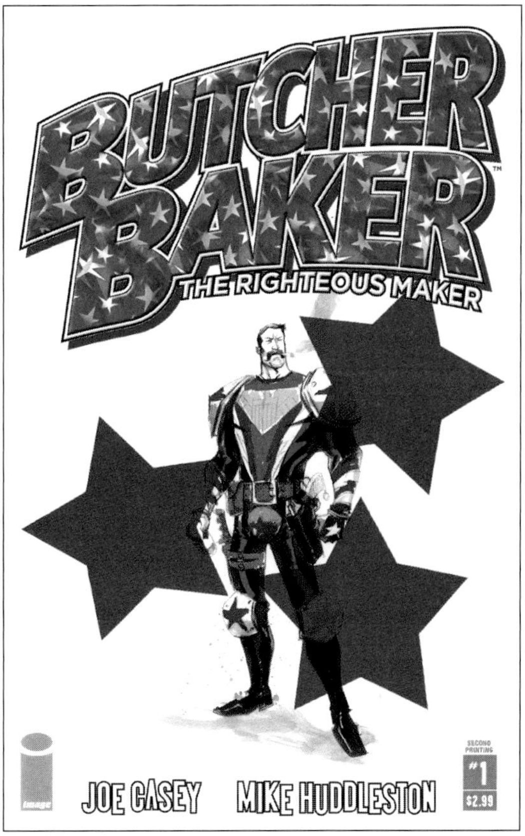

Issue #1, variant cover for second print run.

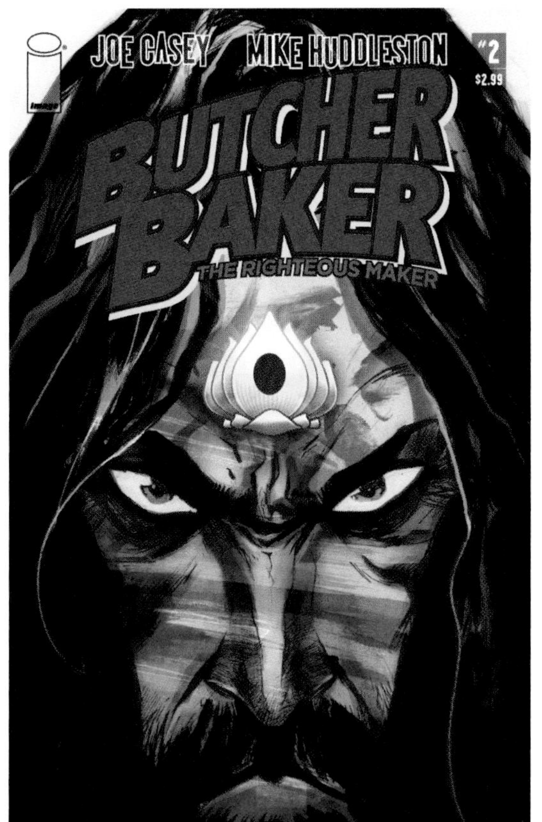

Issue #2

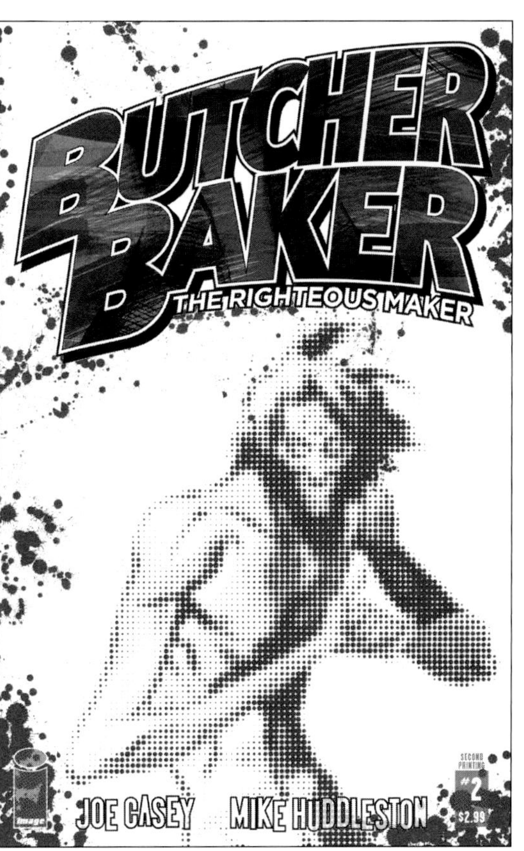

Issue #2, variant cover for second print run.

Issue #3

Issue #3, variant cover for second print run.

Issue #4

Issue #5

Issue #6

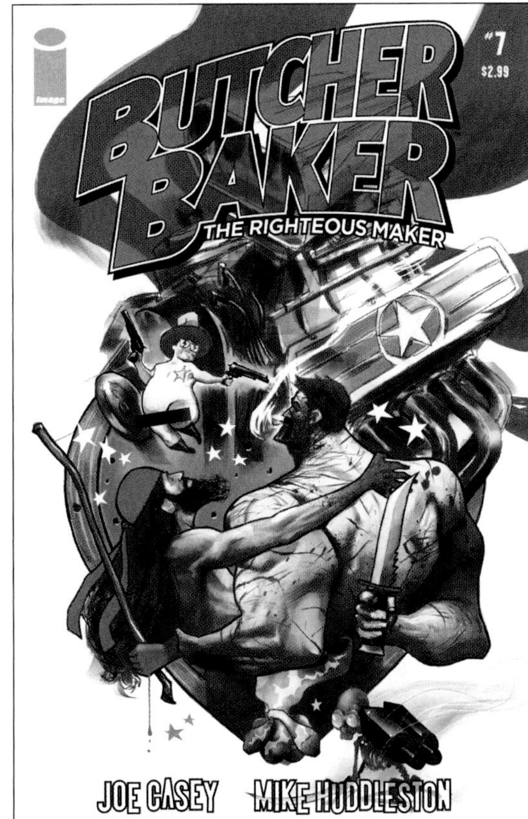

Issue #7

Issue #8

Somewhere, somehow... someone who cannot be identified decided that the early issues of BUTCHER BAKER were going to be "hot" (whatever the fuck that means). That meant early sell outs of the first few issues (on a retail level, it should be clarified), which necessitated second printings of said issues to meet the perceived demand. Yeah, whatever. In any case, we wanted these to be special, and that meant all-new covers to commemorate the occasions. Not to mention, they're fuckin' fun. Viva la capitalism!

Artist Mike Huddleston was hip-deep in actually drawing the book, and we were crunched for time. As some Type-A assholes are fond of saying, we needed new covers yesterday. But this is why you hire a graphic designer that'll jump in and conjure some shit up, seemingly out of thin air. We had some righteous development art sitting on deck, and we grabbed it and went to town. It takes considerable vision to take a mound of ill-formed clay and make a fully-formed statue out of it and, in these cases, designated hitter Sonia Harris had that vision and the results ended up being just as barn burning as any first print covers that graced this series.

As an added-value bonus for all you fucked up process junkies out there, take a gander at the blow-by-blow transformation of the variant cover for issue #3... from a random pencil sketch pulled from the archives to finished piece, ready to jump off the stands and into the hot, little hands of the readers.

Step 1, pencils by Mike Huddleston.

Step 2, invert the scan.

Step 3, color fill

Step 4, begin shading.

Step 5, blur and add noise.

Step 6, add facial contours.

Step 7, lightening background.

Step 8, overlay portrait.

Step 9, finished cover.

They say a hero is only as good as his villains. And, for BUTCHER BAKER THE RIGHTEOUS MAKER, we sure as hell didn't hold back when it came to giving our titular badass plenty of *opposition* to everything that he dared to stand for. Starting with names and concepts and suggestions of superpowers, sketches flew around fast and furious. Knee-jerk creativity mixed with a healthy dose of long standing comicbook tradition birthed a goddamn glorious rogues gallery of mean motherfuckers that -- just in their visual presentation alone -- evoked precisely the kind of twisted world that Butcher inhabited. Just in the ways these guys looked suggested attitudes, relationships, rivalries, backstories, etc.

These are inspired designs, and Huddleston exploded out of the gate with the following full-color representations of each and every villain we came up with. These were used both in the teaser campaign and in the backmatter material. found in the original single issues. Every picture tells a story, don't it?

No *wonder* these bastards were locked up in the Crazy Keep...!

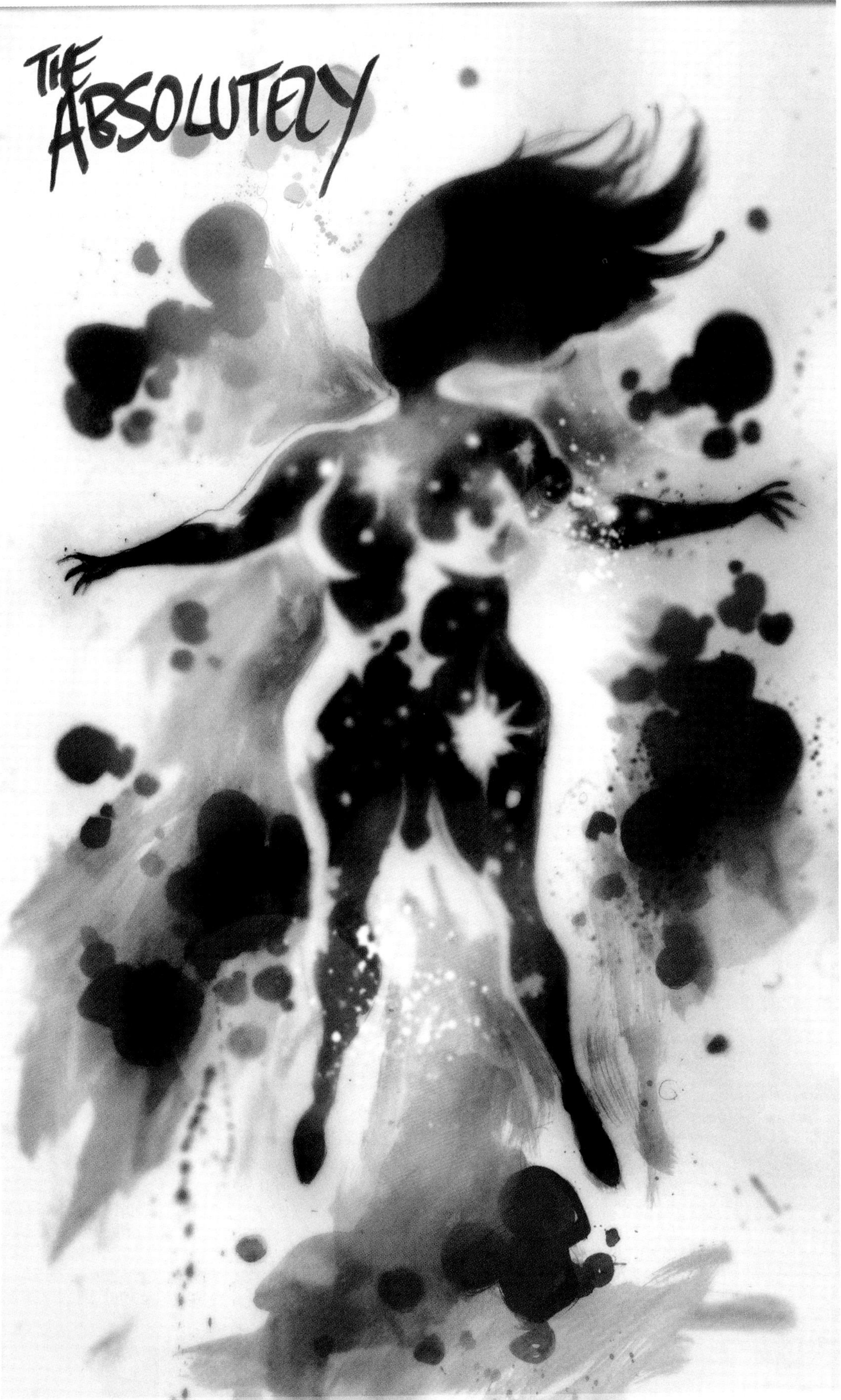
THE ABSOLUTELY

JIHAD JONES

ANGERHEAD

THE ABOMINABLE SNOWMAN

WHITE LIGHTNING

EL SUSHI

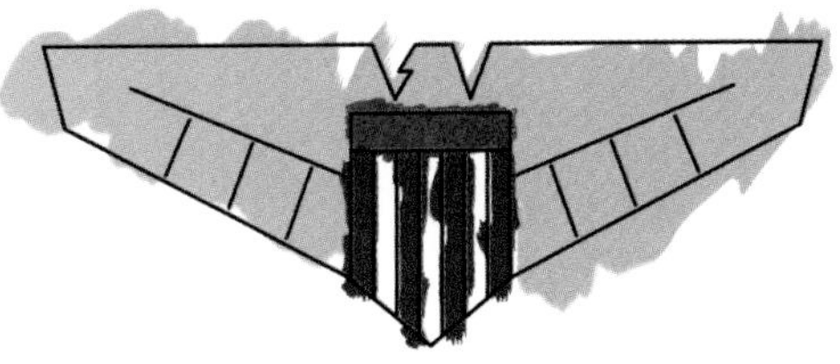

PROTO-BUTCHER... WITH A SIDE ORDER OF ANGST

This was the first -- and only other -- collaboration between my own bad self and artist, Mike Huddleston. It was commissioned by Image publisher, Eric Stephenson, for an anthology series he was putting together called FOUR-LETTER WORLDS that was released way back in 2005. If I'm remembering correctly, I believe it was Stephenson who matched me up with Huddleston in the first place. As it turns out, it was quite an enjoyable strip to do. I was already a fan of Mike's work at the time so I was excited to see what he'd bring to the party.

Oddly enough, this strip, titled "FUNK", ended up being one of the most personal things I've ever committed to comicbook form. It was a moment in time wrenched right out of my own life, one that I decided to try and make some sense of by tackling it in this manner. When I was in my early 20's, I was both incredibly unique and an incredible cliché. I won't bore you with the details, because I think the angst of the strip itself tells the tale fairly effectively. I do remember being quite happy with how it all turned out (aside from the ridiculous name of the lead character, "Taylor Finn". *What was I thinking?!*), and I was proud to contribute to Stephenson's book. It's even cooler to be able to represent it here, in a larger format than it's ever seen print before.

It was the lab experiment where Huddleston and I decided that it'd be worth it to work together again someday. Hard to believe it took another five or six years for it to actually happen.

Feel free to seek out the original anthology book. There's a lot of good stuff in it. In the meantime, for the sake of an artistic completeness that this hardcover collection is attempting to achieve, here's Huddleston and me jamming for the first time...

I STILL DON'T GIVE A FUCK.

FUNK

BY JOE CASEY AND
MIKE HUDDLESTON

LETTERING BY
SEAN KONOT

I DON'T GIVE A FUCK.

I DON'T GIVE A FUCK.

A MAN'S *MISERY* CAN BE HIS ONLY FRIEND.

I LOOK AT IT AS A *FAMILIAR FACE* IN A ROOMFUL OF *STRANGERS.*

MY *OWN* FACE IS A LITTLE LESS FAMILIAR...

TAYLOR FINN. COLLEGE DROP-OUT. CAREER DISHWASHER.

EX-BOYFRIEND.

I GET A FIFTEEN-MINUTE BREAK. I COUNT THE SECONDS.

LIFE IS A SERIES OF *ENDINGS.* SOME THINGS JUST AREN'T MEANT TO *LAST...*

TWENTY-THREE YEARS OLD. I GET THE SENSE THAT I'M NOT INDESTRUCTIBLE.
I STILL LIKE TO TEST IT, THOUGH...
WHICH ONE WILL BREAK FIRST... MY HEART OR MY HEAD...?
AND HOW DO I COPE WITH EITHER INJURY?
I FANTASIZE ABOUT CRASHING AND BURNING IN A MUCH MORE VISIBLE MANNER.
MY LIZARD BRAIN SCREAMS FOR SATISFACTION. INFLICT PAIN TO DEFLECT MY OWN.
I TORTURE MYSELF BY KEEPING HER PICTURE NEXT TO MY BED.
SOMEHOW... EVERYONE SHOULD HURT LIKE I DO.

SHE'S STILL GOT A KEY SO PART OF ME WANTS HER TO COME IN WHILE I'M NOT THERE AND SEE THAT I HAVEN'T THROWN IT OUT.
WHATEVER.
WHY DOES EVERY MOMENT BECOME SO... CLIMACTIC?
YOU GAVE ME SHIT THE FIRST TIME I KISSED YOU IN PUBLIC... WHAT THE FUCK WAS THAT ABOUT...?!
HEY, I ENJOY THE INEVITABLE THAW AS MUCH AS THE NEXT GUY...
THE FIRST TIME YOU DON'T HOLD BACK...
... SMELLS LIKE VICTORY.
I STILL THINK ABOUT THE EXACT MOMENT...
... THE MOMENT THE WORM TURNED.
... I DUNNO, I WAS JUST THINKING ABOUT IT...
... WHAT IF WE WENT ON DATES WITH OTHER PEOPLE...?

AMAZING I CRACKED YOUR CODE, ISN'T IT...?
YOU WERE ALREADY PLANNING ON "SEEING OTHER PEOPLE"...

WHAT WOULD YOU THINK IF YOU COULD SEE THIS, BITCH?!

THEN THERE'S THAT MOMENT. YOU ALL KNOW IT...
... THE MOMENT WHEN YOU JUST DON'T THINK YOU CAN LIVE WITH THIS KIND OF PAIN.

BUT, GODDAMMIT, THAT TURNS OUT TO BE THE EXACT MOMENT...

... WHEN YOU FIND YOUR POWER.

YOU BECOME AS FOCUSED... AS CLEAR-HEADED... AS YOU'VE EVER BEEN IN YOUR ENTIRE LIFE.
YOUR PAIN DEFINES YOU. MAKES YOU WHO YOU ARE.

EVERYTHING ABOUT YOU BECOMES PAIN MANAGEMENT. TURNING YOUR ULTIMATE WEAKNESS... INTO YOUR ULTIMATE STRENGTH.
SUDDENLY, YOU'VE GOT THE KIND OF SELF-DISCIPLINE YOU NEVER HAD BEFORE...
YOUR BODY IS A TEMPLE AND YOU REFUSE TO DEFILE IT.
A TEMPLE OF PAIN.
SOME GO FOR MISERY... THEY DRINK THEMSELVES INTO OBLIVION OR THEY GET WASTED ON WHATEVER QUALIFIES THEM AS VICTIMS OF "SUBSTANCE ABUSE".
NOT ME.
MY FRIENDS ARE ONLY TRYING TO HELP...
I KNOW WHAT THEY'RE REALLY THINKING, THOUGH. THEY'RE HAPPY TO HAVE ONE OF THE BOYS BACK IN THE RANKS.
BUT, DESPITE THEIR EFFORTS, I'M STILL OUT THERE ON MY OWN. FEEDING OFF MY OWN STRUGGLE TO STAY HUMAN.

PRETTY SOON, I'M A WALKING DICHOTOMY. I CAN'T IMAGINE BEING MORE SELF-FULFILLED THAN I AM RIGHT NOW. I'M AN UNTOUCHABLE IRON MAN OF LOST LOVE...
THE BEST VERSION OF MYSELF I COULD EVER HOPE TO BE...
... BUT I HATE IT ALL THE SAME.
EVERY OTHER SECOND... I JUST WANT TO ESCAPE FROM MYSELF...
... WITHOUT BEING OBVIOUS ABOUT IT.
BUT I CAN'T.
I CAN'T RUN FAST ENOUGH TO ESCAPE MYSELF.

AND THINGS JUST NEVER HAPPEN AS FAST AS I *WANT* THEM TO.

SO, IS THIS THE *NEW ME...?*
COLD AS ICE... HARD AS STONE... WALLS BUILT UP AROUND ME...?
MORE *GARBAGE* FILLING UP SPACE INSIDE ME...
IT FINALLY HITS THAT PLACE *BEYOND* "WANTING HER BACK". THAT'S A *VERSION* OF ME THAT'S GONE *FOREVER...*

FACE IT, KID... YOU'RE IN A *NEW* RELATIONSHIP NOW... WITH *YOURSELF.* PAIN IS YOUR PROM DATE.
YOU SLEEP WITH YOUR *LONELINESS.*
THERE'S NO *ROOM* FOR ANOTHER GIRLFRIEND WHEN YOU'RE *THIS* SELF-ABSORBED. AND, FOR A WHILE, I *LOVE* IT...

BUT EVEN THIS RELATIONSHIP DOESN'T LAST.
ALL LOVE FADES... EVEN THE LOVE FOR YOUR OWN PAIN...
IT GETS TOO HARD TO HOLD ONTO IT.
EVERY DAY, I LET ANOTHER LITTLE PIECE OF IT GO...
ANOTHER TINY DEATH...
AND EVERY DAY, THE WORLD REBUILDS ITSELF. NEW LESSONS ARE LEARNED...
START YOUR ENGINE.
GET YOURSELF INTO GEAR.
MOVE FORWARD.
TRY TO KEEP IT ON THE ROAD.
ONE DAY, YOU'LL CATCH YOURSELF SMILING FOR NO REASON
A LAST GOODBYE TO AN OLD FRIEND... AND TWENTY-THREE WILL SEEM A LITTLE LESS NAIVE.
END

JOE CASEY ESCAPED A CHILDHOOD FILLED WITH NOTHING BUT COMICBOOKS, MOVIES AND ROCK N' ROLL... ONLY TO CRASH HEADLONG INTO AN ADULTHOOD FILLED WITH NOTHING BUT COMICBOOKS, MOVIES AND ROCK N' ROLL. NEXT TO BRINGING HIS OWN TWISTED OFFSPRING INTO THE WORLD, FINDING A WAY TO GET PAID FOR HIS INTERESTS IS HIS GREATEST PERSONAL ACHIEVEMENT. AS A FOUNDING PARTNER IN MAN OF ACTION STUDIOS, HE ALSO MOONLIGHTS AS A CREATOR/WRITER/PRODUCER IN THE FIELD OF TELEVISED ENTERTAINMENT.

MIKE HUDDLESTON HAS DRAWN A LOT OF PICTURES, PAINTED A FEW PAINTINGS AND DESIGNED SEVERAL LOGOS. HE'S BEEN HIRED TO DO ONE OR THE OTHER BY ALL OF THE MAJOR COMIC BOOK PUBLISHERS, A FEW MAGAZINES AND ONE GREETING CARD COMPANY. HE CO-CREATED THE COFFIN AND DEEP SLEEPER WITH PHIL HESTER. OTHER WORK, PAST AND PRESENT, INCLUDES DEATHSTROKE, MNEMOVORE, GEN 13, THE HOMELAND DIRECTIVE AND THE STRAIN. FIND OUT MORE AT: HTTP://MIKEHUDDLESTON.WORDPRESS.COM

RUS WOOTON HAS BEEN A LETTERER SINCE 2003, CURRENTLY HUNKERED DOWN IN SOUTH FLORIDA. HE SPENDS MOST OF HIS TIME SITTING AT HIS MAC LETTERING FOR THE LIKES OF JOE CASEY.. AS WELL AS FOR IMAGE COMICS, MARVEL AND DARK HORSE. DRAWING AND WRITING KEEP HIM SANE WHILE DR. PEPPER, iTUNES AND NETFLIX ARE LARGELY RESPONSIBLE FOR KEEPING HIM IN A STATE OF SEMI-CONSCIOUSNESS. HE'S AVAILABLE FOR PAID ENDORSEMENT OF THE AFORE-MENTIONED PRODUCTS AND/OR SERVICES.

SONIA HARRIS MOVED FROM LONDON TO CALIFORNIA IN 1996 AND HASN'T BEEN THE SAME SINCE. SHE HAS DECADES OF EXPERIENCE DESIGNING LOGOS, IDENTITIES, BOOKS, MAGAZINES, COMICBOOKS, WEBSITES, POSTERS, FLYERS, POSTCARDS, ILLUSTRATIONS, AND ASSORTED ADVERTISING. SHE IS CONSTANTLY AMAZED AT HOW MUCH WORK CAN GO INTO MAKING A COMICBOOK LOOK AS IF NO ONE DESIGNED IT AT ALL.

FIND MORE OF HER DESIGN WORK AT: WWW.SOYABEAN.COM

YOU THOUGHT YOU COULD WALTZ IN AN' END US?! JUST LIKE THAT?!
I WANT MY RESPECT!
—FEELS SO FUCKIN' GOOD—
—SUPPOSED TO FEEL SO FUCKIN' GOOD—
I DON'T... GET IT...
THE POP-TAL DRIVER'S... FIGHTIN' FER ME...?
—HERE IT COMES AGAIN—
YOU WANNA' SEND ME TO HELL—
T-TELL MY D-END
PART OF ME WISHES I WAS DOING THIS ONE-ON-ONE...
I'M GONNA HAVE YOU HANGIN' BY YER BALL SACK!
GOTTA' HATE A BLOWOUT.
ASSHOLE.
—GOT A BRAND NEW BOGEY IN THE MIX! NO VISIBLE TAGS!
I AIN'T LETTIN' "ELLE BELLE" OUTTA MY SIGHT! BUT I MAY NEED SOME BACK UP—!
—TWO OF MY LEAST FAVORITE THINGS!
NOW HE'S SAYING SOMETHING...
YOUR TIMING IS, IN A WORD, FORTUITOUS.
I FEEL THINGS HAVE BEEN LEFT UNFINISHED. WHAT WITH MY OPPOSITE NUMBER HAVING SHUFFLED LOOSE THE MORTAL COIL FAR EARLIER THAN EXPECTED.
I'M ON FIIIIRRREEE—!
DOESN'T FEEL GREAT.
NOW THAT'S AN ENTRANCE TO KEEP YER PECKER PLUMP—
—WHEREVER THE HELL I AM...!
FREEZE, MOTHERFUCKAS—!
IF I CROAKED AN' YER JUST NOT TELLIN' ME... WE'RE GONNA GO ROUND AND ROUND...
NOW MAYBE YOU CAN SHOW ME THE WAY...
TO SEE THINGS ON A QUANTUM LEVEL IS TO SEE ALL THINGS SIMULTANEOUSLY.
PAST, PRESENT, FUTURE. THERE IS NOTHING LINEAR ABOUT IT.
"FUNNY TO THINK NOW... HOW MUCH SIMPLER LIFE WAS BACK IN NINETY-ONE. HOW EASY I HAD IT, THEN.
"IT TOOK A FEW MORE YEARS FOR ME TO ACCEPT THE OBVIOUS.
WHO...?
JEEZUS PALOMINO... GUESS I GOT TATERED...
HANDS OFF THE FAT LOSER, JONES...
IN MY NEWLY-MINTED LIBERTY BELLE SEQUEL!
SHE'S JACKED UP WITH METAL FLAKE UPHOLSTERY AN' EVERYTHING ELSE YOU CAN SCAM UNDER A TEQUILA MOON!
LOOK CLOSELY...
LEGITIMATE GRIPE, SUSIE.
"THEY NEVER SEEM TO REMEMBER WHAT
—IS SQUEEZE—
—THE TRIGGER—
GET YOUR OLD ASS FLAT ON THE PAVEMENT
SO I FOLLOW THAT TICKLE IN MY BRAIN...
THE SOUP IS FUCKIN' THICK.
...THERE IS NO DIFFERENCE.
YOUR VERNACULAR HAS A CADENCE I FIND INTRIGUING...
YOU'RE SWEATING ME! IT'S SO OBVIOUS!
I THINK YOU REALLY WANT SOME OF THIS—!
YA' LIKE FUCKIN' WITH MY PONTCHA?
AWWW, NO! NO! THIS...
...SUMMITCH.